EXPIRED BETRAYAL

LAST CHANCE COUNTY - BOOK 8

LISA PHILLIPS

Publisher: Lisa Phillips

Cover design: Ryan Schwarz

Edited by: Jen Weiber

❀ Created with Vellum

1

Lieutenant Alex Basuto knew something was wrong the second he stepped out of the gym. Spring air chilled the sweat on his skin. He scanned the parking lot under the glow of streetlamps but saw no movement in the dark.

The jump would no doubt come when he bent to toss his duffel into the backseat of his car.

Alex pressed the unlock button on his keys and popped the trunk instead. Dressed in sweats, sneakers, and a T-shirt, he had no weapon on him. It was in the duffel, tucked in the side pocket.

He shifted the bag and, as he walked toward the trunk, tugged the zipper down.

That was when they approached.

Alex heard a rush of movement and the shuffle of clothing approach him from the back. He swung the duffel backwards and pulled the gun in one movement.

It fell to the pavement with a thud, leaving him holding the gun on the guy behind him. Three others approached. Two on his left, another on his right.

The guy who'd been behind him had a knife.

"Gonna stab me in a parking lot?" Alex didn't lower the gun. He also didn't recognize the guy or any of his friends. Unusual, considering how long he'd worked as a cop in this town. "Start a manhunt, because you killed a police lieutenant?"

He saw the first flicker of unease in the guy's face. Week-old, unwashed hair, and a growth of stubble on his chin from longer than that. He wasn't in charge, Alex figured, when his eyes flicked to the guy on the right.

"Not here to kill me?" Alex looked over each of them.

"You think I want that hassle?"

"So what do you want?" There might be four, but Alex was the one with the gun. Still, it would be a shame if he wound up killed by these troublemakers. Off duty. Three weeks after he'd been promoted to lieutenant.

His mom had thrown a big party in her backyard and invited basically everyone he knew. She'd tried to set him up with a pretty, dark-haired schoolteacher she knew from church. He'd spent the whole party at the grill, hanging with his nephew. Strategically ignoring both his mother's attempts to introduce him to a woman about five years too young for him, and his boss's side glances. Conroy had been far too amused by Alex's predicament. Not to mention as was everyone else he worked with. Including a bunch of FBI agents present.

A whole group of people who'd find out he couldn't cut it as a lieutenant. Forget being cut down in his prime, or never making it to chief. Alex would die, and they'd finally figure out he didn't have what it took to succeed and be the best cop he could be. And he'd never be rewarded, the way he wanted, with a good woman, even though his mama kept saying it would be, "any time now."

Never mind that it seemed to happen to everyone else but him. To which she always replied, "yet."

After his disastrous first marriage, Alex wasn't so sure that was what he wanted. Still, it was like his heart wouldn't listen to him.

The guy took a step closer. If he had a gun, he didn't get it out. The guy just kept both hands by his sides, thumbs hooked in his pockets. "Where's your brother at?"

Javier.

Of course, this was about Javier. Alex glanced aside slightly, keeping the other three in his peripheral vision. "You think I know?"

"I think you're gonna call him and ask. You can come with us and, when we have him, you can go."

"You're prepared for me to add kidnapping charges to whatever I can bring against you?" Surely someone from the gym had noticed. True, Alex might not have called in before he forced this confrontation. Backup might not be on the way. But that didn't mean an honest citizen couldn't step in. Help out.

He just wasn't about to count on that—and not just because Alex could take care of himself, either.

It was more that he had always been forced to do so, and it was just how life seemed to always turn out for him.

The guy took half a step forward and pulled a gun from his waistband. "Drop it on the ground."

On Alex's left, the two others pulled out weapons. Knife guy in front of him let out a pitchy chuckle.

He leveled his gaze on the guy. He couldn't let on that he'd lost the upper hand. And knew it. "You think I know where Javier is?"

"Cop like you? Yeah, I do. I think you know exactly where your brother crashes, and all the places he crawls into to lay low and get high. Spend my boss's money."

"And the boss wants it back? Wants to get paid? That it?"

The man closed in further. "Thirty grand."

Alex winced.

"So either you tell us where he is and come with us to find him, or Dane here carves you up. And I'll let him get *real* creative."

Another pitchy chuckle.

Okay, not good. This whole situation had gone sideways fast. Three guns—not including his—and a guy with a thing for knives?

He didn't want to know what might happen if a civilian tried to get involved right now.

Problem was, he had no idea where Javier had disappeared to this time. Even Javier's own son Mateo, Alex's seventeen-year-old nephew, didn't know. Mama didn't want to know. Alex tried to keep tabs. The pastor kept Javier's situation permanently on the prayer list, just without including his name, only because Mateo's best friend was the pastor's son.

"What if I don't know where he is *or* where to start looking for him?"

"Cop like you? Guess we'll start cutting and see if that's the truth."

"Liars die." Knife guy did that high-pitched chuckle thing again.

Alex's stomach churned. And not just because he'd otherwise be at home making a post-workout smoothie right now.

He'd lowered his gun but wasn't going to set it down anywhere. A cop never disarmed himself when faced with a threat. No matter if that meant the odds were more heavily stacked against him because he refused to give up the only thing he could use to protect himself.

"Can't tell you what I don't know."

"So get on the phone and find out."

Alex's muscles were already fatigued from the deep burn of a hard workout. Still, his stomach continued to tense. "I'm a cop. You think I know where he is? You think Javier would keep me in the loop?"

If his brother did, Alex would arrest him.

"Pretending you're stupid won't get you anywhere." The guy shook his head. "Typical cop. You'll pick up guys for basically nothing and throw them in jail. But your brother? He gets a free pass 'cause he's family." He let out a sound full of derision. "Figures."

"That's not how it works."

"No? Then tell me where he is."

"If I knew Javier's whereabouts, he'd be in an interrogation room right now."

It had been clear for a long time his brother had intel on other players around town, people who were part of the drug trade. Alex'd had several conversations about that very thing with his chief, Conroy Barnes. The chief had cautioned him to go careful if he did pursue it. After all, if things went wrong, it would break Mama's heart more than it had already been broken.

Then everyone would know where Alex came from, and everything he'd had to wade through to be who he was. There wasn't a woman in the world who would contend with all that, and the darkness he had inside him. Analise had proven that when she'd packed all her stuff and left without explanation. Never mind he still had a tiny flicker of hope that he could have everything he wanted.

Even if it would probably never happen.

"You'd arrest your own brother?" He erupted into laughter. "They said you'd be like this, but I didn't believe it."

An interrogation room didn't mean arrested. Alex figured his brother could at least be a confidential informant for the police department, and at best testify against those who supplied the drugs he sold. People he did cash work for.

"You think I'll let you flip him for the sake of *justice*?" The guy laughed some more.

Alex shrugged one shoulder. Turned out that was a bad move since it drew attention to the fact he still held his gun, though by his side. "No. I think you'll kill him before I can make that happen. Because he's what I think he is to you. A liability."

"They said you were smart as well as bullheaded."

Alex figured that was probably accurate but didn't indicate it to these guys. "You're gonna try and make a deal with me?"

"Nah, they said you'd never go for that."

"You tip your hand, indicating he owes your boss money and do it, knowing you'll get nothing from me? How do you expect me to believe that's the whole story?" Alex didn't think that made sense. Except for one thing.

The guy shifted slightly. He wasn't in charge. Alex's hunch had been right—there was a boss above him.

Knife guy half stepped toward him. "I'll get blood."

"One slice of that blade and I put a bullet in you." Never mind that the others would possibly—probably—kill him for it. He looked at the guy to his right and tried to gauge the level of loyalty between these guys. Not to mention whether their orders were different than what they claimed. "I don't know where Javier is. Tell your boss that. And leave now, so this doesn't get more difficult."

It was a reasonable request.

The guy didn't accept it. "I'm leaning toward blood."

Had they been given orders to kill him? Or maybe just cut him up a little?

"You think I'll let it go after that?" Alex shook his head. "Not likely. Unless all of you leave. Now." He could recall enough he'd be able to write detailed descriptions of all four of them. Then he'd spend the rest of the night looking at mug shots on his computer at the office, identifying each of them.

The guy hesitated a second.

That was when Alex knew this was a fishing expedition, not a murder attempt. And not just fishing, but this had been designed to distract him.

The other realization he had was that he was clearly doing well as a police lieutenant if they felt they needed to waylay him so he couldn't respond to...whatever was going on someplace else. Someone was being hurt or taken. A person Alex cared about.

That was a short list if it included whether or not the person could take care of themselves. The vulnerable in his life consisted of Mama and Mateo, though Mama had a shotgun in her hall closet and Mateo was a linebacker on the high school football team. His brother Javier didn't want help.

"This ends now." He swept his gaze through all four of them. "Get out of here."

"Dane." The guy to his right flicked two fingers.

Dane lunged. Before Alex could squeeze the trigger now under his finger, Dane backed off laughing. Nothing but a fake-out.

Alex watched them go and pulled his phone from his pocket. No new texts or calls. Whatever it was, it hadn't been reported yet. He might not be on duty tonight—he'd worked six this morning until eight tonight already—but the new dispatcher would contact him regardless.

He called his mom's number. She didn't pick up.

Mateo did on the second ring, his voice muffled. "Yeah."

"You okay?"

"*Tío* Alex?"

"Yeah. Go check on Mama. Make sure the house is secure."

Mateo groaned, but it sounded like he was only protesting getting up. Totally asleep. Considering it was just after eleven-thirty on a school night, that was a good thing. Or at least it meant the kid didn't have a paper due tomorrow. He lived with Javier on occasion but mostly slept at his Abuela's.

A couple of minutes later, Mateo said, "She's asleep. The house is quiet. All the doors and windows are locked, and no one's messed with the alarm."

"Good. Go back to sleep." Alex hung up.

He slid into the driver's seat of his car and frowned as he tried to figure out who the target was. Someone he would rush in to protect without a second thought.

But not his family.

Was this just about him being a cop and the fact he'd respond to any call about a citizen in danger?

The image of a little boy with bright blue eyes flashed in his mind. A child he'd helped just days ago, along with his mother. Packed them up and took them to Hope Mansion, a refuge in town for women and children.

His phone rang.

Yep. The name on the screen: *Maggie.*

2

Sasha gripped the phone. "I'm not doing it."

"…another job after—wait—what?"

"I'm out." She stared at the curtain hung over the attic window. "I'm not taking any more jobs."

Silence. "For how long?"

"The foreseeable future."

He sounded incredulous. "Babe—"

"Don't. I'm not going to change my mind." Sasha had never liked working side jobs while being fully employed for Millie at the accountant's office. But the pay couldn't be beaten and she was one of only a few people in the world who could—or would—do the type of work they needed. Her retirement accounts were fully funded by now.

For weeks she'd been staying here, at Hope Mansion. Her refuge.

Before this, her job had been working at the accountant's office with Millie and Bridget—and their colleague Clarke, who'd betrayed them all before being arrested.

Considering the company hadn't had anything to do with accounting, the stakes had been high. Their client list consisted of high-level government assets, former spies, and even a few

Special Forces soldiers. People who needed to start over with a clean ID that would keep them safe.

Even though she'd signed a non-compete with her legal employer, Millie Cullings—the wife of an FBI agent—Sasha had still done the side work. Taking government contracts, private contracts, or she-didn't-ask-who contracts had never sat well with her. But only because she didn't like lying to Millie. Considering she didn't have a job right now, it probably wasn't the time to cut all her sources of income. But Sasha was looking for a new path. A fresh start of her own.

After all, this path had put her on the FBI's Most Wanted list.

The feds didn't know half of what she'd done—for Millie, or even before that. Or during those years. Or since.

On top of all that, the fed leading the charge was Special Agent Eric Cullings. Her former boss's *husband*. Talk about complicated.

Sasha sighed. Half the time she didn't even have the mental energy to wade through it all, and yet she'd lived it.

A muffled thud came from downstairs. Sasha strode to the window, which gave her a crow's nest view of the parking area out in front of Hope Mansion. Two trucks had been parked haphazardly on the grass.

"Spread the word," Sasha said. "I'm out until I say otherwise."

She hung up on him. Her "handler" for those jobs. She didn't trust him much farther than she could throw him. Then again, there were only two people in her world she did trust—neither of whom were speaking to her right now. Millie, her former boss, and Bridget, her former colleague. Both came from Last Chance, but Bridget was the only one living here right now.

She was also the one Sasha felt an obligation to make things right with. More than she needed to figure out what she was going to do with her life next.

That was probably the real reason she was still here in town.

Face it. You're a sucker for forgiveness. Friendship had made her soft, and now that they'd discovered the subterfuge she'd perpetrated six years ago? Radio silence.

Sasha passed her cot and opened the trap door. Wooden stairs lowered into the opening so she could climb down to the upstairs hallway. She rarely used them, preferring instead to climb down herself, silently.

"Don't lie to me!" A man's voice rang out, carrying up the stairs and to the hall below her.

Another thud. Someone hit. A woman cried out.

Sasha dropped through the opening into a crouch, then stood. A little boy gasped. Dark hair, dark eyes, and thick brows. He huddled against his mother's side, his face against her abdomen. She stood in the doorway of a room on the second floor which could house up to thirty, though comfortably it was more like twenty-two. Currently, there were sixteen residents: nine women, and seven children. Maggie, the homeowner and manager of Hope Mansion, lived downstairs on the first floor.

The woman in her doorway whimpered. Tears gathered in her eyes, glistening beside the ragged scar down the side of her face. "He hit Maggie with his gun. She's bleeding."

Sasha nodded while her heart twisted at the thought of Maggie being hurt. A woman who did that much good should never have to suffer. "I'll take care of it."

None of these people needed to endure more than they already had. She possessed many scars similar to theirs, and only some couldn't be seen—even in a bathing suit. Because those scars were on the inside.

"Where is he?!"

The little boy started to cry.

Sasha neared them. "Go in your bathroom. Lock the door. Bar it with anything you can find." She turned to the others who'd come out. "Everyone get out of sight. Closets, bathrooms, or under your beds," she whispered. "Hide and don't come out until I tell you the coast is clear."

She headed for the stairs and looked over the railing.

A man trotted up, heavy coat on and a gun in one hand. Sasha stepped to the side. She grabbed a kid's backpack hanging by the wall and tested the weight. Good, there were a couple of books inside.

The man neared the top.

Right as he reached the last step, she swung out, making solid contact with his left shoulder. He tumbled back down the stairs and hit a companion on the way. They both rolled end-over-end to the bottom and landed in a heap with a grunt and a yell.

"There's someone up there."

Before they could race to her, Sasha stepped out. She strode down the stairs as though she had every right to be there, which essentially, she did. Sasha had lived at Hope Mansion for eight months the year she turned seventeen. After she'd given birth to a baby boy, she'd left town and hadn't returned until a few weeks ago.

Now it was like she *couldn't* leave.

She stepped off the bottom stair. "Not someone. Just me."

A big man stood over a woman, holding her by the hair. On her knees. Crying. One eye was already swollen and her face had reddened from being hit.

He shoved her away.

The woman fell to the carpet and curled into a ball.

Sasha looked away, not wishing to remember precisely how that felt. She didn't need to go back there. And yet, given there were five men in the room, how could she not? Five to one wasn't good odds on her best day, armed to the teeth. She had on yoga pants and a tank top, along with running shoes. Not an abundance of places to stow a weapon.

The last time she faced down odds like this?

Yeah. Not a place she wanted to revisit, even being back in Last Chance where all her triggers resided.

"You wanna get involved?" The man took a step toward her.

It was probably supposed to look tough. She was a woman, so cowering was what he'd expect. Instead, she looked around. Maggie wasn't anywhere in sight. Was she somewhere else, bleeding? She returned her gaze to the man like he was nothing to her.

Other than that, Sasha didn't move. She only lifted her chin slightly. "I'm thinking, *yeah.*"

He sneered. "Not a good idea. I wish I had time to explain a few things to you, but *she*—" He pointed at the woman on the carpet. "—is gonna go get my son. Then I'll be leaving."

One of the others chuckled.

"You want your son? I'm guessing you should go see a lawyer." After all, there were few reasons a woman and her child would have sought refuge at Hope Mansion. And the reasons this woman had were kind of obvious. "You aren't taking him."

The quicker she could get this resolved, the better. Sasha was on the FBI's Most Wanted list and her physical features currently weren't perfectly disguised as they would be if she were out on the street in Last Chance. Her picture was out there. This guy might've seen it, and she figured he wouldn't mind causing trouble for her.

Or, he wouldn't after she did what she was going to do next.

He took another step.

Two of his guys closed in. Not the two she'd tumbled down the stairs. They were licking their wounds and probably already plotting their revenge.

She swung out and grasped his wrist—the hand holding the gun—and brought up her knee between his legs.

He doubled over. Such a tough guy.

She didn't get the gun in time, so she kicked his face with her tennis shoe. He dropped to the floor unconscious, just as someone grabbed her from behind.

Sasha flung her head back and heard the guy's nose break. Never mind that it hurt the back of her head like few other things did. He let go, so what did she care?

The next guy already had his gun up, but hesitated. Questioning whether or not he wanted to kill a woman he didn't know. She kicked his stomach and grabbed the gun. One of the guys who'd tumbled down the stairs rushed her.

She shot his thigh.

The other pulled up short, hands raised, but she saw the glint in his eye and spun. A knife slashed down from the man behind her.

Boy, it'd been a few weeks since she'd worked out like this. She was kind of rusty. If Zander found out, she'd never live it down. He would put her in a month-long training program until she passed to his satisfaction.

Sasha twisted and felt the fire of the blade as it nicked her shoulder. She hissed out a breath, grabbed his arm and kicked his knee, then slammed the gun down onto his temple. She raised her gun to the only man standing.

A dark blur slammed into her. Sasha hit the wall, and they dropped in a heap together with his shoulder smashed against her cheekbone.

She shoved at his shoulders and chest.

He pulled her under him, and the back of her head slammed onto the bottom step of the stairs. She heard someone laugh.

Hands wrapped around her throat.

Sasha's whole world swallowed down in a rush of memory.

Laughter. Hands. Pain.

She shoved at him and tried to get purchase, not just to push the memories away, either. She tried to fight back. To remember who she was. A grown woman, not a teenage girl with no skill and no training.

She got her feet under him and kicked.

He barely moved, not even slightly dislodged by a ram powered by her strong legs. He was too heavy.

White spots flickered and sparked at the edge of her vision.

Someone screamed. The other woman.

Sasha got her hands up and pressed her thumbs into his eyes. No hesitation.

He cried out and let go enough that she could gasp a breath. And slam her hand into his throat. He coughed, and she scrambled out from under him. Toward the gun.

She brought it up and pointed it at him from her supine position.

"Whoa." He raised both hands, then coughed once. "You got spirit. But you're not why I'm here."

"I'll make it why."

He nodded to one of his buddies. "Get that gun. Then tear this place apart. Bring me my son."

Red and blue lights flashed against the wall through the open curtains.

"*Now!*"

The woman started screaming again. She begged him to leave them alone. To not take her son.

"Shut up!" He turned from her to his wife. Sasha nearly put a bullet in his back. Any other time, or place, she probably would have.

A booted foot kicked her in the head. She rolled, fighting unconsciousness. So that was what that felt like? Yeesh. How many times had she kicked someone in the head? She blinked and realized she'd rolled all the way to the wall.

"Police!"

Hands grasped her.

"Leave it. Let's go." The man added an ugly curse word, referring to the woman. His wife. "This ain't over."

"Last Chance Police!" Pause. "Maggie? You here?"

Sasha pushed off the floor but had no energy to stand. A man was inside, and he was a cop. She had to get out of here before she was seen. There was no time to tell this woman to not mention her presence here. It was going to come out.

Sasha would be discovered.

The woman whimpered. Tears rolled from her one, good eye. The other was still swollen shut.

"Where is he? Your son?" Sasha could at least make sure the child was all right.

She sucked in a choppy breath. "Upstairs with Marta."

The cop, whoever it was, was in the foyer. She could hear his boots on the wood. Sasha pulled in her feet and stood with one hand braced against the wall.

She could still feel hands on her, the crawl of sweaty palms. A slap. Thick fingers on her throat.

She swallowed against the sensation.

"Ma'am? You okay?"

The other woman was led to a couch and settled there. Sasha's vision blurred. White stripes flashed on the man's workout pants as he made his way to her. Gun in one hand. Broad shoulders. Nausea roiled in her stomach.

He touched her shoulder. "You'll need to get that looked—"

Sasha slapped his hand from her.

"Whoa. Easy."

She lifted her gaze and gasped.

"Sasha Camilero." The way he said her name didn't sound like a good thing.

Memory swallowed her even farther back. Bare feet, racing through a field. Ice cream. Locking their bikes to take a nap in wildflowers. She could still smell them.

"Alex." She said his name on a sigh. Why couldn't she forget it all? Why did she have to remember everything?

He reached for her. "You're under arrest."

Sasha shoved at him.

He stared at her like he had no clue who she was. Like he'd never seen her before.

Sasha turned and raced up the stairs.

3

"Hey!" Alex watched her flee, frozen to the spot.

He should have run after her, but all he could see in his mind were those dark brown eyes. He'd seen those eyes before. Somewhere. Who was she, other than a woman on the FBI's Most Wanted list? This wasn't that.

He knew her.

Alex couldn't quite place where he'd seen those eyes, but it was safe to say they triggered a response. His heartbeat pounded in his ears. Sweat beaded on his forehead, and down his spine.

He knew her.

Who was Sasha Camilero, really?

"Alex."

He spun to the muffled voice and found Maggie in front of him. She frowned. "Are you okay?"

Behind her, the injured woman sat on the couch with her wide eyes on him. Great. He was scaring both of them. Alex needed to get a handle on himself. And yet, everything in him was freaking out like he was having an anxiety attack.

He'd seen it before in others. Felt it before in himself. Years of therapy later, and he'd taken for granted how long it had been since he'd been back there in that panicky state. It seemed strange to be remembering the sensations now. All because of looking into that pair of dark brown eyes. With both hands, he squeezed his temples, willing his mind to cooperate. It was like his mind was willing him to remember details he'd shoved away. Then, without warning, his mind flashed to *that* night.

His teenage brain had blocked out most of the images, something that'd concerned his mother at the time. The therapist had reassured her it was likely for the best and was helping him deal with the lingering issues.

Seeing those eyes now, when his adrenaline levels were already jacked? It felt like he was in an unrelenting tailspin.

Alex glanced around, rolled his shoulders, and assessed that they were all safe here. For now. "One second." He turned and headed upstairs after her.

"Lieutenant!"

He ignored Maggie's call and reached the top step. Where had she gone? There were plenty of places to hide, but he didn't want to go barging into people's rooms and freak out everyone who lived here. Most were victims of domestic violence. Some were simply women who needed somewhere to stay. They didn't need a big-shouldered guy muscling into their rooms.

"Sasha! Come out!"

Every door remained closed. He heard a shuffle and then a door cracked open. A little boy peered out. "Lieutenant Basuto?"

"Hi, Simon." He didn't like pumping a kid for information, but he had to at least ask. "Did you see a tall, dark-haired woman run up here?"

Simon shook his head.

"Okay, thanks. Let your mom know those men are gone, okay? It's fine to come out, but there's gonna be cops downstairs for a while." He patted Simon on the shoulder and stooped down to his level. "Everything's gonna be okay. You hear me?"

Simon nodded silently and closed the door.

Basuto headed back downstairs. Maggie sat beside the woman on the couch. He said, "Where is she?"

Maggie raised one brow. She had red hair and had to be in her fifties, at least, though she didn't look it. Trim, like someone not unaccustomed to physical activity. She wore jeans and a sweater, despite the late hour, and had fluffy socks on her feet. She was taller than him but didn't use that to make him feel small.

Alex was five-seven. Sure, that was average height, but he didn't always appreciate it when people towered over him. Sasha was at least two inches taller. In heels, more than that.

She'd been taller than him years ago, too.

"What is it?" Maggie approached, a wary look on her face.

Alex pushed aside foggy memories. Why did his brain insist on going back there? Sasha had nothing to do with his past.

"Emily?" Maggie motioned to the woman beside her. The victim. "You're the one who brought her here."

"Not Mrs. Perkins." Though, he shot the woman a soft look so she'd know she wasn't in trouble. "I'm talking about Sasha Camilero. The fugitive you're harboring." He folded his arms because it would help him feel steadier. "How long has she been staying here?"

"Who?"

Maggie was going to play it like that?

Alex lifted his brows. "I'm going to find her. The FBI is looking as well. If you've been hiding a wanted woman, that makes you an accessory to every crime she's committed. You know that, right?"

"This place is a sanctuary for anyone who needs refuge."

"To escape justice."

She sighed out her disappointment with him.

"I'm not harming anyone." Alex wasn't going to back down. "To be honest, it's you who is doing harm by allowing her to stay here in secret when the police and FBI are both looking for her."

"That's your assumption." Maggie lifted her chin. "Maybe she walked in the back door to confront those men? Maybe I haven't seen her since…"

He waited, but she didn't say more. "Since what?"

She frowned. "You don't remember? You were in the hospital."

There was only one time in his life Alex had been there overnight. "What does that have to do with a wanted fugitive?"

"I'd think you, of all people, would have compassion for her. Considering."

Alex squeezed the bridge of his nose. "I have no idea what you're talking about."

Sasha Camilero was wanted by the FBI for her involvement in three suspicious deaths of prominent foreign businessmen, two thefts of priceless art that had been traded on the black market, and for questioning as a person of interest in countless other crimes.

And he was supposed to have compassion for her? Considering what?

Alex didn't know why on earth he would, except for the fact she recognized him. Knew his name. She'd fled because he was a cop, and she was a suspect. A wanted criminal.

No other reason.

"You really don't remember who she is?"

"I know exactly who she—"

Maggie shook her head.

Before he could finish, two uniformed cops strode in. Aiden Donaldson, with brand new sergeant stripes on his arms and an equally shiny gold band on his left ring finger. With him was Officer Frees.

Alex winced. "Sergeant, I need statements from everyone. Frees, check around outside and make sure there are no stragglers."

"Copy that, Lieutenant." Frees, with his gruff demeanor and imposing stature, headed back outside.

Alex turned to Maggie. "You said they all fled?"

"Sasha took care of them."

It looked to him as though she'd been in a hard-won fight— if she'd won at all. He wasn't so sure that was the case. And Maggie seemed content to be on her side of this battle. If he brought the manager of this house to the police station to answer questions, the FBI would want to speak with her.

Some cops might want to protect her by keeping her name out of it. He'd learned the hard way to do the right thing. Always.

Uphold the law. Operate within the bounds of his sworn oath. The alternative was that people got hurt and criminals went free.

In a situation like this, where a woman had been terrorized, it was better to let the sergeant take over while Alex looked for Sasha.

Aiden, who had a daughter, and was well known around town as a longtime single dad, had since married the child's mother. The residents here were more likely to trust his baby face and his reputation.

Alex had other things to do right now. He turned to Donaldson. "Please speak with Mrs. Perkins."

Aiden didn't move.

"Sergeant Donaldson."

He frowned. "You okay, Lieutenant?"

Alex didn't have time for this. "I'll look around upstairs."

"You think one of them hid up there?" Donaldson glanced in the direction of the stairs.

If they had, there would likely be a ruckus for anyone to hear, but there wasn't. Even so, he shook his head. "I'm just making sure."

He didn't offer more of an explanation or bring up the fact Maggie had been harboring a fugitive. He just headed upstairs again. Something he'd seen before didn't want to let go of him. A hunch, the kind he usually chased down.

Like the one that had led him to explore deeper into his brother's life years back. He'd found both drug paraphernalia and a roll of cash at the trailer where Javier made his home. It hadn't taken long to ascertain that his brother was likely dealing.

He just couldn't prove it, then or now.

"You aren't going to tell Aiden about…" Maggie glanced back, and then quietly whispered, "Sasha."

Alex stopped at the top of the stairs and turned to her. "I have no evidence and no proof. Mrs. Perkins can inform him of her presence here. After that, I'll back up what she says."

"Then you'll call the FBI?"

"She needs to face what she's done. That's what this is about. Justice."

"Justice without mercy isn't justice."

"We should simply allow criminals to go free, because of mercy?"

Maggie lifted her chin. "Sometimes it's about more than what a person has done. It's about why. About the extenuating circumstances." She leveled him with a stare. "I know you know what I mean."

"This isn't a woman presently abused, forced to confront her attacker with lethal force. And circumstances are for her lawyer to argue."

"The justice system—"

"I know it's not perfect, Maggie. That's why I do this job. Why I won't bring anything to the FBI without evidence to back it up."

He half expected Maggie to argue that Sasha had never killed anyone. But she didn't, and neither did she defend anything else about the woman. "You're harboring a fugitive. That puts me in a sticky situation."

"Look around." Maggie lifted her chin. "I have nothing to hide."

That only meant she didn't think he would find anything.

Alex knocked on the first door. "This is Lieutenant Basuto.

It's safe to come out now."

It opened. A young Asian woman peered out but said nothing. Maggie patted his arm, and he moved to the next door. Before he knocked, he glanced back.

The woman looked at Maggie, and then up to the ceiling.

Alex gave her a small smile and saw Maggie was talking to the woman. He went to the next door, glancing surreptitiously up to the ceiling as he moved. The door to the attic was up there.

Was that why Maggie was so sure he wasn't going to find anything?

Alex ducked into the bathroom and came out with a vanity stool. He stepped on it and reached for the trapdoor, shoving it aside.

"Basuto!"

He gripped a ladder inside and pulled it down, then shifted the stool out of the way.

Maggie rushed over. "Please don't—"

"You can't protect her forever. The FBI will find her." If he didn't do it first.

The attic was dark. He had his gun out and waved one hand as he walked carefully. The light cord swayed. He pulled on it, illuminating a bare bulb. Bare floor. One cot. Sleeping bag and pillow. A rickety wardrobe in one corner. Curtained window.

The pane had been shoved up and was still open four inches.

Maggie climbed up behind him.

"You let her escape."

She gasped, and it sounded completely fake. "Someone has been living up here. I can't believe it. I had no idea."

"Nice try."

He strode to a tiny pedestal sink in the corner. Above it was a mirrored cabinet, the inside barely big enough for a modern stick of deodorant. Sasha had been living up here. Like this? Plenty of people lived in sparse conditions, for any number of reasons. He helped out at the food bank, and visited a few elderly people in town regularly, so he knew how deep poverty ran in parts of this community.

For some, these would be luxurious conditions. Everyone saw their world differently, and others would view it based on preconceived ideas of "need" versus "want." He tried to help without passing judgment.

Hanging on the corner of the mirrored cabinet door was a gold chain. At the bottom hung a butterfly. One wing had broken off, leaving it a fragment of what it had been.

The last time he'd seen it.

Alex held it in his palm. "Melina."

"So you do remember her."

He squeezed his eyes shut as the past rolled back like a wave and crashed over him. "No. That's not Sasha. It can't be. That doesn't.... It isn't.... The FBI would *know.*" There was no way the feds wouldn't be fully aware if Sasha used to live in Last Chance. Everyone would know. He'd have been briefed.

"You didn't recognize her."

"You can't harbor her anymore, Maggie. She needs to turn herself in." *Lord.* Was this really Melina? He hadn't seen her in years. He didn't even remember her face from back then. Just a few sensations—the sun, and grass under his feet. That necklace. The therapist said he'd blocked most of it out because of the trauma of what had happened.

"You remember her now. Don't you?"

Alex strode past her. "If she comes back, call it in." He double-timed it downstairs to where Donaldson spoke with Mrs. Perkins. "How long has Sasha Camilero been here?"

His sergeant coughed.

The woman blinked. "Who?"

"Sasha. She was here when I got here, and then she fled up the stairs. Where would she have gone?"

The woman shook her head. "There was no one else here. I'm the one who fought off those men."

4

Sasha climbed out of her car and zipped her coat to the top to ward off the evening chill. For twenty-four hours she laid low and waited for the cops to show up because someone had turned her in. Alex's face rushed her in her sleep—dark dreams where he slapped her in cuffs and threw the jail cell door closed.

She shivered and stared at the yellow lit basketball court where a contingent of teen boys played a rough game of pickup. The kind of competitiveness that wouldn't fly in a school game, but which she heartily approved of. Life didn't play by rules. The world was a wild place, and anyone who had the skills to protect themselves would survive a whole lot longer than those who didn't—or who expected others to fight for them.

Her phone vibrated in her pocket. She slid it out, half expecting the caller to be Millie or Bridget. Either one of her friends would probably turn her in right now. Maybe they'd apologize out of a sense of nostalgia, but they'd do it.

Sasha had no intention of explaining to them the "why" of everything she'd done in her life. After all, there was no reasoning for all that'd happened to her. She could argue her actions were nothing but a reaction. But how did she know?

The injustice that had been done to her was simply wrong.

Horrific and wrong. No explanation. No justification. She'd sought her own brand of justice...and found she could do it. She'd survived. Then the government had found her, trained her, and set her loose in the world. These days they'd deny ever knowing her.

Didn't matter either way.

The feds weren't wrong about what she'd done. Or, at least she figured they weren't. Sasha didn't know what the actual charges would be when they caught up to her. If they caught up to her.

She had begun to formulate a plan. Not so she could get away with any of it, but so justice could be brought down the way it should. No mistakes.

She'd heard years ago the story of a former assassin who'd been relocated. One of those legends. A rumor, and nothing more. A place where those whose faces were recognizable could go, like witness protection for the famous. The dangerous.

But she didn't need a sanctuary.

Sasha didn't deserve to be free, and she would never find a happily ever after. That didn't happen to people like her.

The phone quit ringing.

She blinked down at it and realized she'd gotten lost in her thoughts and never answered the call. That wasn't good. Not for someone like her, with a target on her back. She fingered the stun gun in her pocket.

She wasn't going to carry a gun. That wouldn't look good if she was caught before the plan was complete. And she wasn't going to zap any cops, but she did want to be able to protect herself if necessary. Coming up against those guys had been nothing but luck. It had to be that. If there was a God in heaven, He certainly wouldn't do her any favors. Never had. Why start now?

Her phone rang again.

The caller ID displayed a series of numbers. She wasn't

going to assign a name in case anyone ever got ahold of her phone. "Hey, D."

Dorian was…she wasn't even sure. An old friend. She didn't trust him because she didn't trust anyone. That wasn't a slight against her acquaintances, like Maggie or the two women she'd worked with. Just that it was better to not be surprised when people acted in their own interests.

"Are you kidding me with this?"

She bit the inside of her lip. "Does that mean you won't do it?"

Silence filled the line. Finally, Dorian said, "This is unbelievable. I can't even…"

"Get over it."

"This is not a bad plan. Per se."

"So you'll do it?"

He sighed, long and loud.

They'd served the US government together and done a few mercenary jobs as a team since. He looked out for her. She tried not to get in his way. There wasn't a better sniper that she'd ever met or heard of. Even the rumors. He charged the most money of anyone, but that was because he was just that good.

"You know…" He sighed again. "I'd do the same thing." That was as close to affirmation as she was going to get. "But make sure it's a week. No sooner. I've got a thing this weekend, and it's time sensitive."

She knew better than to ask what it was. "Thanks. I knew I could count on you."

He grunted and hung up.

One week. He might not want this to happen any sooner, but Sasha wouldn't wait much longer. Still, she had a number of letters to write by then. After she was done, she intended to go out on her terms.

Dear Millie,

I know I lied.

She'd kept the truth from her former boss. Withheld way too

much information, and pretended she was a good person who wanted to do the right thing. Eventually, the truth had bled in. Sasha wasn't the kind who deserved a good life even if she wanted to try and have it.

She was going to make sure her end wasn't going to come by the electric chair because the government denied any knowledge of her employment. Or extradition to some country where she'd be tortured and thrown in a pit.

Been there. Done that.

Not fun.

But she'd survived, and she'd earned the right to dictate her future.

Dear Bridget,

I know you'll never forgive me.

To protect both Bridget and her child, Sasha had lied. She'd done the only thing she could think of, what she'd thought was right, and given the child to a father who loved and doted on her. Aiden Donaldson, now the police sergeant, had given back to Bridget everything Sasha had taken. They were all three now safe because of what Sasha had done. Never mind the pain, the lost years. Everything had turned out amazingly in the end.

Because they were the kind of people happily ever after happened to.

While she lived with pain of her own every day. Pain she would never be free of.

Sasha stood at the fence and peered through the chain link. One of the boys was a little taller than the others. The line of his shoulders was familiar.

Dear Jonah,

I know we've never met.

He might have been the result of the worst few days of her life—even with everything she'd been through since then that still ranked highest in terror. Seventeen-year-old Melina, the girl Sasha had been back then, hadn't been ready for it. No one would've been, but she'd thought she was so tough. Little had she known.

Out of that fire, Sasha was born.

Melina died on the floor of the barn that night. Taken. Stripped. Abused. She would never apologize for the things she'd done since. She also wasn't going to pretend it had been a result of her trauma. She'd been broken that day. But she chose every action since, and if there was a God up there, then she would answer to Him.

Sasha was done with this world.

The boy turned. Saw her standing there. He returned his attention to the game, but not before she got to absorb all that he was. The promise of the man he would become, plainly there in his face. She would savor the image of him later when she was alone. When she needed to shore up her defenses. To remember this was the proper thing to do, putting everything right again in the only way she could.

By telling the truth.

I know we've never met.

She probably wouldn't even send his letter. What would it help? Turning his world upside down wasn't going to benefit him. He would only realize he'd lost something he never knew he didn't have.

No, she wasn't going to let him know.

But she could tell Bridget. Her friend would understand, and maybe she would visit him for Sasha. Help out if he needed something. Or Alex could. She didn't want to think about him, or the fact he didn't even seem to remember her. He was a cop now. He'd forgotten. She might be angry about that if she had emotional energy left over, but she didn't. Sasha was completely drained.

She wasn't going to waste energy on a cop who had no emotion for her except to be disappointed. He wasn't wrong.

She sighed to herself. A tiny slip of emotion, completely unhelpful and only vaguely satisfying.

The boys had stopped their pickup game to watch some-thing. Some*one*. She glanced over toward the street where they watched a man get out of a compact car with a duct-taped back bumper. In front of it, a big truck had been parked.

Two men met on the sidewalk. It didn't look like a happy conversation.

She watched the boys for a moment. Tension lined two of them, Jonah and another kid his age. Hispanic heritage. His coloring reminded her of Alex, but the world was such a melting pot kind of place. People were different, and it was often hard to tell where someone was from.

If this became a problem—and it seemed to be given the stress it birthed in these boys— Sasha would wade in. She'd done it at Hope Mansion. That didn't turn out so well, but every situation was different. She needed to recon first. Assess what was happening.

Jonah's buddy was upset, and he had taken on a reassuring stance.

Yeah, Sasha was going to get involved. There wasn't much she could do for him, but she could do this.

The two men crossed the street, headed for an alley. One had a beanie on. He also wore jeans and a threadbare sweater with a hole on one side of the hem, by his hip. Work boots. Paint on his jeans. The other guy had more spare cash to spend on clothes. She'd guess he had a business—maybe a few. Legal or illegal, she didn't know. The latter, likely, given how he scanned the street. Making sure no one saw them.

Innocent people don't check their surroundings like that. He wasn't watching for a threat so he could protect himself. This guy wanted privacy to conduct business.

Sasha paused by a van, then continued to the end of the side street at the corner of the building.

It didn't matter if the boys saw her. They'd never know who she was, and they'd never see her again.

She itched under the edge of the knit cap over her forehead

and leaned against the corner of the building. Phone out. She snapped a photo of both men just as the business guy shoved the other one against the side of the neighboring building and pulled out a gun.

A hand grasped her arm and hot breath brushed her cheek. "You're under arrest."

Sasha braced. Alex. He didn't present a threat, but tell that to her racing body. Didn't matter who it was. The squeeze of his hand. The press of his body. "Don't touch me."

He wasn't even paying attention to what was unfolding right in front of them.

The man in the alley cried out against his attacker. "No! Don't shoot me!"

She shoved Alex away and saw he wore his police lieutenant's uniform of a dark suit and blue tie, white shirt. A police shield on his belt. Gun and cuffs in his hands. He was on duty.

"Were you following me?"

He frowned at the men in the alley. "Javier."

"Who—?"

Alex strode past her. "Police! Drop the gun!"

The man turned. She read his intention in the line of his body. The set of his jaw. He squeezed the trigger and, without a second thought she slammed into the cop beside her.

Fire blazed across her hip, and they hit the ground.

5

No other shots came.

    Basuto held onto Sasha while he looked down the side street. A man fled. His brother, the other guy there—the one who'd screamed for the shooter not to kill him—stood with his back to the wall.

"Javi!"

His brother jerked around. Too far away for Alex to read his face.

Sasha groaned in his arms.

"*Tío* Alex?" Two boys ran from the basketball court.

"Mateo. Jonah." He pushed out a breath. Mateo might be his nephew, and unfortunately not unaccustomed to stuff like this with his dad—who Alex stared at warily in the alley. The other kid, Jonah Daniels, was his best friend and just happened to be the local pastor's son. That wasn't going to go down well. Alex didn't want to see Mateo lose his best friend, which might happen when his parents found out what they'd witnessed tonight.

"I'm good." But still lying on the ground with an injured woman in his arms. "Sasha?"

He heard her suck in a breath through clenched teeth.

"Fine." She lifted off him and sat up.

Alex glanced at the two boys. "Help her up." He didn't see any blood on her, though he thought she'd been hit.

As he climbed to his feet and brushed himself off, he saw her flinch and realized his suspicions were confirmed. She twisted to touch the side of her hip and her fingers came away wet with blood. "How bad is it?"

"I liked these jeans." She frowned. "Now there's a hole in them."

Not to mention a bloodstain. "Don't go anywhere. I'm calling this in."

He turned away, otherwise he'd have to contemplate the fact she'd taken a bullet for him—right before having to arrest her. Alex sent a text to the dispatch number and asked for a squad car. Sasha would then be put in cuffs, arrested because she'd saved his life. Probably. Maybe. Before it had even occurred to him to move, she had already begun tackling him to the ground.

Faster reflexes. Probably because she'd spent years wading through the criminal underworld. She'd need to be able to react like that. It'd likely saved her life on more than one occasion.

He strode to his brother, who looked ready to bolt. "You're not going anywhere."

"Alejandro—"

"Don't bother." He lifted a hand. "I don't wanna hear it from you. Only who that guy was, and why he wants you dead."

Those men from the other night, the ones who'd waylaid him outside the gym, might have been distracting him. That had been their intention, after all. But they'd also asked about Javier. So maybe that wasn't a lie.

"Do you owe money?"

His brother scrubbed at the stubble on his chin. "I've got it covered."

"Yeah? Thirty grand, is that it?"

Javier winced.

"I can help you, *Hermano*."

His brother barked a laugh. "Right. Roll over on them and put Mateo in danger—all so you get a conviction. Meanwhile, my life is *over*."

Alex had been trying to get his brother to turn confidential informant for years, but the drug habit he didn't seem to want to let go of meant he didn't always think straight. He needed to get clean and do the right thing. "It's because of Mateo that you need to do this."

"They roughed up *Mama*."

Alex got in his brother's face. "What did you just say?"

"Chill, okay? She's fine. Just a bruise, no big deal."

"*Talk*. And do it fast." An officer would be here in minutes, and he had to get Sasha locked down so this didn't go sideways. Who knew how she'd react to him arresting her?

Part of Alex didn't even want to do it. He quickly locked that feeling down, considering it was nothing but unhelpful emotion. Not a benefit in his job. Feelings got in the way of doing the right thing. And doing the right thing was what would get him what he wanted. Peace. Happiness.

He'd seen it over and over with his friends and colleagues. Good people, blessed with relationships that overflowed with love. Meanwhile, Basuto went home alone and then frequently got called out to haul his brother's behind out of one situation or another.

Because he hadn't yet done enough to earn what they all had.

Javier sighed.

Alex glanced at the boys. Sasha was nowhere to be seen, and the teens were both looking to the side. Talking low to each other. Watching something.

Someone.

He spun back to his brother. "Go in with whoever shows up. Tell them *everything*."

If this cost Javier personally, Alex was going to have more of a problem with him than he already did. And it was already huge. The risk was on his brother, not because Alex was doing the right thing.

Javier muttered something Alex didn't have the time to respond to. He picked up his pace and passed the boys. "Where is she?" His hip protested the movement, but he ignored it. Probably bruised from Sasha's tackle.

While she'd taken a bullet for him.

He spotted her over by a blue compact car and stretched out his legs to a long stride as he ran to her. "Leaving?"

She turned. Her face paled, and she started to fall.

"Whoa." Alex caught her. "You moved too fast, and the blood loss…" Did he need to explain this to her? "You caught a bullet for me."

"That wasn't the plan." She grasped his arms and held on to push off, but swayed.

"Easy."

"I need to get out of here."

"Yeah, to the hospital." The patrol car he'd requested wasn't here yet. If he left, he'd lose Javier for sure. But Sasha needed to see a doctor. The wound could be worse than he thought.

He shifted her to the side and opened the back seat. "Lie down." Then called back to the boys, "Tell the officer that shows up I'm taking her to the hospital."

Mateo nodded. Alex climbed into the front seat of her car. "Keys?"

She held them out beside his shoulder. He heard her shift and the moan that escaped.

"You okay?"

"Call Zander."

"You're going to the hospital."

Her chuckle sounded almost vicious. "No." She patted his shoulder with a cell phone. "Call Zander. I might need his doctor."

"He has a doctor?" Of course he did. Zander was a local guy and the senior member of a team of private security specialists. Their home base was in Last Chance. Usually, as was the case right now, they were off on some mission or job—whatever it was they did, and however they referred to it. "He's out of town."

"Just call him."

Alex wondered how she knew Zander but didn't ask. He didn't actually want an answer, because it would probably implicate him as an accessory in something. "I'm driving to the hospital."

"I'd rather you just shoot me right now. Tell Conroy you thought I had a gun. No one will question it. Execute me right here, and I might not wind up with a sentence of lethal injection."

His stomach flipped over.

Alex put the car in Drive and pulled onto the main street, then dialed Zander from her contact list and put the call on speaker in the cupholder.

It connected. "Yeah."

"Zander?" Two muffled explosions rang across the phone line.

"Basuto, that you?"

"Yes." He explained what'd happened. When Zander said nothing, he added, "She wanted me to call you."

A loud explosion rang out. Alex flinched. Zander came back on. "Kinda busy right now, and too far away to help. Sasha?"

She called out, "Yeah," from the backseat. She sounded a breath or two from passing out.

A second later, the other man said, "Get her somewhere safe."

Alex figured Zander was talking to him. "Like the hospital?"

Zander said, "If she even gets a whiff that the feds are closing in, she'll bolt and you'll never see her again."

Alex clenched his back teeth. "So why is she still here, where we all recognize her?"

"Do you?"

He knew now for certain that she was Melina. He still couldn't believe Sasha, of all people, was the girl he'd known. The girl who had gone through such unfathomable pain. They both had been changed that day. His entire life since that day had been destroyed by what they saw. Stripped of innocence and riddled with trauma and therapy. Even now, he couldn't think about what happened or he'd be unable to function. But Sasha—Melina—had endured much more pain than he was even willing to think about.

"Just tell me where to take her."

"Figure it out. But you take care of her."

That had sounded suspiciously like an order. But what struck him was the fact she was the kind of woman who inspired loyalty from a guy like Zander. "Who is she to you?"

There was a pause, but no explosion. Then Zander came back. "She's my ex-wife."

The line went dead.

Alex stopped at a red light. He squeezed his eyes shut and gripped the steering wheel. He was going to take her in. That was the right thing to do, and he didn't doubt his oath. Sasha was wanted by the feds.

But still, he could make sure this was done the merciful way. After he made sure she was patched up, he could convince her to turn herself in quietly.

Alex drove to his mother's house and pulled into the drive. He hauled Sasha's unconscious form from the car and carried her to the front door. He'd convinced his mom to lock up even when she was home, so he waited until she answered the door. Considerably smaller than him, she wore pressed slacks and a blouse, her hair a slightly different shade than last time.

Her eyebrows rose.

"Javier said you have a bruise."

"And you're carrying an unconscious, bleeding woman."

Fine, she wasn't going to explain. "You have a first aid kit, yes?"

She stepped back. "With Mateo in the house? Of course."

When he stepped in, she said, "Wait. Is that who I think it is?"

"Depends." He carried Sasha to the couch. "Are you going to mention the FBI Most Wanted list, or will you use the name Melina?"

"You know?" She studied him warily.

"Why was I the only person who didn't?"

"You didn't remember it." His mom hesitated. "You knew she'd been there with you, and you wouldn't let it go when the police found you. Screaming about how she was gone. So, when they got her back from…I told you she was safe now. Because she was."

"And I just forgot all about her?"

"They had you on a lot of medications." She winced. "You weren't well."

"I was so traumatized I forgot all about her?" He remembered pieces now. Back then was just a blur.

"Alejandro—"

He cut her off. "Can you just get me the first aid kit?"

He'd figure what to do about Sasha soon enough. After all, he had to. There was no way he could say he was headed to the hospital with an unnamed woman, never show up, and not have to explain to his boss, Conroy Barnes, the chief of police, exactly what this was.

The bullet had torn a hole in the hip of her pants. He widened the hole and got a look at the ragged wound in her skin. It seeped blood. His mom handed him gauze in a paper packet. He tore it open and pressed it against the injury.

Sasha moaned. Her eyelids flickered.

Alex squeezed antibacterial cream on it and managed to stick down enough of a bandage to cover it.

"Will she be okay?"

He stared at Sasha rather than look at Mama. She would see

the feeling on his face, and he wouldn't be able to hide the truth of it from her. "Zander vouched for her."

"You're not going to—"

Sasha blinked.

Alex pulled cuffs from the back of his belt and slapped one on her wrist.

"Alejandro!" Mama gasped.

Sasha's gaze flicked from him to his mother, and back to him. "So this is how it's gonna be?"

"This is how it's *got* to be."

"Don't make me regret saving your life." She frowned at him. "Please just give me a little time. Then I'll come in. I'll even do it so you get all the credit for arresting me."

She thought that was what he wanted? "I can't let you go. I'm a cop, and you're a fugitive. The FBI wants to talk to you."

"No, they want a scapegoat they can pin on whatever will stick. It doesn't matter what it is."

His phone rang in his pocket. Alex straightened and stepped away to answer it. Conroy, his boss, was calling. "Basuto."

"Clarke is dead. He was shot tonight outside the courthouse in Denver right before his arraignment." The chief's tone rang with frustration. "No one was supposed to find out, but *somehow* Sasha did because he's dead. She killed him."

Cold settled in him. "When?"

"Two hours ago."

Alex hung up. There wasn't enough time for her to get back here from Colorado if she'd actually done that. Before he could figure out how he'd tell Conroy and the feds that, he turned to look at her to make sure she was doing all right—though he had no idea why that even mattered to him.

But when he turned around, she was gone.

And Mama had an amused look on her face.

"What did you do?"

6

Sasha grasped the wheel and moved her foot from the brake pedal. A palm slammed the window beside her face.

Her foot slipped off the pedal and the car started to roll back. Down the drive.

She hit the brake, put the car in Park, and pressed the button for the window. Lieutenant Basuto glared at her as it rolled down. "Where are you going?"

She sighed. "Where do you think, *Lieutenant?*"

If he wanted to do this, then it would happen as cop and fugitive. Not as a man and a woman, or two people who'd been friends once.

"The feds want to talk to you."

He was still on that? It was like listening to a broken record. "You heard Zander. I'm not going to let them get me before I'm ready for it."

"And how long will that take?"

"All depends on you." She motioned to him with her index finger, a little bit satisfied by how confused he was. "I'll be in touch."

He again slammed a hand down on the open window frame. "Not so fast."

"You have to let me handle this in my way, Lieutenant." It was easier to think of him like that. Not a friend she'd had at seventeen, the last summer she'd been in town visiting her uncle and step-aunt. Probably her only friend back then. That bond hadn't survived what they'd witnessed together, but then neither had anything else about Melina, so it wasn't entirely surprising.

"It's Alex. You knew that the first second you saw me."

"And why did I get the feeling you didn't even recognize me?" She lifted her chin. "Am I supposed to believe you don't remember?"

He shook his head. "Pieces have come back. And what I recall of the...incident is pretty cloudy. I even blanked out your face. There's just the blood. So much blood." To his credit, he looked pale. Otherwise, she might not have believed he was serious. "The therapist said it was a good thing. My mind's way of protecting itself."

"Nice for you." Her tone sounded as deflated as she felt. That was the most major thing he'd been through that summer, and it was bad enough she supposed. Her experience had been substantially different, but he had no clue what she'd been through.

"I was the one who told the cops he took you when he left. But they told me later that they got you back. What else is there to remember?" His gaze searched her.

She wasn't about to explain that what'd happened in that time frame between her uncle being sliced up to the absolute destruction of the girl he'd known. "Maybe it's better you don't remember her. That girl is dead anyway."

Sasha hadn't fared much better in the years since. Melina had been weak, and for that reason, she didn't get to live. But the woman Sasha was now was too far gone. The years had finally caught up to her and she could no longer skate out from under the FBI or the justice department, or whoever else had a telescope pointed at her. Nor did she want to. Everything had consequences, and she would face hers. But she could put as much to rights as she was able to before that happened.

"You need to come in."

"I will." She stared out the front window. "When I'm ready."

"That call I just got?"

Sasha looked at him. He seemed troubled. Doubting. A wayward soul in need of reassurance. She kept her mouth shut since the last thing she needed right now was to connect emotionally with this guy. It would cloud everything and make all this that much harder.

"Clarke was shot."

Sasha flinched. "He—what?"

"Yeah. Two hours ago, while you were running around here in Last Chance, your former colleague was shot by a sniper outside the courthouse in Denver." He paused. "He was headed to his arraignment, escorted by US Marshals. They think you did it."

She swallowed against the lump in her throat and lifted her chin. "Who else would have?"

"I think you know. You were here, even though you told Bridget you were going to kill him."

She nodded. "I was mad."

"Unless you have a jet I don't know about, you couldn't have killed him. There wasn't enough time for you to get there and back between the time I saw you earlier yesterday and then again at the alley."

"If I had a jet, I'd be in Aruba by now."

"I can help you."

Because he'd been confronted with reasonable doubt that she might not be precisely as guilty as the feds thought? "Don't go soft on me now. They don't know half of what I've done. I probably *should* be in jail."

Sasha shoved the car in reverse and peeled backward down

the drive, spun the car around, and headed down the street at breakneck speed.

He'd be on the phone by the time she turned the corner onto his mom's street. His *mama*. What kind of a guy took a wanted criminal to his mother's house? It wasn't like he owed her anything for taking a bullet. She wasn't even killed. Just mildly inconvenienced. If he'd been shot, the world would have lost someone who'd actually made a difference.

It was a simple choice.

Only now he'd have the cops all looking for her car. She needed to ditch this compact somewhere. Didn't matter where. So what if they found it? That would just ensure they didn't waste more time than necessary watching for it.

Sasha dialed her phone at the first stoplight. It rang as she pulled away.

"Yeah?"

"Dorian?" She probably should've called Zander, but he'd seemed busy. Plus, he'd told Alex—Lieutenant *Basuto*—that they were married years ago. Unbelievable. Sasha was pretty sure no one else who knew either of them had any idea about that, especially because it'd been a hot second, seriously years ago. Their relationship had exploded right away. Like a grenade, it burned barely long enough to do any damage—except to the two of them. There was nothing left between them but debris.

Hardly worth talking about, even if they did still care about each other.

She was grateful they'd managed to forge a kind of frosty friendship that meant they traded business favors occasionally and helped each other if needed. While keeping score, of course.

"What's up, Sasha?" He sounded distracted.

Her sometimes partner. Her occasional avenging angel—maybe demon.

"Did you kill Clarke?"

"That was fast."

She turned another corner. "Did you? Because my safe house has been burned, a cop has seen the car I'm using, and now they think I killed Clarke. I have nowhere to go. No way to get there, and I've got to prove I didn't do this, too. It doesn't help that I told Bridget that I was going to take care of Clarke for her."

"You didn't, though. Kill him, I mean. And you told Bridget that weeks ago."

"The only reason I didn't kill him was because you told me not to." He'd shown up and convinced her that waiting on killing Clarke was the best course of action, and she'd gone along with it, even knowing that time would dampen the urge to get revenge. But not so *he* could do it later. Some kind of "favor" she didn't want or need.

He'd said he had a job to do. Was that it?

"You said it yourself. Betrayal means death." Dorian paused. "It's what I'd expect to come my way if I were to betray any of you, and I know Clarke felt the same." Dorian chuckled. "He looked at me like he knew, too. Caught his expression through the scope. He understood what was coming. So I gave it to him."

Sasha pulled over while her stomach roiled. Probably only because she'd been grazed by a bullet, hadn't eaten all day, and now it was nearly ten at night.

"Tell me I'm wrong."

"Millie and Bridget wouldn't agree."

"They're about the light," Dorian said. "You and I? We inhabit the dark places good people don't want to know about. We do the things they can't."

Sasha shivered.

"You didn't need him *or* all the leverage he had on you that could've been spouted to the feds, messing things up for you... This is about getting clear, right? You know Bridget is never going to forgive you."

"So it's a pipe dream being here." Sasha stared at the night sky, half watching for a cop car to discover her pulled over on the side of the street. "I should do…what?"

She honestly didn't know, and he might have an idea.

She wanted to be free, but the only freedom she'd be able to find was in death. And given what practically everyone she knew believed about the afterlife, even that wasn't going to mean she was done. No way could someone like her find peace in eternity.

It didn't work like that.

Frustration burned inside her. They'd say she only had to confess. One prayer and all of it would be washed away. But that didn't wipe the slate clean. How long would she even feel better for? An hour. A week, at most.

"Fine." He sighed. "Your plan isn't a bad one. I think I'd be inclined to do the same thing."

"So you're still good with being part of it?" The idea he could still double cross her didn't sit too well. She had betrayed others and been betrayed herself enough times to know the surprise just birthed a ton of extra problems. Ones she didn't need.

"I'm good. Don't worry about me. I'll take care of everything."

"Thanks." She nearly choked on the word.

"Yeah. Gotta go." He hung up.

She told herself it was just the wound on her hip making her less capable of containing her emotions. Pain was a trigger and things were a lot closer to the surface.

She rubbed her hands down her face and tried to sort through it all in her head.

But all she could think about was Alex.

His *Mama*. Sasha shook her head. What kind of guy did that? Like there was some personal connection he felt with her that existed years later. He honestly thought his mother would be safe with a wanted fugitive in her home.

Her mind wanted to conjure up images of Jonah. How close in proximity he'd been to her. How concerned he'd seemed. The bridge of his nose, which looked like hers used to look before it had been repeatedly broken. His jaw. The thickness of his hair.

Her son.

Today was the closest she'd ever been to him since the day she had given birth to him in Maggie's back room with only her and a midwife in attendance. After they'd cleaned him up, Sasha hadn't even looked at him. Saying goodbye would've been too hard.

The pastor and his wife had been waiting in the foyer.

Maggie had handed the baby over.

As soon as she'd been able to walk on her own, Sasha Camilero left Last Chance and never came back. Not until a couple of months ago.

Now it seemed like she *couldn't* leave.

Everyone was so worried about her and what she'd done that they weren't seeing the problem in front of their noses. That guy, the one earlier with the gun, could have hit any of those teen boys and killed any one of them when he'd shot at Basuto. It was only luck, or providence, or whatever anyone wanted to put it down to, that no one died. Then there was the guy who'd invaded Hope Mansion with his men. A thug with no concept of consequences—or kindness.

That kind of recklessness wasn't going to go unanswered.

Sasha had time. It would take a few days for her to get everything done so she was ready for Dorian. Until then, she would take care of this. Jonah would be as safe as she could make him.

And then, she would be done.

Dorian would put a bullet in her head the way he'd done with her enemy, and Sasha would be gone from this world.

On her terms.

7

Alex didn't knock. He strode into Conroy's office and held the paper file in one crushing grip.

"I've gotta go." The chief replaced the handset of his phone on the base. "What happened?"

Alex shook his head. The words wouldn't come out. His thoughts ran to where he'd been weeks ago when he'd talked Aiden through a stressful time. The now-sergeant had discovered his former girlfriend—the mother of his child—was actually alive. Not dead, as he had been told and for years believed. The shock that had been on Aiden's face that day must match the shock Alex now wore on his face.

Now he knew what it felt like to be on the other side of it. He couldn't even remember if what he'd told Aiden in reassurance was even sound. It didn't feel like any amount of words could take this sting away.

Alex bent nearly double and pressed the file against his legs as he breathed.

Conroy pushed his chair back. "Tell me what—"

He straightened, open palm raised.

Conroy didn't back off. He took the file from Alex's other hand and flipped it open while Alex stared at the painted mountains framed on the wall. The previous chief had decorated in plaid and animal trophies. Conroy's stance was more of a cele-bration of Last Chance and all it represented.

"Why are you reading this again now?"

He squeezed his eyes shut. "Sasha…"

"The woman the feds are chasing? Eric emailed me this morning. He said they've been hearing chatter that Sasha has a hit out on her. They think she might be at risk of being assassi-nated by one of her enemies."

Alex blinked.

"What does she have to do with—" Conroy waved the file. "—what you witnessed as a teenager?"

Alex stumbled to a chair and slumped into it where he ran his hands down his face. "Special Agent Cullings needs to know this."

Eric had a personal connection to this town. He was also the FBI agent at the head of the task force currently hunting Sasha. Not only that, but Sasha had previously worked for Eric's wife at her company. Alex wanted to kick himself. He'd arrogantly dismissed how difficult it was to remain impartial. He'd seen the look in her eyes when he said she was under arrest, and now he was past wondering if a personal connection might not be a good thing.

Conroy slapped the file on his desk. "You're gonna tell me first."

"Melina Vasquez *is* Sasha Camilero. It's her."

"How do you know?"

"I've seen her a couple of times in the last few days."

Before Conroy could launch in and chastise him, Alex continued, "She was involved with the incident at Hope Mansion. I saw indications she might've been living in the attic. And last night she took a bullet that was aimed at me. Javier owes money to some local guy. She and I both stumbled on whoever he owes trying to get their cash. At least, that's what I think happened."

Even besides updating the task force in charge of looking for Sasha on this new information he could provide, there was still a pile of work to do. From the guys who'd accosted him outside the gym, to the shooter from last night. The guy at Hope Mansion.

Alex waited for the recrimination.

"What you saw back then…"

Alex didn't want to think about it, but he had to. "She was right beside me, and I didn't even remember her face. So what else don't I remember?"

"That's not a black mark against you. Seeing that at fifteen? Even now, you or I, with all of our field experience, would have an issue stumbling upon someone cutting baggies of drugs from a man's stomach." Conroy shook his head, his expression almost too much to look at. "You had no frame of reference and no way to process seeing something like that."

"He was her uncle."

"And she was your friend. So when the guy took his drugs, and she tried to fight him off—"

Alex shut his eyes. He'd forgotten that, too. But apparently, Conroy already knew the file front to back. Melina had screamed and launched herself at the man over what he'd been doing when they walked in. Her uncle. Down on his luck, he'd agreed to be a drug mule to get heroin from Mexico. He'd died after one of the bags exploded in his stomach, and the dealer had shown up to retrieve his merchandise. They'd walked in to find her uncle laid out on the dining table with a man performing a macabre surgery on him.

He'd seen a lot in his life as a cop. A lot of awful things, and some truly horrendous. But not like that. Conroy was right. Nothing could've prepared him for it.

Or for the fact the man would take his drugs in such a barbaric way—along with seventeen-year-old Melina.

"I told the cops he took her."

"And that was the last you spoke for days. You were in shock."

"They told me they got her back." What they hadn't told fifteen-year-old Alex Basuto was what happened to her in the two days during which the drug dealer—and his friends—had kept Melina. The rest of their payment for the drugs they would never recover.

Bile rose in Alex's throat.

"They did get her back. She lived for nearly a year with Maggie—probably why she's sought refuge there now. And then she was gone. Chief Ridgeman asked around, but no one knew where she was, and Maggie told him she was fine." He paused for a second. "Basuto, you were fifteen. Cut yourself some slack."

"I should've…" He didn't know what.

"You barely survived as it was."

"From shock. Which means I did nothing."

"You had a concussion."

Alex frowned.

"It's in the report. Chief Ridgeman added a few notes after the fact, along with one to himself so he'd remember to swing by your mom's house and check if you were going to be okay to play football the next season."

"Really?"

Conroy nodded.

So much of those months afterward were a blur. He'd had a concussion? Along with the way his brain had protected itself from the trauma, it was a wonder he'd mentally qualified to be a cop. But there were a lot of years in there. Plenty of counseling and time spent getting space from what'd happened. There didn't seem to be any lingering issues.

Or there hadn't been. Until Sasha.

"You think you'll see her again?"

"I have no idea." Alex shrugged. "She's run away from me twice now." He stared at his clasped hands, between his knees.

He wanted to help her. And why not, when he let her down so thoroughly? They'd been friends. It was like he'd forgotten all about her, so wrapped up in his issues.

Melina had been…fire. Two years older than him. He'd followed her around like a puppy begging for scraps of attention. She'd been taken. He'd been hospitalized. And he hadn't found her later. Or if he'd asked, he was told to leave it alone. He didn't remember which it was. Maybe Maggie knew.

But what was the point dredging all that back up? The past was in the past, and they were both such different people now than the two kids who'd witnessed something horrific that day.

"Does the task force even know about her connection to Last Chance?"

"If they did, they'd be here looking for her."

Basuto had figured out that her aunt still lived in town, though he didn't think they had a relationship. "She's a survivor."

"She's still a criminal."

"That's where it all started." Alex motioned with a finger at the file on the desk. "Chief Ridgeman wrote it up like a rival gang came in and killed the three of them. The others were still there, and he arrested them. He had some theories about who it might've been."

"Why do you sound like you're thinking Ridgeman lied?"

"Because I think she got ahold of a weapon and killed them."

"Based on?"

Alex shrugged. He didn't want to go over the photos or other evidence that'd been collected from the three dead men. Or the fact they'd been found in the room with a very bloody and traumatized Melina Velasquez. A gun on the floor.

No one had even checked it for prints.

He'd thought he had the monopoly on drive and ambition. He'd practically worn it like a badge of honor. And yet, under it all, he'd gone through something like that and forgotten all about it. He'd used his passion for justice to justify going full bore in everything being a cop entailed. Test scores in the academy for fastest times, and best shot. Most arrests. Highest case closure. Youngest sergeant in the department. Now the youngest lieutenant.

He shook his head at himself. *So blind.* Maybe it wasn't realistic to think he'd have been able to do anything. Even in simply being her friend later. But that didn't mean he shouldn't have at least tried.

They'd absorbed the same blow, and he thought his experience equaled hers. He'd had no clue what she went through after. But now he did.

Conroy studied him. "You think self-defense justifies decades of breaking the law?"

Alex pressed his lips together. "It just sheds a new light, that's all."

"Be very careful here, Lieutenant."

"I need to be the one to bring her in."

Conroy caught himself. "That wasn't what I thought you'd say. But I'll still caution you to be careful. Don't put everything you've built in jeopardy."

And yet, in a sense, Melina—Sasha—and what'd happened back then had made him the cop he was. The kind who was going to bring her in peacefully to face the consequences of her actions, whether she liked it or not. After all, what they'd shared made him the one who could show her the most compassion. Especially now that he knew the whole story.

What she'd been through?

He wanted to rage. Throw a chair through the glass window that separated Conroy's office from the main bullpen.

Conroy stood. "I have to go. Mia has an ultrasound appointment." His boss tugged on his suit jacket. "Call Eric. Tell the FBI taskforce everything you know about Sasha. They'll probably set out for Last Chance the second you hang up with them, so prepare. We're about to be invaded by feds." Conroy gave him a pointed look.

Alex nodded. If he could convince Sasha to turn herself in or bring her in himself before the task force could drive up from Denver, that would be the best outcome.

And now there was chatter about a hit out on her?

He should've checked his email before he came in, but he'd been too absorbed reading about what had happened after they saw her uncle dead on his dining table.

Alex could picture the face of the man cutting into him, retrieving his drugs. But he couldn't remember what Sasha looked like back then. No doubt that image haunted her dreams as well—and for much worse reasons.

He ran his hands down his face again.

"I'll be back in an hour."

The door closed behind him, leaving Alex alone in his boss's office. He wanted to scream. Maybe even cry. But the emotion wouldn't come, and that was almost worse than being able to exorcise all the anger and pain.

"Lieutenant Basuto?"

He twisted to see Kaylee, their receptionist, in the doorway. "There's a kid at the desk asking for you."

Alex went to the counter, where a boy in a beanie and a blue jacket held a manila envelope. "Hi."

The kid lifted the envelope. "She said to give this to you."

"Who?"

The kid shrugged.

"She pay you?"

"Five dollars." The kid eyed him like Alex might object and demand the payment be handed over.

"You should've asked for ten."

Kaylee laughed. The kid's gaze flicked between them, and then he scurried out the door. She was still laughing when she said, "He'll be grifting within a year. By high school he'll have four streams of income."

Alex didn't find much that was funny about that. He had work to do, and it didn't include random mail deliveries. He had to call the feds with this update, then find Sasha and convince her to come in. Preferably before they got to town.

"What's in the envelope?"

"No idea." He tore open the flap at the top and pulled out a stack of a few pages of lined paper. All had been written on by hand. At the bottom of each page, it had been notarized.

This is my statement regarding the death of French Ambassador Theodore Terraine. All details included are true to the best of my knowledge.

"Whoa." Kaylee peered over her shoulder. "That guy was assassinated, wasn't he?"

"They never found the killer."

The signature on the last page of the document belonged to Melina Vasquez, also known as Sasha Camilero.

8

The sign out front read *Will and Hollis*. Around back, the door to the rear entrance had been propped open with a rock as long as Sasha's foot.

A security camera blinked, high on the wall. It wouldn't take long before she met resistance. Assuming someone watched the feeds constantly. This was a diner, so security might not be a high priority. Fry sauce, though? As far as she was concerned, that was top-tier priority. Not so much random people walking in the back door.

According to the county website, the place was owned by both the "Will" and the "Hollis" named on the front. One had lived here all their life. The other was a former FBI agent. Not just that, but an undercover agent.

He was the one Sasha worried about. But she'd seen him leave seven minutes ago and drive away with a paper cup of coffee in one hand. If he was coming right back, he'd have waited on the drink.

She snuck down the hall to the kitchen where the air seemed laced with that grease smell that all diners had. The kind that lingered on clothes even hours later.

Sasha leaned against the door frame to get a better look, out of sight of the counter and the window to the diner's main room. The place bustled with people. If someone knew where to look, any one of them could see her face and call the police, or tell someone later that she'd been here and who she'd been talking to. Then she wouldn't be the only one with problems.

Sasha studied the man at the grill. He'd filled out, in a good way, since the last time she'd seen him. Given that he had been involved with a South African gang and two rabid dogs, she wasn't going to hold it against him that he'd seemed a little emaciated. They hadn't fed him all that much during that time. Not exactly a captive, but she'd had to rescue him since they weren't about to let him leave.

Stuart was married now. No longer an operative for a private company spearheaded, it turned out, by a sociopath and conman.

His wife worked for the police department as their receptionist. They'd been through enough pain together, and now they were happy. No, Sasha wasn't going to bring additional trouble down on them.

An onion flew across the room.

Sasha caught it one-handed. "Better luck next time."

He chuckled to the grill. "You just gonna stand there and stare at me all day?"

"Trying to figure out what your wife sees in you."

"Next onion's gonna hit you in the forehead." Stuart glanced over with a grin on his face.

She stared. Everything he'd been through. The things she knew he'd seen, and things he'd done.

They were gone. His face held a relaxed sort of peace. She might even venture to say he looked happy.

"What?"

Sasha pulled the house key from her pocket. "Thanks for letting me stay at the cabin."

He eyed her. "Keep it. Unless you're leaving town today?"

She shook her head.

"Then you might need it again."

"So you can double-cross me and have the feds raid it in the middle of the night?"

"Now I know you weren't paying attention. You think I'd do that to you?"

"No." Nausea rolled in her stomach. "I'm sorry."

His whole body twisted to face her. "What's going on?"

She shrugged. "Other than the usual?"

"Are you dying?"

Sasha pressed her lips together, biting them between her front teeth.

"Tell me right now."

She shook her head, dismissing his request. "Thanks for letting me use the cabin. I do appreciate it."

"It's a lean-to. Kaylee won't even step a foot in it because she's a 'lady,' and she refers to it as a 'hovel.'"

Sasha felt the corners of her lips curl up. She liked Kaylee already. "It's cozy. So there's no running toilet? I don't see what the problem is."

Stuart tipped his head back and laughed.

The door from the diner swung open and a heavyset woman rushed in, her cheeks flushed. "What…" She spotted Sasha, and her eyes widened. "Oh. Uh, hi."

Her name tag read: HOLLIS.

"I won't be here long."

Hollis shook her head and waved a hand, then turned to Stuart. "Just make sure Will doesn't see her. If the FBI asks, he won't be able to lie." She glanced back to Sasha. "And give her some soup. If you're hungry?"

Sasha didn't want to admit she was starving. People who'd lived like the two of them had, and been the places they'd been, ate when it was available. Otherwise, they would often go days with no food if the mission called for it. That was what survival was.

"Feed her." Hollis disappeared back through the swinging door.

Stuart plated a cheeseburger and fries and put it on the counter. He spun the metal frame that held the orders with a magnet and then tossed two more burger patties on the grill. "Chicken soup or chili?"

She couldn't get over the change in him.

"Hollis will be cool. So don't worry that she went to go do something like call Conroy—"

"Who?"

"The chief of police in town."

Oh. "Alex's boss."

Stuart frowned. "Oh-kay. Hollis is good, though. She comes from a long line of criminals. Her whole family. She clawed her way through the fire—literally—to something good and beautiful. So she gets it."

Sasha turned her gaze to the swinging door. But she didn't kid herself that Stuart missed the sheen of tears in her eyes.

"Alex?"

She shook her head.

"Then tell me about Clarke."

"What does it matter what I have to say. The FBI believes I killed him, right?"

"How would I know?" Stuart waved his spatula. "I'm not an operative anymore. I'm a cook."

"Not even a chef?"

"I hardly create culinary masterpieces. And I have no qualifications."

"You always were good with knives."

He loaded a burger patty with two kinds of cheese, smiling.

"I told the Last Chance Police about Ambassador Terraine." She didn't want to mention Alex again. Not when Stuart would be able to see right through any story she came up with to dismiss the significance of Lieutenant Basuto and how he fit into her life.

Nothing but an annoyance. The man trying to arrest her.

An old friend…who'd grown into a handsome man.

No pushover. Someone who fought for family, even when they didn't fight for themselves. Who protected people. Who trusted his mother.

She didn't know what that kind of life felt like but guessed she'd be happier in a life like that than he seemed to be. In their brief exchange, she had gotten the feeling he was trying to grasp at something but couldn't quite grab hold of it. What did he want out of life?

Stuart broke out of his quiet. "Good. They should know about Terraine."

"I'm going to tell them everything."

Stuart nodded slowly.

"I'll leave your name out of it."

He shrugged.

"That's it?" She was a wanted fugitive. Meanwhile, he'd made a life for himself here. People thought he was a good person. And maybe he was…now. Sasha didn't have the same luxury. There was no one in her life to stick around for. No relationship that would settle her, suddenly transforming her into a homebody. A wife. A mother.

As if she could have any of those things.

What little she'd been given, Sasha at least had the right sense of mind to know she was no good for it. So she'd given her baby away, and he'd thrived here. And after she was gone for good, he would continue to thrive. With no help from her.

"What do you want me to say?"

Tell me not to do it. She respected him. If he thought her plan was a bad one, she wouldn't do it. That was how much weight she placed on his opinion. One of the few men in her life she'd managed to develop some semblance of friendship with. Though, she would never admit she cared for him.

At least Stuart still tolerated her presence.

Unlike Zander.

She was surprised her ex had even picked up the phone when Alex had called him from her number. He usually ghosted her.

"Are you going to tell the cops it was Dorian who killed Clarke?"

Sasha shouldn't have been surprised. Of course he knew. "They think I did it."

"You told Bridget you would."

"I did." She sighed. "Dorian talked me out of it, Clarke was arrested by the FBI…"

"And you disappeared."

She shrugged. "I needed a break. It was a crazy few weeks."

"You were running. Bridget was mad at you, and so was Millie and both their significant others. You wanted to meet… what's her name?" He glanced at the corner of the wall. "Right. Sydney." He shook his head. "Unicorn milkshake."

"What?"

"I squirt syrup around the glass." He shrugged. "Her idea. She brought all her little first grade friends in last week. They all got one. I ran out of sprinkles."

"What does that have to do with—"

"You know you want to meet her. She's your best friend's daughter."

"Bridget isn't my—"

"Don't bother lying. Just because she's never known y'all were best friends doesn't mean that's not how you feel about her." He shot her a look, then plated the two burgers. "You think of me as your brother, right?"

"Yeah. The annoying kind."

He grinned and gave her a short bow, then ladled chili into a bowl which he handed to her. "At your service." The glimmer in his eyes dissipated, the humor gone when he said, "Dorian isn't your friend."

"It's a business arrangement."

"Not for him."

"He isn't going to double-cross me. I know too much."

"He could say the same about you."

She leaned against the door jamb and spooned chili into her mouth, trying to look like a lady and not a starving lunatic.

"He's a wildcard you should have cut loose a long time ago."

"More than once I've thought the same about you. And yet, here we are."

She waved a hand, trying to add levity to the conversation. But there was no levity with Stuart. Even now that he seemed happy. At peace. Despite the laughter, he was still a man who had seen some of the worst the world had to offer. He'd taught her how to deal with her stress reactions. Without Stuart, she didn't know who she would be, or where she'd have ended up.

"Dorian is..." She wasn't sure how to explain. "It just is what it is."

"Because you don't think you should have good people in your life. You think you deserve what you've got now. That it's best for you. Or all you should expect."

She squeezed her eyes shut. She didn't want better. She just wanted *peace*.

"I know you don't want to hear it."

She wandered over and handed the bowl back. "I'll be careful."

"Why does that sound like a goodbye?"

What could she say to that? "Be happy."

His eyes flashed. "Sasha." Her name was a warning.

She shook her head. "I might see you around."

He followed her to the back door. "This doesn't have to be it."

"You know it does." She hugged him.

"No, no, no." He shook his head. "This is bad. So bad." He looked like a nervous boy, reminding her of another certain dark-haired teen.

"Don't worry about it." She stepped outside. "Everything will be fine."

"You said that to me before. Then we both had to jump off that cliff in Norway into that fjord with the name neither of us could pronounce, and we still managed to get hypothermia anyway."

Sasha couldn't help the laughter that bubbled up. "You made me watch that awful movie and I made you hot chocolate, and we laughed so hard marshmallows came out of our noses."

"Yeah, and Zander walked in on us in the middle of it. He nearly committed both of us to a psychiatric facility."

She swiped a tear from under her eye. "That was a good time."

"He'd have killed me if he hadn't already divorced you."

She grinned.

"Still," he said. "Best New Year's Eve I've ever had."

Sasha lifted her hand to wave and say goodbye to the only brother she'd ever known. A man who was no relation, but still family to her. More than any genetic relation she'd had.

A crack sound splintered across the parking lot.

Her whole body snapped taut, and she saw Stuart topple back inside.

Sasha screamed.

9

"After that, she ran off."

Alex twisted to the tree line, where Stuart indicated. He'd been in the office when the call came in and figured anything concerning an active shooter and shots fired meant Sasha had something to do with it.

He turned back to Stuart who sat on the back step of the diner holding an ice pack to the side of his head. "And Hollis called it in?"

She stood behind Stuart, her anxious gaze scanning the tree line. Did Hollis and Sasha know each other? Hollis seemed concerned about her. Or was this just about a shooter and her diner? Her employee, and a woman she didn't know.

Neither said anything, so he asked, "Why was she here?"

Hollis shook her head. She didn't know.

Stuart studied him for a second. "*Alex.*"

"What?"

"Nothing. Explains some things, though." He seemed to debate for a second. "Sasha and I have known each other…a while."

"You know about Zander?" If Stuart really had "known her

a while," then surely he would know the private security team leader was her ex-husband.

"Our friendship post-dates her thing with Zander."

"Rebound?" The last thing Alex wanted was to be confronted with yet another ex of Sasha's, but life was life. He had no claim on her and no right to form an opinion of her prior romantic relationships.

It wasn't like they were ever going to have one.

"It was never like that." Stuart lowered the ice pack. "She's more like my sister. And a good friend, though we don't see each other all that much. In fact…" He didn't finish.

"Tell me."

"As a cop, or as a man who wants to know about Sasha?"

Alex frowned. "What does that matter?"

He didn't have anything to do with Sasha. Not considering how thoroughly he'd abandoned her. Despite the fact he'd had no tools back then to help her through a situation like the one they'd both endured, he still felt like he'd let her down. As though he could've fought through his trauma and done something. Or that he *should* have.

Hollis gasped. "Stuart. Are you saying they're..?"

"I guess we'll find out."

Alex flipped his notebook shut. "Does one of you want to explain what you're talking about?"

Stuart looked like he wanted to smile, but he didn't. He was far too stoic for that. Alex had only ever seen him soften enough to smile at Kaylee. If he and Sasha were friends…

"It seemed like she was here to say goodbye." Stuart paused while Alex absorbed that, then continued, "If that means anything to you."

Alex shrugged. "Why would it?"

He turned to the tree line. Searching for her. Or, at least, it would appear so.

Instead, his thoughts roiled. The envelope, a statement from her point of view detailing the assassination of that French ambassador. She'd been in the car at the time, simply a bystander there on an operation—though she hadn't given details of what the job was, or who had hired her. The car had been overrun with gunmen on a street in New York City, and the ambassador had been taken.

She hadn't been able to stop that many hired guns. However, she'd given detailed descriptions of physical features, tattoos, and any other discernable thing under their black fatigues and knit ski masks. She'd even deemed the brand of their boots relevant enough to include.

The ambassador's body had washed up days later. No witnesses. No evidence. No leads.

Now, because of her statement, they were able to close a file the FBI had listed as a cold case. They had never attributed it to Sasha, or her presence in the car, and had no new leads in the last eight years as to who might've done it. The case file didn't mention a woman being present at all.

Yet she knew.

She'd been there.

What else had she seen or done over the years since she disappeared from Last Chance, and more recently, when she'd reappeared?

He wanted to contemplate the idea. But how was it relevant? Sasha was a wanted woman, hunted by the FBI. He was a local law enforcement officer. The two didn't mix. And he certainly shouldn't get involved in anything regarding a case against her. He was way too personally connected to be impartial.

Because of their shared history. Seeing her uncle like that.

Not because he had any kind of feelings for her. Even if he did, that shouldn't play into what happened to her now. He would compromise the FBI's case through interference, not to mention jeopardize his career and fall prey to being swayed by his emotions.

Right now, he needed laser focus. That was the only way

he'd know he had earned anything good that came along in his life.

"Guess that's why she came to see me," Stuart said. "Because you don't mean anything."

Alex winced. He didn't turn around. It wasn't an insult, but it felt like one all the same. Another way he'd failed, even if this wasn't something he wanted to succeed at. "Do you think she'll come back?"

"With Sasha, who knows? She'll do what she thinks is right."

He turned then. "Is that true? Like some kind of criminal code?"

"It doesn't matter if you believe it's real or not. We all have principles."

"You mean situational ethics." Changing your morals and values depending on the circumstances was something he saw frequently. Alex's principles were unwavering. Good things came to people who earned them. Being a criminal got you killed, eventually. Truth and justice were the highest good.

Stuart shrugged. "We all get to decide what we believe in and what we think is important."

"The *law* is important."

"There it is."

Whatever that meant. Even Hollis bristled.

Alex glanced again at the trees. "I'm going to look for the shooter." And Sasha.

"He's long gone, whoever he is." Stuart leaned against the door frame, his eyes slightly glassy. Not surprising since he said he'd hit his head on the floor when he fell. "I'm not going to bother arguing for compassion because I know it won't penetrate. But I will say this. Sometimes we find our justice. It doesn't always have to be imposed upon us."

Alex frowned.

"She sent you the statement, right? Ambassador Terraine."

He nodded, unsure where Stuart was going with this.

"That means she trusts you'll do the right thing with it."

"If it's true, sure."

Stuart winced. "She chose you for a reason. Her survival dictated she reach out to someone she thinks she can trust. That's why she came here, and in her own way she let me know she wasn't going to last much longer. I don't know what she's planning, but you're a part of it whether you want to be or not."

Before he could say anything, Stuart continued, "You make her vulnerable."

Alex wasn't about to be bullied into anything. "She's going to leave. After she's enacted whatever she has planned to conjure up more sympathy. The injured party. A wanted fugitive, wrongly convicted of crimes. She has intel no one else has and provides that to the police. Then, when we're all feeling serious doubts about her guilt, she disappears. Never to be seen again."

The idea coalesced as he spoke aloud.

Had he been harboring the idea at the back of his mind? Not once thinking it through, and yet part of him seemed to believe she had no intention of coming in to prove her innocence or face her guilt. Perhaps this was nothing but a game to her, and Sasha enjoyed giving the feds—and Alex—the runaround. Stringing them along.

After dropping the bomb about what happened to that ambassador, she was probably long gone now. Pretending as though her life was in danger, she'd paid someone to shoot at her and sell the concept of being on the run.

Stuart stepped past him, bumping Alex's shoulder a little in the process. "There she is."

Sasha strode toward them. He could see the slight limp in her stride, a result of the gunshot wound on her hip he knew was there. Did Stuart know? He doubted anyone else would notice it, the movement was so minuscule.

Why was she still here?

Stuart glanced over his shoulder at Alex. "You think it's smart to approach a cop in broad daylight? She could be seen.

You could take her in at any moment, and you likely will. So, she's either counting on it, or she has a plan so that doesn't happen. But she's still here, and she's approaching you. As I said, you're part of this whether you like it or not."

If it was him, he'd be in Aruba as she'd said earlier. That she wasn't had nothing to do with the fact she had no plane of her own. It wasn't all that hard to get a fake passport and book a ticket. She could have disappeared weeks ago. Instead, she'd been living in Maggie's attic and hanging around town.

Alex couldn't figure her out at all. The woman made no sense to him.

He didn't need Stuart repeating himself, trying to get the concept to penetrate Alex's thick skull. He was perfectly capable of absorbing different opinions. It wasn't helpful to be so bull-headed as to never consider other ideas.

That left no room for change.

"The shooter?"

She shook her head in response to Stuart's question. "Long gone by the time I got to the spot where he'd set up."

Now there was no evidence of a shooter left? Even someone with her supposed skills hadn't caught whoever was there. If anyone had *been* there. Maybe she'd set up a remote system on a timer to pull a trigger with some kind of mechanism. The illusion of a shooter trying to kill her.

A good sniper didn't miss often.

She hadn't been hit and neither had Stuart. Could be she'd only planned for this to seem like an attempt on her life. When the truth was that it was nothing but subterfuge.

She was cunning. He wouldn't put something like this past a woman like her—one on the FBI Most Wanted list.

Stuart approached her, tearing open a packet. Alex realized that while he'd been seething with conspiracy ideas about her, the other man had rummaged through the first aid kit Hollis had brought for him.

Stuart lifted whatever he'd retrieved, raising his hand in Sasha's direction.

Her hand whipped up and grasped his forearm. They faced off. Two people accustomed to sparring with each other.

Stuart's voice was soft. "You have a cut on your cheek."

"Probably a branch whacked me." She released his arm. "I was running." Stuart let her take the wipe from him, and he stepped back. She tried to clean the cut herself but didn't get all the blood.

Alex moved to her. "You missed a spot."

She allowed him to take the wipe and held still while he dabbed. She only winced a fraction. Not much at all, even when he edged the scratch on her cheekbone.

Alex was careful not to touch her. He'd have laid a hand on her shoulder, or maybe even steadied himself with a hand on the back of her neck, his fingers threaded in her hair. If it had been anyone else.

He'd read through her file and now knew what had happened to her. Though, even much of that had been implied by the former police chief and not overtly stated. The state she'd been in when they found her. The injuries she'd sustained and the fact the rape kit results had returned four separate semen samples.

Alex dabbed too hard. Sasha frowned.

"Sorry."

She studied him. There seemed to be a lot of that happening between them, and even with Stuart around.

Alex figured that was because this woman remained a stranger for the most part. He was intrigued by her. Alex could admit that much to himself.

He even wanted to help her.

10

H e *knew*. He had to know, considering she'd figured it out. It wasn't that much of a stretch to conclude there was someone in town trying to kill her. Sasha exercised situational caution all the time. She never let down her guard unless she could help it. All that got you was deep in trouble.

So, yeah, someone was trying to kill her.

And that had nothing to do with the arrangement she'd made with Dorian, which didn't come into effect for days.

Alex offered her a tiny packet of antibiotic ointment.

She shook her head. "Is it bad?" She'd been slapped by a few trees while she ran through the woods around the diner. Seriously, this was a terrible place to live. There were so many spots a sniper could sit and never be seen, it was ridiculous.

"You okay?"

She sighed. "Whoever took that shot is going to hang around and try again. He'll hole up in the trees for days. Maybe even weeks."

"We'll find him."

"No, you won't. This guy is a professional. I saw the spot where he set up." She glanced at Stuart. He would know exactly what she meant.

"Clean?"

She nodded. "Two impressions for the stand, a depression in the grass where he lay."

Alex said, "But he missed."

"Or he tried to hit *me*." Stuart tipped his head to the side. "Could be one of my enemies."

"You think?"

"No. But this is a free exchange of ideas, right?"

Sasha shook her head. "Not if they're unhelpful. No one is here to kill you."

"What makes you so sure about that?" Alex asked.

"Because I have an alert out with all the major brokers. People in our circles who contract that kind of thing. Act as the middleman. If someone wanted Stuart dead, I would know."

Alex's brows rose. It had occurred to her that he was a handsome man. The cop badge—or shield, or whatever they called it—she'd usually shy away from. But he made it work. The fabric of his suit jacket stretched across his broad shoulders. He had a stocky build and average height, nothing special. *Keep telling yourself that.* She didn't study his eyes too closely. Sasha was liable to get distracted from reality if she did that.

His lips parted in a tiny smile.

She huffed. "It isn't Stuart. It's me. We can't go looking for him. He *won't* be found."

Alex shrugged. "We can call someone better. Like Zander."

"The Last Chance police does that? They call a professional team of security experts every time they get in a bind?"

"No."

Great. So he was just about making exceptions where *she* was concerned. Or he figured Zander would care enough to wade in. Which was doubtful.

Sasha set a hand on her hip. "Did you get my package?"

He nodded.

"And?"

"Why'd you send it?"

As if she wanted to get into the nuts and bolts of her plan. She turned to Stuart. "Are you okay after..?"

"Bumped my head."

"Concussion?"

He shook it, then winced.

"Yeah. Might want to curtail that for a while." She grinned, and he returned it.

Alex said, "I don't know why you think you have any reason to be amused. Nothing about any of this is funny."

"You have to find joy where you can." To Stuart, she said, "I'm glad you're okay. Tell Kaylee I said hi."

Stuart nodded. "Bye, Sash."

There was a weight to those departing words. As Sasha headed for her car, she shoved that weight away because she didn't want it on her shoulders. This was going to be hard enough. There were people in this world she cared about. And ones who would genuinely mourn the loss of her.

Sasha didn't want to think about it.

The priority here was making sure she stayed alive long enough to finish everything she wanted to do. And to accomplish that, she was going to have to remain vigilant every second. Scan the vicinity. Keep all her instincts aware. She could feel eyes on her, the way she had many times before.

That instinct had let her down when she'd been talking to Stuart. Lulled into a false sense of security, distracted by their friendship and saying goodbye, she'd allowed the shooter to strike.

Not again. This was too important.

"It's good you aren't unaware someone tried to kill you today."

She didn't turn to Alex but kept walking. He would say what he had to say regardless.

"A lot of people can't comprehend it, so they dismiss the idea and act like it's not a thing. Then they wind up getting hurt."

"Great." She reached her car and turned to see him eyeing it.

"Stolen?"

"Run the plates." She folded her arms. "Find out for yourself." He was on the job, after all. Buttoned up. Investigating crime and safeguarding innocents. She knew where she fell in the scope of those things. "I'm guessing if I'm dead, there will be less paperwork. Case closed and all that."

"Why don't you just come in. You'll be safe." He leaned in for long enough to say, "Case closed."

As if. "The FBI has already made up their minds about me. What is there to say when they're not going to listen to a thing?"

"You'd plead your innocence, is that it?"

"I'm not clean. I've never lived clean."

"That's not true."

"Fine. *Sasha* has never lived clean." She wasn't going to kid herself that he hadn't figured out exactly who she was by now. If he hadn't, then he wasn't half the cop she thought he might be. "They'll find plenty to pin on me."

She could argue she'd had scruples. The sanctioned kills she'd undertaken for the government might have been controversial ones no one else would do. She'd vetted each one and found that the black mark put on her soul was well worth getting scum like that off the face of the earth. Too many deserved to die.

She wasn't the judge, the one dispensing justice. She was simply the executioner. A nameless, faceless killer who enacted the will of those in charge.

Sure, when she'd been in fifth grade and had to write that paper about what she would be when she grew up, it certainly wasn't this. She'd wanted to be a dance teacher. But plans changed. She'd rolled with the opportunities life had given her and made some money doing things she could live with.

There was already plenty in her that kept her up at night. She didn't need to add to it. That was why, when the black grew too big for her to handle, she'd quit and gone to work for Millie at the accountant's office. She'd spent the last several years doing good in the world. Helping people who needed to find peace.

Even if that would never happen to her.

"I know what happened to you, Melina."

Shame bubbled to the surface, but she shoved it back down. "Don't call me that."

Alex took half a step back and winced as he moved.

"I'm not her."

"She wasn't weak." He frowned. "And she didn't deserve what happened to her."

"I know both of those things." She wanted to scream. To shake sense into him and make him drop it. But why would she do that when she could simply walk away from Last Chance and never look back? Sure, the FBI would hunt her forever. She would never be able to live free and wouldn't be able to end her life knowing she'd done all she needed to do.

Sasha took a step back. "Melina was unprepared for what was coming. But Sasha won't be."

Alex started to speak but caught himself.

She waited. He genuinely seemed torn. She spoke up, "You should just let me go. Don't get involved." There was plenty in his life to worry about. She would send him three more envelopes he could pass on to the FBI, and that would be it.

There was no time for regret.

He reached out but let his hand fall back by his side without touching her. "I'd like to help you."

"I don't need pity. And I don't need allies."

"Yet you've managed to build a group."

"They don't interfere." She could confirm that for sure when she talked to Dorian to find out if he knew who had fired at her and Stuart today. "They accept that I make my own choices. And I know what I'm doing."

"You think it's good they just do their thing and never put their necks out for you? That's not friendship or loyalty."

"You don't know any of the things they've done for me."

"And yet—" He lifted his chin. "—your best friends don't show up to speak for you. They don't come when you need help, or work to protect you."

"I don't need protection."

His expression softened to one of sadness. "And if I try to help, whether you agree or not?"

He wouldn't...

"I could talk to the FBI on your behalf. Negotiate for you to say what you need to say, and even make sure you get a fair shake in the judge."

"You don't have that kind of pull."

"Maybe not, but I can try. Or you could call whoever you know that does have the weight to make a deal for you, and they could get something worked out. But you won't do that, will you?"

She didn't answer. He already knew.

"That's what I thought."

"Being self-sufficient isn't a bad thing. And I *earned* my independence."

He spoke with a soft voice, "I know you did. I know you don't owe anyone anything, and you don't bank favors to use later. But I want to owe you. I feel like I should. And I want you to ask me to help you."

"Not if it jeopardizes your job. What if I ask too much, and you can't, or won't, do it? What's the point? You want to negotiate, but the fact you wouldn't cross a line is something I respect about you, even if that by-the-book thing infuriates me."

His lips curled in a smile.

"There's nothing funny about this." She repeated his words from earlier, but in a far snootier voice.

He chuckled.

"Before you get busy helping me, maybe you should work on

getting your own house in order." Sasha folded her arms. This was why she didn't have family entanglements.

Alex frowned. "What do you mean?"

"That guy from yesterday. And the kid. They were your relatives, right?"

He nodded. "My brother Javier, and my nephew Mateo. The other boy is my nephew's best friend, Jonah Daniels."

"Javier is in trouble, and if he's not careful, the boys are going to get caught up in the crossfire. And if you're not there to help out? Which you won't be if you're doing favors for me with the feds. What then?"

"You don't want my help, then? Fine."

"Doesn't mean I'm making this up." She wanted him to make sure Jonah would be okay, as well as his best friend. She'd seen guys like his brother Javier before. He needed help before he got in much deeper with whichever gun-wielding sniper sent that bad shot.

"Maybe I need *your* help with Javier." Alex shrugged. "We could help each other out."

She was about to tell him where he could go stick his offer when her phone rang. That was probably for the best. She slid it out and recognized the number from Hope Mansion. "Maggie?"

She sounded out of breath. "Sasha, it's bad."

"What happened?"

"Those men came back. Mr. Perkins and his friends. Emily was already torn up. They knocked her out and took Ian. He was screaming." Maggie pushed out a breath. "Lord, he was screaming so loud."

"Did you call the police?"

"Dean is on his way for Emily. I'm calling them next."

"Why did you call me?"

"Sasha." Maggie quieted. "You saw those men. It's different. He's a little boy. That man might be a monster, but he doesn't want to hurt his son. At least physically." The implication he'd hurt the child in other ways was clear. Emotionally. Psychologically.

Sasha could only guess.

"And he was asking about you. Who you were."

She looked at Alex and that questioning gaze of his. Without thinking too much about it, she said, "Tell Emily we'll find Ian."

11

A lex jabbed a finger at the screen on the dash of his patrol car. The call connected and he answered, "Basuto."

"It's me." The screen read Chief Barnes, and the voice came through the car speakers. "I want an update."

Alex pulled out of the drive of Hope Mansion where they'd spent the last hour figuring out what had happened. "I just got done speaking with Maggie and some of the residents."

In the passenger seat, Sasha sat completely still. Her mouth in a tiny O shape, she even breathed silently. Nothing was going to induce her to make a noise and alert Conroy to her presence in the car.

It was also seriously cute.

Sure, she was a wanted woman and shouldn't be in his patrol car. He was breaking the law even just having her up front and not cuffed in the back. But if she could help find Ian? Her skills. Her connection to Hope Mansion, and the fact she'd seen those men, while he hadn't? That made her an immediate asset.

Legally he could be in the clear if she aided this investigation. More so if she helped secure the child and then gave herself up into his custody.

"Emily had her head slammed against a door frame. Dean got her to the hospital so she can be assessed. There was major head trauma, but I hope we'll be able to talk to her more. She was shaken up and didn't make a whole lot of sense. The others filled me in enough."

"Thomas took Ian?"

"Yes."

Conroy was silent for a moment. Sasha shifted in her seat. She pulled out her phone and started texting. The FBI didn't know about that phone or they'd be tracking it for sure.

"He was in and out quick. Overwhelming force. More guns than last time."

Conroy said, "He probably thought Sasha would be there again."

Out the corner of his eye, he spotted a flash of Sasha's white smile.

"Probably." Alex nearly grinned, but he was also well aware he was sharing a moment of amusement with a criminal he was supposed to, if found, hand over to the FBI. What would Conroy say if he knew? "But she wasn't. And either way, it's good no one else was hurt. They're all terrified enough."

"What about Maggie? She's been known to stand at the door with a shotgun if need be."

Alex winced. He'd seen that with his own eyes. She had the right to protect herself and those who lived in her care. But gun ownership and use should never be taken lightly. By anyone. It might be a right, but it was also a privilege. Anyone with the ability to hurt another person—physically or otherwise—should be cognizant of that very fact.

Alex said, "It was likely good she wasn't there." If she had been, they might've killed her. "Maybe they planned it that way."

"I'm thinking the same."

In the passenger seat, Sasha shook her head.

Alex agreed with both of them. "If they waited until she left, then moved in, they'd be assured of less resistance, even if Marta was on duty." She was much older and might still be spry, but they were talking about six gunmen.

He thanked God it hadn't been a blood bath. He'd seen more than one of those in his life, though Melina's uncle had been the worst by far. He didn't need the therapy bill it would bring from having to relive it over and over again.

"And with Sasha gone as well——"

Conroy cut him off. "I won't ask if you've seen her since. The FBI can deal with that. We have a child to find."

Sasha shifted in her seat. The tilt of her head conveyed surprise, something he didn't think she experienced often.

"It's my understanding," Alex said, "that Maggie may have called Sasha to aid with the search."

Sasha smacked his arm, but not with much force. He shook his head. Should she turn up, or be spotted by someone from Last Chance PD, it made more sense if he was the one who'd laid the groundwork. Yes, they might now be keeping an eye out for her. But if it was clear she was helping, things could go easier.

"If that's true, I can tell the FBI when they get here," Conroy said. "Catch her in the act. But that might jeopardize Ian's wellbeing, and I'm not a man or Chief of Police who's okay living with that on his conscience. So I'm with the judge now. I'll have the warrant ready by the time you get to the Perkins's primary residence."

"Copy that."

The chief hung up.

"Is that it?"

Alex took the turn for the highway to head for the Perkins's house before he answered her question. "The chief won't exactly be happy when he finds out I aided you when you shouldn't be free. But it's the FBI's problem to deal with. I might get temporarily suspended or put on administrative leave." He shrugged one shoulder. "Ian is the priority."

"Agreed, which is why we should part ways. You'll only get in trouble. And I can just call you if I get any intel."

"Careful. It almost sounds like you care about what happens to me."

That got him another light slap and a flash of her smile. "You know what I mean." She looked out the window. "I don't like children being in danger."

"Neither do I." He wanted to squeeze her hand and offer some kind of physical comfort but didn't. They pulled up at a stoplight. "Help me find him, Sasha."

She turned to him. So independent. Strong and capable. These glimpses of the vulnerability in her touched him. She might not need or want protection, but he would always want to give it to her.

"Sasha—"

"The light's green."

He hit the gas.

"No one would honk at a police car. But they *will* think you're just looking at your phone." She smirked. "Being in the front seat of one of these things is weird. Can you imagine me as a cop? What a terrible idea."

"Maybe a private investigator."

"Hmm. Like Tate." She pressed at the material of her black pants above her knee. "And he already skirts the edge."

"Zander never asked you to join his team?"

She shook her head. "I think he was about to, right about the same time it was clear we should just get a divorce. It seemed more amicable than one of us killing the other, or one of his team guys killing both of us. We were all miserable. I went back to work for the government after that, but—"

"You worked for the government?"

"I thought you read the FBI file."

"I did. There's nothing about the CIA in there."

"It was off-book. More secret than the Agency wants to admit to."

"Huh." He pulled onto Perkins's street. "I had no idea. But finish what you were saying."

"I didn't like it. It didn't make me feel good about myself." She stared ahead as he found the house. "The guy in charge was new and made me feel weird. I can't work for someone who makes me feel uncomfortable, even if he never did anything overt. And I didn't like the jobs he was giving me, so I quit and went to work for Millie."

"Huh."

"I'm not a good person. I've done a lot of awful things, but my actions aren't all that condemns me. Doesn't the Bible say we're, like, evil to the core, or whatever? Thoughts. The things we say. Not just what we do. Even what we believe can be a sin. Or doing nothing. Or saying nothing."

"Okay." He put the car in park and twisted to her. "So where's the hope?"

"I haven't found it. Yet. I'm not just going to pray some prayer and let it all get wiped away. I have to pay *something.*" She shook her head.

"I always figured that when I finally earned it, the peace would just appear. It would be right in front of me." And yet, despite everything, and even though he hadn't yet felt like he'd earned anything in life, she made him feel...calm. Content. Even while the rest of the world swirled around them.

"Like a gift? But one you earned. That's what you've been looking for?"

He shrugged. "I am the kind of person who has to earn it, even if it is freely given."

"I don't think I get that."

"I want to be worthy of it."

"Maybe you already are."

He wasn't so sure, especially if she was right that the Bible said no one was a good person. That wasn't even the point of any of this. "I think I would know. Wouldn't I?"

His phone buzzed in the cupholder. He spotted the email address and the subject line. "Conroy." Alex swiped through to make sure. "We have a warrant to search the house."

"So backup is on the way?" She looked around as though she was expecting to be swarmed with cops at any moment now.

"Nope. We're spread thin. You think he's hiding his kid back at his own home?"

She frowned. "The house does look pretty dark."

"Let's go make sure." He cracked his door, and she met him at the driveway.

"I'll take the back door."

Alex didn't argue. It was a good idea, and she had training. "Just don't shoot me."

"Tempting. But I'm good."

He knocked on the front door, smiling at her words. They brought out a lightness in each other that he enjoyed. It seemed strange, but he didn't fight it. *Thank You, God.* He didn't say that enough. He was too busy striving to be worthy or trying to convince everyone—and himself—that he was sufficient to receive what he wanted.

The door swung open by itself, not properly latched shut. Alex wandered through the living area.

"Clear!"

He found her in the hall.

"Isn't that what you guys say?"

"Yes. No one's here?"

"Not that I found." She turned. "Place is a mess."

"Yes, it is." He found a bedroom, the master. Bedclothes were askew, drawers open. The closet had been trashed as though whoever lived here had grabbed everything on hangers and pulled it all free in one grab. "Suitcases? A duffel bag?"

There was an empty spot on the floor of the closet where it looked like those were normally kept.

"They left in a hurry."

"So he's rushing, not planning. Or he already had a place set up they can go to." Alex scratched the stubble on his chin. "Maybe Emily has an idea where that might be. A favorite place, or a cabin he owns."

"You think he told his wife that stuff? Maybe while he was beating her?"

Alex decided to leave that topic alone. "Then we'll check financials. See if he owns property anywhere."

"I'd stay with friends." She narrowed her eyes on the dresser, which looked like a tornado had blown through it. "Or get an RV. In someone else's name. Or cash, and register it on a fake ID. You'd never find me."

Alex stared until she looked at him.

"What?"

"Maybe you could write this down," he suggested. "The cops in this town need those kinds of out-of-the-box ideas to consider when they're working cases."

She shook her head. "No way I'm telling a bunch of cops my secrets."

And yet, she was telling him.

Alex got on his phone. Conroy answered quickly, and he explained the state of the house. "They left in a hurry."

His boss sighed. "Thomas and the kid's stuff both?"

Alex moved to the room that belonged to a child, though not one who was doted on. He had few toys and not much stuff. Things didn't mean love, but kids had to be able to play with *something.* "Nothing here for either of them." He mentioned the property idea.

"I'm running that now. And when the wife wakes up, we can ask her more questions."

"Copy that."

"I'm alerting state police. Thomas and the boy are in the wind. And I'm informing the FBI as well because I'm not messing around with this. The case is now federal." Conroy hung up.

Alex turned to Sasha, so he could tell her what his boss had said. But she wasn't in the hall. Or out front.

She was gone.

"He said to ask you for ten dollars."

Sasha grinned at the kid. "Is that right?" She pulled out an additional five and handed both over.

The boy hugged the envelope to the front of his jacket.

"If the lieutenant isn't there, hand it to the woman at the front desk. Kaylee."

"I know her. She gives me root beer suckers."

Sasha watched him walk across the parking lot. The kid's paper route took him down this street. She'd clocked him a few weeks ago, established a relationship, and had no problem giving him ten dollars instead of five.

He disappeared inside the police department with the second envelope for Alex. This one was a recounting of the apparent murder-suicide of two prominent Senate aides. She'd been offered the job but turned it down. She had, however, made a point to know who had taken the job and who had been contracted to have it done. Both were included in the statement.

The killer's career was the stuff of legends. Different mode of operation every time, never discovered. Later she'd followed up, just to make sure she wasn't wrong. It was his handiwork that'd killed them. She'd included information for Alex so that he could have access to the email account and find the message and its reply in the inbox. She'd scrubbed everything else.

Those two kids—twenty-something, smart, going places, trying to make the world better—hadn't deserved to be cut down like that. Not when the real culprit had never been discovered. Justice had never been served.

But she could make sure the FBI had what they needed so it did, finally, and so their families could know the truth.

She turned away from the police department and headed for her car, parked on a side street. Yes, she'd ditched Alex last night. She'd heard what Conroy said about the FBI. Sasha couldn't be anywhere near the hunt for that boy without being seen. That meant she'd be arrested. If she was going to help find him, she had to do it her way.

She'd also maybe, kind of, freaked out about that little boy's bedroom. She was at least willing to admit that to herself.

Just the sight of it had brought back so many childhood memories of her mom's trailer. She'd rushed silently out the back door so she could cry a bit and try not to scream in the backyard. Not that anyone would see her do it back there.

After that, she'd headed to her attic at Maggie's, figuring no one would look for her there given the location had been burned. She'd spent the night scouring the local county website and their postings of mug shots. Finally, she found the man who had shot her in the alley, even though she'd been looking for the men with Perkins.

Don Evers had been arrested for being in possession of narcotics. Not for shooting at her.

He was out on bail awaiting his court hearing and had no intention of ceasing his favorite pastime. That being waving his gun around and threatening people with it, before actually using it on them. Or a bystander, like her.

It made sense now that he'd tried to shoot Alex. A guy like that, one who'd go straight to jail with no chance of bail this time around didn't want to get caught. He was willing to kill a police officer to avoid going to jail.

But she had no idea where to find him.

The person she was going to talk to was the man he'd threatened. Javier Basuto, Alex's brother.

She wanted to know if Evers had any dealings with Perkins and if he'd know where to find Thomas. Which meant she needed to know where to find Don Evers. It was a rabbit trail, sure. But she investigated in her way. Ran down leads. Figured out people's patterns of behavior. She'd done a few jobs that'd involved gathering information on the target—she'd figured it was so they could either be killed or so the person paying could threaten them. Blackmail. Intimidation.

Those were the things she understood. Because she had been taught by her mom, of all people, manipulation, survival, and how to abandon the people you were supposed to care for when they needed you most.

She was done grieving and had been for a long time. Jonah was healthy and happy, and even though she'd given up her maternal rights, she had a plan to do the right thing one last time. She could show Jonah love in the capacity that she was given.

The house Javier owned was a single-wide trailer, and so similar to the one she'd grown up in that Sasha stared at it for a few minutes. Then she rolled her eyes and got out. February drizzle filled the air, with not even enough strength to call it rain. It reminded her of the weather in England. Gray skies and dampness everywhere. Mild temperatures. So blah it was no wonder nearly everyone in the country escaped for warmer temps every summer.

The TV was on. She crept through the trailer and saw the bedroom was empty. No one was in the bathroom, and it smelled. It was bad enough she didn't even want to go in there and check that no one hid behind the shower curtain.

A man's boot stuck up from the end of the couch. Javier

Basuto lay there, jacket and shoes still on. Drool on his stubbled chin. Dirty jeans. Empty beer cans on the table.

Sasha found a disposable cup on the kitchen counter and filled it with water.

She poured it on his face and crossed to sit in the recliner as he sat up.

"What…" He glanced around. "Woman—"

She held up the hand not holding the gun so that he could see her open palm. "Don't even start with me right now."

He slumped back. There were no weapons visible, but that didn't mean he had no access to one without getting up. It could be in the back of his belt. Or in his boot.

She kept the gun on her knee, not pointed at him. Finger away from the trigger. He eyed it. "What do you want?"

Sasha took out her cell phone and showed him the screen. "This is Don Evers, but I figure you know that already."

He shrugged. Probably knew him by another name—some kind of street name, or a nickname, she figured.

"I was shot the other day because of you, so I'm feeling *super* charitable as you can imagine." She waved the phone. "Tell me where to find him."

Javier was probably younger than Alex. She maybe remembered a little brother but wasn't sure. Still, the life he had led—drugs and alcohol, rough work and stress—meant the lines on his face were far more pronounced. If she hadn't known their family, she'd have guessed he was older than Alex.

Alex might not live a perfectly healthy life, and he certainly had his fair share of stress, but he clearly worked out and kept himself in good condition.

Enough it distracted her now to think of him.

"I don't know that guy. Never met him before."

"Really." She'd figured he would try this tactic. "And if he'd hit your son with that bullet? Or the other boy? Would you know him if your kid was in the hospital right now, fighting for his life? Or dead in the morgue, while you're making funeral preparations." He didn't need to know that she was fully aware of who Jonah Daniels was. Pastor's kid, running with the screwup's son. "Gone, because of you."

It was a test of his measure, and she studied him carefully. There were feelings there, but still other things in his life he counted as more important than the health and wellbeing of his son.

"You were with Alejandro." He leaned forward a fraction. "I'm sorry. *The lieutenant.*" He used a high-pitched voice. "Who are you, a cop? Maybe one of those detectives at LCPD, all women. They hire you?"

So, either he had no idea who she was, or he was a fantastic liar.

"Tell me where to find Evers."

"I have no idea." He flashed a smile, pleased with himself.

"A little boy is missing. Even though you don't care much about your son, maybe you'd care about a seven-year-old kid who right now is in danger, and is probably more than traumatized from being ripped from his mother's arms by his father." She felt the hot burn of tears about to gather but steeled herself against the sensation.

The last thing she needed to do was get all emotional in front of this guy.

He'd think she had a heart.

"Though, maybe you don't care about him either." She glanced around so he'd think she was passing judgment on his living situation. "Maybe in your case, it's *you* who's the dangerous parent."

"My son can take care of himself."

"Because you taught him he had to." She eyed Javier. "You taught him he had no choice. After all, you weren't going to do squat."

He stared at her.

"Tell me about Thomas Perkins."

"That's who you're after?" He laughed. "No. No way. I give him up to you, I'm dead. Perkins doesn't mess around."

"That's who you owe money to?" She watched him for a reaction. "Evers works for him?"

Given the flex of the skin around his eyes, she was right.

"Where would he go if he was on the run? I'm talking about safe houses. Maybe a cabin somewhere. A place he'd hide to lay low."

"Are you kidding? He'll be long gone if y'all are looking for him."

Sasha wasn't so sure. Not given what Maggie had said about Thomas asking about her. She hadn't known what to make of that and still didn't. But if he was interested or wanted to get revenge, then she planned one hundred percent to use that to her advantage.

If it got Ian back, she would use *anything*.

These people lived in a world she knew well because she inhabited the same place. Alex might know it. But he didn't live here the way she did. He was on the periphery as a cop. Alex had pulled himself away from it while Javier walked right in and stayed there. Perhaps he thought he'd had no choice or was stuck now.

Sasha had walked right back out. She owed no one, that was the difference.

The world Alex lived in was one where people did the right thing. Where they followed the law because it was good. She saw more gray areas than black and white. Always had. It was going to get her picked up by the FBI if she wasn't careful. As much as she might like to believe otherwise, Alex wasn't her ally.

"What did Evers say to you before Alex showed up?"

"*Alex.*" Javier sneered.

"Answer the question."

"So you can run to your cop boyfriend and tell him I spilled? Do you know what Perkins does to rats?"

"I can imagine."

"You have no clue."

"You'd be surprised." She paused. "Now tell me what he said."

"Give me the money, or else."

"Creative." Though, she didn't know if it was even true. "Tell me where to find him."

"The bar on Lexbury. He works out of it."

"And when they come for their money again, what are you going to do about that?"

The fallout of Javier's death, or whatever they had planned for him, wasn't something she wanted his son to have to face. Even if she didn't know the kid. She knew what that felt like and wished it on no one.

He glanced to the side, a tiny smirk curling the corners of his lips. A tattoo peeked out the collar of his shirt. Something generic with no imagination. Trying to be a tough guy.

"Not scared? I guess you don't get what Perkins does to people who don't pay."

He smirked, his attention now on the TV. As though payment was the farthest thing from his mind.

Cold settled in her stomach. "What did you do?"

13

E ric Cullings, FBI Special Agent and head of the task force
assigned to hunting Sasha, got up from his chair. It rolled
back a foot and he lifted his hands, lacing his fingers behind his
head. Elbows splayed out as he paced. "This is unbelievable."

"If it's true." An agent still at the table leaned back in his
chair.

Alex shot the guy a look. Was that helpful? "Why wouldn't it
be true?"

"A murder-suicide of two senate aides? Come on. Please. I
don't buy into conspiracies." The agent lifted his hand and
started counting his fingers. "She's blaming other people for
things she did so we go easier on her." Another finger lifted.
"She's distracting us with different cases so we're spread thinner
looking for her." Another finger. The middle one.

He lowered his hand, but not before his intention to flip off
Lieutenant Basuto in the middle of his precinct was clear.

Before Alex could say anything, Eric stepped up to the table.
"Get out. That was uncalled for, and I won't tolerate it. You just
bought yourself lunch duty. Go fetch us all sandwiches, because
you're of no use to me right now."

The agent gathered his coat and stomped to the door. He shot Alex a dirty look before the door shut behind him.

"Nice team." Chief Conroy Barnes sat at the table.

"I don't wanna hear it." Eric held up a palm.

They'd worked with the feds, specifically Eric, several times now. Their rapport was solid. Eric's wife was a Last Chance native, and her brother was the town's private investigator, Tate Hudson, who just so happened to be married to a detective here, Savannah. It was the circle of life and relationships.

The team Eric had brought with him was new. Last time, during the hunt for Clarke, one of their agents had been compromised. Eric had been given a whole new group, all extensively vetted by their boss.

"She didn't kill Clarke."

Eric turned to him. "So who did?"

Alex didn't know what to say.

"Perhaps you could send a note back, via this boy who delivers her envelopes. Ask her if she knows who did."

Alex was aware of his boss's study of him. Conroy likely knew he'd been in contact with her, just not exactly how much. He figured Eric's suggestion might help the case. Especially if more of Sasha's statements were admitted as evidence in the case against her. She would be heard in the way she'd assured him she would not be.

Conroy studied the screen on the wall. "Who did she say hired out the hit on those two aides?"

Alex had been so concerned with the assassin's identity, the one who'd staged the deaths to appear as a murder-suicide, he'd glossed over that. None of the agents present, of which there were four, and sandwich guy was the fifth, plus Eric, had even thought to look at it as anything other than what it appeared. But all of them knew of the deaths. It had been the lead news story for a month after it happened. Public knowledge. There had even been a movie made of it, piecing together the truth from emails and texts. Interviews. All presented as an elaborate Romeo-and-Juliet tale.

Little did anyone know how far that story was from the truth.

Eric held the evidence bag in front of him, studying the paper copy of the statement. The envelope could be seen inside the evidence bag as well. Alex looked at his photocopy. Before he could find the name, Eric said, "The Mayor of Richmond, Virginia."

Conroy blew out a breath. "That's some implication. Does she have evidence to back it up?"

"It'll have to be corroborated, but yes. There's enough here to go on." Eric glanced at him for some reason.

Alex didn't know what to say.

"We should post someone, cop or agent, to sit on the kid. See if she approaches. These two statements were days apart. Maybe she's working on a timeline, and it's a pattern she's sticking with. When she contacts the kid to deliver the next one, we can swoop in and get her into custody."

"We need everyone focused on finding Ian Perkins right now." Alex waved a hand at the file on the table. "This is all good, and I'm as uncomfortable as you are that she's still roaming free. But the priority here is the missing child."

"I agree." Eric folded his arms. "I also disagree. There are enough of us we can multitask. Two of my agents are already at the cabin Thomas Perkins owns. If there's anyone there or any leads as to where he might be with Ian, they'll call in."

"And in the meantime, we stand around here doing nothing?" That didn't sit well with Alex.

No one who was actually responsible for that child was currently involved in the search for him, just a bunch of cops doing their jobs. The mother—the boy's most promising advocate—was unconscious in the hospital. The father was their suspect. The kid had no living grandparents within two thousand miles. Ian Perkins had been let down by everyone who was supposed to care for him.

Which left the job to the cops.

He looked at Conroy, pleading with his boss. "Sasha should not be the priority right now." Even she agreed with that. She'd gone with him to Perkins's house before she'd ditched him.

He'd wondered for a few minutes that she might've been taken as well, like Ian. Or arrested before he could... He realized right then he didn't know what he would've done if she had been arrested right in front of him. Not stop them. Maybe help, and make sure she was treated fairly and with respect, as anyone who was arrested should be.

"We'll have to agree to disagree about that, Lieutenant. I have agents not assigned to working the missing child case. Their priority will be Sasha Camilero."

Alex figured that was fair enough.

Eric addressed Conroy. "What about the wife? What's her status?"

"Unconscious, per the last update from her doctor. They say even if she does wake up soon, she may not be in any state to speak with us. She suffered a serious head injury, and they're worried about bleeding in her brain."

Alex blew out a breath. All for trying to protect her child. Emily Perkins had been hurt more than enough, even before this. Now the child had been torn from his mother's arms, taken by the person who hurt her.

He slumped into a chair.

"I have a question, Lieutenant."

It was one of the other agents. Alex lifted his head and indicated for her to go ahead.

"Why did she pick you?"

"Sasha?" That had to be who she was talking about.

The female agent nodded. "Ms. Camilero addressed this statement to you, specifically. Why would she do that?"

Alex wandered to the laptop plugged into the TV on the

wall. He'd scanned the contents of the file for this exact reason, digitizing the pages as PDFs so the FBI could be made aware of what might be extenuating circumstances for some of the accusations against Sasha, or at least give a broader idea of her history. As far as he knew, they had no idea of what was in her file.

"Sasha Camilero was born Melina Vasquez."

Several people in the room gasped.

Alex glanced over at Conroy, who seemed amused. Then he continued, "We knew each other in high school. She used to come here each summer and stay with her uncle and aunt." Alex swallowed, sitting on the edge of the cabinet against the wall. He didn't need to look at the screen. "You can read the details of the case, but suffice it to say the two of us witnessed the grisly aftermath of her uncle's murder. And that wasn't the end of it for her."

Eric took a step toward Alex, sensing the tension in his body language, along with a whole lot of fury. "You should have told me."

"I didn't remember her—at first. It was Sasha who actually remembered me, and I put it together afterward. I had no idea she was back in town. Or that her name is now Sasha."

"How can you not remember her?" The female agent sat back in her chair and shook her head. "If you were friends."

He nodded. "Friends who, together, experienced a trauma that ultimately put me in the hospital. I blocked out a whole lot of what happened. Including her. A kind of stress reaction." He paused before continuing, "She eventually moved away, and when she showed up here again, I didn't recognize her. Until recently."

"Are we supposed to buy this?" one of the agents asked. "You know her. You were friends. We're supposed to believe she hasn't twisted you, or compromised your ethics in some way." He shrugged. "If you've seen her since and recognize her now, you should have arrested her immediately."

He turned away to the laptop and emailed the pages to each of the agents. They needed to read what had happened to Melina after her uncle's gruesome death. He didn't think he could say it aloud. He wouldn't be able to pass her off as some stranger, a victim he didn't know personally.

The first time he'd seen her recently, at Hope Mansion, she'd freaked out and run from him. Injured from her fight with Thomas Perkins.

Then she'd been shot, and he had to help her. It had been a compulsion. Only, why had she been watching Javier in the first place? He realized he hadn't asked her how she'd come to be there.

The most recent time he'd seen her, she'd been willing to help him. The pain in her eyes, and the compassion for a boy she didn't even know and certainly wasn't responsible for. Both of those things had induced him to overlook the right thing. Instead, he'd utilized her skills to help find Ian Perkins.

While the agents read the pages and discussed their contents, Alex pulled out his phone and sent her a text with her number she'd finally decided to give him.

WHY WERE YOU WITH JAVIER?

While he waited, he wondered if she'd ditched the phone. Or if she'd given him a wrong number so he couldn't use it against her.

Then his phone buzzed.

IT'S PERKINS HE OWES MONEY TO.

Alex frowned. She couldn't have known that days ago. He didn't even know the identity of the man who had fired at them, and he hadn't had the chance yet to talk with his brother. Had she?

WE NEED TO TALK. YOU SAID YOU'D SHARE INTEL.

The reply came quickly.

BUSY.

Alex stowed his phone. Conroy was watching, but Alex wasn't about to lie and make up some story about his nephew being the person he was talking to. He'd crossed plenty of lines recently but lying wasn't going to be one of them if he could help it.

"Instead of the mail delivery kid, I'm leaning on *you* being the bait to catch Sasha."

Alex had no idea what to say to Eric. "That's…" Crazy. Inspired. Infuriating. Invasive. Probably going to work.

"We can push your history. Have you go to the place where she was held, maybe. If she's keeping tabs on you, she might show up. We can take her down." The agent lifted his phone from the conference table. "I'll call HRT."

The Hostage Rescue Team was the FBI's version of SWAT. They would only be brought in if a suspect was armed and dangerous, and they thought they needed that level of firepower to ensure no innocents were harmed. As though Sasha would take hostages and make things difficult.

Alex ignored the knot in his gut. "She's giving you actionable intel. That makes her a potentially valuable asset."

"She's a dangerous woman."

"One who could help you." If they got over their need to punish anyone deemed a criminal and allow her to tell them what she knows.

Eric spoke in a low voice. "You're walking right into being compromised. This woman will undermine your work here, and you could lose your job."

Alex looked at Conroy. "Would I?"

The chief laced his fingers on the desk. "The people in this community need to be able to trust you. You're willing to give someone the benefit of the doubt. That's an asset, not a liability. But, even so, the trust I have in you has limits. Be very careful."

The FBI would note it, for the record, if a local cop worked on the suspect's behalf. It wouldn't look good for him.

Alex didn't want to take his boss's trust in him for granted. "I'm just asking for a little compassion and understanding. Fewer flashbangs and noisy takedowns."

Conroy answered his phone. "Barnes."

A second later his eyes flashed, and he informed the room, "Shots fired at Don Evers's house."

The guy he'd seen harassing Javier? The one who'd shot Sasha?

Alex hadn't even had the chance to talk with him before he was processed, arraigned and released on bail.

"Neighbors report a woman waving a gun around and disturbing the peace. They think she's gonna kill him."

14

———

S irens could be heard in the distance. Sasha had overstayed
her welcome.

Evers flashed a mouthful of bloody teeth that had seen
better days. He needed to lay off the drugs. "Time's up."

She should shoot him. It was tempting, but instead, Sasha
said, "Tell them where Tom took his son."

Evers laughed at her. "Or what?"

Sasha didn't answer. She headed for the back door at a fast
clip. He didn't have a weapon, at least not one he'd taken out
during their conversation, even after she'd fired her gun at the
ceiling to get his attention. She was unwilling to mess around.

Still, he could shoot her in the back as she left. Just in case,
she turned back at the door. He was gone from his spot.

She jogged down the backyard and wiped off her gun. She
dropped the weapon in the bushes and hauled herself over the
fence, hoping she hadn't left even a partial on the metal of the
weapon.

If the FBI tried hard enough, they could probably corrobo-
rate Don Evers's story about her being here. But that wasn't her
biggest concern right now.

Ian was.

The boy and the intel Evers had grudgingly given her.

She crouched by the fence and scanned around her. Side street. She'd be exposed if not for trees and houses on the other side of the street. Sasha ran down the line of fences. When a car passed on the street, she crouched by one of those cable connection boxes in the grass. Not quite big enough to hide her, but she made it work.

It didn't appear as though she'd been seen.

Still, she waited there to be sure. Just not too long, or agents searching the area would find her. Even though they wouldn't know it was her since she was wearing a blonde wig, it still wouldn't look good. She'd have to think of a clever excuse as to why she was out here hiding at this time of night. Then she'd be on the run again and would have to find a whole new disguise.

Her core still rocked at what Evers had told her. Thomas Perkins had no intention of leaving town anytime soon. He was here, with Ian, and he was asking everyone who knew anyone the identity of the woman who'd been at Hope Mansion.

When he'd been choking her, she'd left an impression on him. That was nice. Sasha rolled her eyes and kept moving along the fence line. She moved at a measured pace, trying not to trip or roll her ankle. She needed to be able to ambulate, while an injury would prevent mobility.

Not so she could run from the cops. Though, that was what she was doing. Arguably Don Evers was a bigger criminal than her, but it didn't work like that. They had a bee in their bonnet for her.

Not for the first time did she wonder why.

Who of the higher-ups at the FBI decided to push this case, signing off on the money—for a task force of all things? It wasn't like she'd committed a crime in the last few years. Sasha was old news.

Which meant it could be down to an old grudge.

She needed intel on that as well. But with a missing boy, she was hardly the priority.

Thomas Perkins was trying to find her? He wanted to know who she was so they could talk. Or whatever else he had planned. Options she didn't want to think about.

An idea formed as she moved, borne of the blood pumping fresh oxygen into her brain. She always went for a run when she needed to think. Ideas came when she was moving. Whether that was running from the cops, or not, didn't matter.

If she contacted Perkins herself, or put out the word that she wanted to talk, she could find out where Ian was. Sasha could even offer to exchange herself for the boy. Would he even go for that? She didn't know if she was of high enough value to him to make that kind of trade. Evers had said Perkins had a thing about her. Whatever that meant, he hadn't wanted to elaborate except for a few lurid suggestions that weren't helpful. More like they were painful reminders of something she'd tried to forget for decades now and didn't need to be brought back up.

She would never be over it. What was the point in trying? Sasha turned the corner and headed to her car, a few streets over. The roads were empty except for a patrol car that had pulled over. Right behind her car.

Out of reflex, she reached for the gun she'd dropped earlier in the bushes, while at the same time, turning around to make sure no one was behind her. She didn't need to be snuck up on.

Sasha instantly regretted disposing of her gun but instead found her backup weapon. It was non-lethal, but she would use that if necessary.

A familiar, suited cop bent to peer in the back window of her car, a flashlight in his hand.

"Snooping?"

He straightened as she approached and lifted the flashlight to point at her face.

She covered the beam glare with her hand. "Seriously?"

Alex sighed, then flipped the light off. "Neighbors called in to say that you yelled your intention to shoot Don Evers. That will go in the report."

"Along with my arrest?" He wasn't going to let her go, not this time. Her chances had run out. And she hadn't even been able to finish her statements. There were three more she needed to write, and after that she would contact Dorian. Start the ball rolling.

He would go dark.

Her life would end.

She would finally find her peace, however that came about. She was content to leave that in God's hands. Sasha was too tired to fight Him. Just so long as the pain stopped.

He took a step toward her. "What's wrong?"

Then it was like he caught himself. Straightening up and backing away. She'd have believed his attention was to toy with her emotions if not for that. She figured it was likely he still planned to arrest her but wondered if he'd told the FBI about her car. His knowledge of the car she drove now was what had brought him here.

"You should be talking to Evers about what he knows of Ian's whereabouts."

"You don't need to tell me how to be a cop, Sasha. I can do my job." The dark of night, even lit with streetlights, didn't allow her to see his expression. She could make out his face, but all she normally saw in his eyes was obscured. She would have to take his word for it.

"Nice wig, by the way."

She didn't respond to that inane comment. He was learning all her tricks, and she needed a new car now. Probably a new phone, too. Instead of cataloging all that, she got back on topic. "Then go do your job. Find that boy." If he did that, she wouldn't have to worry about Perkins's apparent infatuation with her. Or whatever it was. Could be revenge, considering she was just guessing as to what his intentions might be.

"And you? What will you be doing while the police department is distracted by the search for Ian Perkins?"

Finding him her way. "I have things to do. Did you get the second envelope?"

"Yes. Are you planning any more?"

She nodded. His shoulders were so broad. She wanted to know what the feel of his arms around her would be like.

And at that thought, she knew she had to take care of this. And soon.

She was getting attached.

"The feds had no idea the case was anything other than what the write-up said. It was good you told them. It will put things to rest." Almost sounded like he was proud of her. Yet, if she was smart, she would remain skeptical about his intentions. He could be manipulating her. Simply lulling her into a false sense of security and then—BAM—he would arrest her right on the spot. Yes, if she was smart, she'd keep her wits about her.

She took a step closer, so he would think it was working. "I know I have no leverage, but I need a favor anyway. I have to ask."

She saw the flick of his head. "What is it?"

Simply asking gave him power over her. Like he didn't have enough already. Still, she wasn't willing to jeopardize the people whose lives she had decided to safeguard. He would know there was yet another vulnerability he could use against her. Didn't matter.

"I need you to take care of Jonah Daniels." Before he could ask why, she said, "Make sure he stays out of trouble. That kind of thing."

"The pastor's kid."

She nodded because it was somewhat of a question. Mostly he just sounded confused. "Your nephew's friend."

"Who is he to you?"

"Someone who seems like he needs a nudge in the right direction." That was true enough. He was flirting the edge. She could see it in the way he dressed and how he held himself. The genetic predispositions she'd given him, that darkness in her bleeding through from him. "Just promise me you'll keep an eye out for him. It shouldn't be that hard when he's your nephew's friend. You've established a relationship, so it won't be weird. You're a cop doing your cop job."

She tried to make that sound like she didn't consider it a demerit.

"Jonah Daniels."

"Alex, you need to pay attention. I have to go." She started to move. He reached for the cuffs on the back of his belt. He was going to arrest her?

She moved closer so there was only starlight between them. "Who I am, and what I've been involved in? That already puts me at risk. There's someone in town watching me through a sniper scope. And since then, I've discovered I'm now on Thomas Perkins's radar."

His body snapped taut. "You're *what?*"

"He's asking around about me. He'll find out who I am, eventually. This is a small town and I tried to keep it quiet, but he'll put it together soon enough. So you need to watch out for Jonah."

His shoulders softened. "It's important to you."

"There is nothing more important to me."

"I'll do it. I'll watch out for him. For you."

It was coming. She could feel it in the air, a change in the wind, if she even thought that kind of thing was real. But her senses were going haywire. Sasha closed the gap between them and touched her lips to his cheek. "Thank you, Alex."

His hand reached for her wrist. She felt the curl of his fingers. Heard the clink of the metal cuffs.

Sasha pressed the button of her stun gun and touched it to his side. Between the vest he wore and his belt.

Alex stiffened. She had to step back a fraction. He dropped the cuffs with a hiss, all that electricity going through him. "Sasha." His voice was a growl. He'd had training. He knew what this was and how to fight the effects.

She didn't let up.

He slumped to the ground.

Sasha stepped back, the taste of him still on her lips.

No one was on the street with them. She opened his passenger door and used the radio on his dash to call in an officer down. The last thing she wanted was to walk away with him vulnerable like this. He could get hurt.

Sasha left him there. Everything she could have had in her life if things hadn't turned out this way. If the course of her life hadn't changed so drastically and left her torn apart. Destroyed, in one of the worst ways that could happen to a person.

She climbed into her car and drove away. A patrol car passed her, lights and sirens flashing. Sasha shifted the blond locks of the wig over her cheek and turned her head so her face wouldn't be visible.

She needed to stay free long enough to find Ian Perkins.

15

Conroy stepped into the observation room. "Did she really stun you?"

Alex lifted the hem of his T-shirt. He should be home now, but they were all working until Ian had been found.

Conroy winced. "Ouch."

"Yeah." He rubbed the back of his head where he'd presumably hit the ground. After Sasha zapped him with her stun gun. Sure, he'd been about to arrest her, but was that the point? "Dropped my cuffs. Couldn't bring her in. Gotta give her credit, though. She gave me a good story for Cullings."

The door to the interview room opened and Eric walked in. Special Agent Cullings looked every bit the senior FBI agent he was as he approached the table where Don Evers sat, taking the seat across from him.

Eric introduced himself as he opened the paper file and slid a photo across the table. "Was this the woman in your home?"

Alex watched Don. "She was wearing a blonde wig." It had seemed bright in the moonlight. At first, he hadn't realized it was her, but he'd caught on quickly enough.

Don peered at the photo. "She was blonde, but yeah. It was

her that tried to murder me in cold blood." He started to stand up.

Eric motioned to the chair. "Sit back down, Mr. Evers. You're out on bail, and you shot at a police officer three nights ago. You aren't going anywhere."

"So arrest me."

"Sit down."

Evers sat.

"Before I read you your rights, you can tell me what you know about Thomas Perkins." Eric's voice remained steady. "And before I arrest you for attempted murder, I want to know what you might know about the whereabouts of Ian Perkins. Then maybe I'll speak to the DA about what the charges might be. See if we can't clear up some of your...indiscretions."

"He can't be serious." Alex turned to his boss. "Did you know the feds were going to offer him a deal? He tried to kill me."

Conroy shrugged. "He's got the weight of the bureau behind him. If the DA goes for it, there's nothing much we can say. They want the bigger fish. Perkins and Sasha." When Alex shot him a questioning look, he continued, "They've done homework on Perkins. They'll give me something I can make stick. I'll facilitate them taking Sasha in."

"And in the meantime, a guy who shot at me and could've hurt a bystander goes free. Or gets a slap on the wrist."

Sasha had been right when she'd pointed out the fact Evers could have hit one of the boys. Mateo.

And Jonah.

Was that the reason she'd been there that night? Alex asked Conroy, "What do you know about Jonah Daniels? He's one of Mateo's friends."

"Where'd that come from?"

"Humor me."

Conroy said, "Pastor's kid. Seems like a good kid, and we've never seen him in the station, right?"

"Far as I know."

Conroy shrugged. "He's either clean, or he's quiet."

There had to be a connection. It couldn't just be his association with Alex that interested Sasha. Sasha wanted Jonah
protected. Watched out for. She was right that it wouldn't seem
strange for him to look in on the teen, even just to check that he
was doing all right. Not given his family connection to Mateo, or
his position in the community.

If she was otherwise unable to, he'd do her that favor. It was
the right thing to not leave a kid hanging if he might need help.

His brother Javier was the one Evers shook down for
Perkins's payout. If Evers worked for Perkins, then it stood to
reason Perkins was the one Javier owed money to.

A man who took his child from a safe place.

What would he do to Mateo, or even Jonah by association, if
he thought he could send a message? Or get his pound of flesh.

Back inside the interview room, Evers had perked up at the
mention of a plea deal. "I know plenty."

"That remains to be seen." Eric would need him to prove it.
That was how deals like this worked. "For example, where does
Perkins have his son Ian?"

Don's face fell. "I don't know that."

"Don't waste my time, then. Honestly, we've been here too
long already, and you've given me absolutely nothing." Eric
stood this time. He flipped the file closed on the photo of Sasha.

"Hold up," Don called him back. "I know stuff."

"Nothing that counts, far as I can see." Eric, still standing,
leaned in closer and grasped the edges of the table with his
hands.

Alex asked Conroy, "He's going to leverage Evers to get
Perkins?"

"Seems like it. Trying to, at least."

Evers said, "That woman you asked about."

"Sasha Camilero."

"That's her name?"

"What about her?" Eric leaned against the wall.

Don twisted in her chair. "She was at Hope Mansion the first time Thomas tried to get the kid back. She got in his way. Got his *attention*, if you get what I'm saying. Now he's asking around about her."

"I'd think he'd be more concerned about keeping his son than some random woman who crossed his path."

"He don't let anything go. Once he finds out who she is, he'll send someone to grab her. Or kill her. Whoever owes him the most. That's what he learned from his daddy."

"Javier," Alex muttered his brother's name.

"What's that?"

He shook his head in answer to Conroy's question while the idea coalesced. Was the amount of money Javier owed big enough that Perkins would trade Sasha as currency?

If this guy was even telling the truth, Alex could use that information. Get Javier to give Perkins the money he owed him. Control the fallout. The FBI would want to do a sting, catch both of them in the process. He didn't want to think about the ideas the agents on the task force would have about allowing Sasha to be taken, or hurt, so they could ensure the leverage they'd need to be able to nab Perkins when they moved in. At this point, he assumed Sasha was dispensable to them. That, or she was their primary concern.

Sasha might not be so deserving of compassion, but he didn't want her to get hurt. It wasn't on him to pass down judgment.

But first, he'd have to get Javier on board.

He turned to Conroy. "I have an idea, but I have to speak to my brother. I'm gonna go do that, and if I can get anywhere with it, I'll text you. Okay?"

His boss nodded.

Alex signed out of work and headed to Javier's trailer. The

front door was unlocked as usual. He knocked as he stepped in. "Javi!"

His brother emerged from the bedroom area as Alex shut the door. Wet hair. Droplets of water on his bare chest. Jeans on, thankfully. Looked like he'd just taken a shower. His brother walked past, dismissing him, and headed for the kitchen. "What do you want?"

Alex leaned against the door frame by the fridge while his brother made a pot of coffee. "Everything okay?"

"Because I showered?"

"That, and it's night and you're not drinking."

"I figured you wouldn't say yes to a beer."

He'd be right about that. "And nothing happened recently?"

Javier continued making the coffee. After he hit the button, he turned, leaning his hips back against the kitchen counter.

"It's Perkins you owe money to, right?"

He said nothing.

"He took his son from Hope Mansion."

"That's why she was here." Javier glanced to the side. "The woman you were with."

"She got shot because of you."

"Doesn't mean I owe her. I've got enough problems of my own."

Alex tried to gauge if he was sober. Mostly, he figured. Enough to pass for it, even if there was still enough alcohol in his system he probably shouldn't be driving. Should he even offer this scenario? What if Eric had thought of the same thing and now had Evers calling Perkins to inform him of Sasha's identity? They might even now be setting up a meet. A sting.

Alex was the only one who could get her there.

By double-crossing her so she'd be arrested by the FBI.

It didn't sit well, but it would still be the right thing. The two statements she'd already given the FBI might be enough to sway a judge into listening to anything else she had to say. She could get a deal of some kind, possibly.

That would be good for her.

Alex wasn't going to feel bad for doing the right thing. He also thought Sasha might not be inclined to hold it against him, either. Even though she seemed to want to fight to do it on her terms.

He still didn't understand, but now he at least knew Jonah Daniels was somehow related.

"Why are you here, Alejandro?"

"I want you to call Perkins. Tell him you know who the woman is that he's looking for. I'll give you all the information. Say you'll bring her to meet him. See what he says, cause he either wants her or he's willing to offer to wipe your debt by having you kill her for him. We can work something out if you help us bring him down and get the kid back with his mother."

Javier's eyes flashed. Alex knew well his impression of the police. He likely wasn't jazzed about working with the cops, but the idea of having his debt wiped? That was a whole different story.

"You aren't going to kill her. She's wanted by the FBI. They'll take her, Conroy will get Perkins, and the kid will be safe."

"You'll probably get another promotion out of it."

"That's not what I'm after here."

"No? *Alex.*"

"What?"

Javier smirked. "You're low, bro. Burning a woman who likes you, and for what? For your job. Even I didn't know you were that hardcore."

"That isn't what's happening here." Though, he would likely be awake several nights while he thought it over. *Likes you.* She'd kissed him right before she stun-gunned him. Javier would likely consider that hilarious if he ever decided to tell his brother what'd happened. He wasn't going to.

"Are you going to do it, or not?" Alex got out his phone so

he could fill in Conroy. "Get yourself out of some of this trouble you're in."

Javier turned to the coffee pot. "Fine. Want a cup?"

He figured it was going to be a long, frustrating night, so he said, "Sure."

Conroy messaged back quickly. Eric had the same idea but had hit a roadblock with Don Evers since the guy refused to say much after Alex had left. He outlined his idea and told Conroy to have the feds ready. There wasn't enough time to get a warrant for the phone that would contact Perkins. They'd have to wait and see what Alex came up with.

He and Javier drank two cups of coffee each while he went over the plan and wrote notes for Javier to use.

"You're really burning this woman?"

"It's not like that."

Javier said nothing.

"She knows what it is." And yet, it occurred to Alex that even if she wasn't surprised by it, she still might be hurt by his actions. "I'm not going to abandon her, but she knows I have to do my job. It's the right thing on both ends."

Javier got his phone and called Thomas Perkins. He put it on speaker.

"Yeah."

Thomas answered the phone. In the background, Alex could hear a little boy crying.

Javier glanced over. Alex nodded his encouragement. "It's Javi."

"Talk."

"Her name is Sasha Camilero. And that's not all I know."

"Is that right?"

"Yeah. It's right." Javier sounded so different. Alex realized he was seeing his brother's "street thug" persona. "What I want to know is what you want me to do with her."

"Bring her to me."

"Tell me where, and I'll do it."

Thomas chuckled. "I'm not unaware your brother is a cop."

"So when I bring in the woman, you'll know he has nothing to do with me. I just want my debt clear, that's all."

"Where highway twelve meets Candlewood. Noon tomorrow. I don't care what condition she's in, I just want her breathing." He chuckled, and the line went dead.

16

Sasha heard the whole phone call. She'd cloned Javier's phone with her own at his place during their conversation. Now she knew exactly what was going down.

"*Alex.*" She gritted her teeth.

This was nothing but an attempt to catch her *and* Perkins. Both of them in custody would be a huge prize for the police in town and the federal task force. It had to be a setup. Of course. What else would it be, considering they'd made sure to involve her?

They'd handed her identity over to Perkins, so sure their way was the best way to deal with everything.

She didn't believe Javier could have figured this all out on his own. Even though she'd been to see him—and he'd realized her slip using Alex's first name—he couldn't have put it together. Not this fast.

At least not without Alex's help.

So when her own phone number rang a short while later, she didn't answer. Instead, Sasha called a contact of hers.

"I need a GPS location for this phone number." She recited the digits.

Silence answered her.

She was about to prompt him when he said, "I do this one favor for you. For old times' sake. Then we're done."

"Explain."

"You've been burned." He hung up.

Burned. Sasha stared at the phone. "What does that mean?"

It was one thing for a spy to be burned. Her job with Millie and Bridget at the accountant's office where they'd worked with that traitor Clarke had been about helping burned spies get new IDs and find somewhere safe to live. They'd worked with all kinds of people who needed to disappear. Most because their lives, and the lives of their families, were in danger.

But that was another lifetime ago.

Sasha slid the new statement she'd written into the envelope. This one wasn't going to be notarized. She didn't have time, and by now they knew what she had to say held weight. They'd verify it, sure. But she didn't have to do anything other than tell what she knew.

The future would take care of itself.

No way was the FBI or police going to succeed in taking her down before she found Ian Perkins. They were grasping at straws. She didn't begrudge their efforts. Bagging two key criminals in one swoop would be a serious win for the department. But she'd have preferred to not be one of the key criminals.

Sasha took the envelope and went downstairs.

Hope Mansion had been quiet since the night Emily was attacked and Ian taken. The residents were understandably freaked, more so since they found out firsthand what that kind of terror felt like when the threat was directed at them.

She found Maggie in the kitchen. "Hey."

"Leaving again?"

Sasha held out the envelope to her. "I need you to deliver this to Lieutenant Basuto at the police department."

Maggie studied her with those bright green eyes. Her red

hair, threaded with gray, pulled back into a bun. She'd lost her daughter several years ago, the whole thing a mystery. It was no wonder she found a daughter in every woman—and became an aunt or grandma to every child—who crossed the threshold of this house.

Even Melina.

Maggie took the envelope. "It's not a bomb, right? Or Anthrax?"

"You think I want to kill him?" All she figured was that the delivery boy's involvement wasn't going to work anymore. The feds had likely caught onto it, and she didn't want him to get in trouble.

"It's not Alex's fault you never saw him again."

"You think I *wanted* to see him?"

"I know you said you didn't."

Maggie started to speak, but Sasha cut her off. "Don't bother trying to tell me something good came of it."

"Didn't it?" Maggie was so sure.

Now Sasha had seen Jonah up close, she wasn't sure she could argue that at least some good *had* come of it. Still, she said, "Only if I can get Ian Perkins back from his father."

"You could do that?" Maggie paused a second. "Never mind. I don't want to know."

She saw too much. Always had.

Back when Maggie had taken Melina under her wing after the nightmare she'd been through, there had been no point lying or hiding anything. Maggie understood it all. Melina had left when it was time, and became Sasha, but she remembered well enough how this wise older woman had brought much-needed peace into her life.

Maggie had sat beside her bed when she woke in the middle of the night screaming. Held her hair back when she deposited her most recent meal into the toilet. Maggie had gone with her to doctor appointments. Suggested therapy. Made her smoothies. Watched kid cartoons with her. Invited her to the Bible study she held here weekly.

She'd done everything a single person could have. She'd done more than enough.

But it hadn't taken away what had been done by those men. That was why Sasha had left. She would always remember if she stayed in Last Chance. And yet, leaving hadn't made her forget, either.

She'd tried to push the memories away the same as she did with her emotions.

It was all still there inside her. A deep, dark well. The kind found in horror movies with unspeakable things at the bottom. What was the point of trying to clear it out when there was no getting rid of it?

"Please just deliver the envelope."

"I'll do it. If you go and see Bridget." Sasha started to shake her head. Before she could argue, Maggie continued, "She's your friend and your family. It's time."

"She has a family. She doesn't need me."

"I'm sure there are things she would say to you if she saw you."

"Yeah," Sasha said. "She said all those things last time. Said that I overstepped my bounds. We worked together, and we were friends. Then she found out. I did what I had to do to protect her child. Now she has Sydney back, and they're all together. One happy family."

Her best friend had married the police officer who was also the father of her baby.

The baby Bridget had thought she'd lost at childbirth, all because Sasha had told her she'd died.

If she hadn't done it, Bridget would've lived a terrorized life protecting her baby from a powerful man trying to kill her. Instead, the child had been raised by her father, Last Chance Police officer Aiden Donaldson—now the sergeant—and recently reconnected with Bridget after the threat was over.

"Perhaps she regrets her words and has come to understand that you did the right thing—the only right thing you could think of at the time." Maggie's expression held entirely too much.

Sasha didn't want to talk about her triggers. Or how she occasionally reacted in the moment, full of emotion, while failing to check herself before she set upon a course of action.

She'd been working on that.

The emotion part, at least.

"You won't know if you don't go to her and find out. You could meet Sydney. See what a wonderful girl she has grown into. Cutest seven-year-old princess you've ever seen, I'll tell you. Bridget is glowing. I'm pretty sure that after that whirlwind of a wedding, she's pregnant." Maggie smiled. "You really should see her. She's happy, and she owes that in part to you."

"Well, I'm not going to go tell her, 'I told you so.'"

"At least not until after you find Ian Perkins."

Sasha grinned. "Now you're getting it."

Voices in the hall broke through the quiet.

"I should go." She didn't want to put anyone in the position to lie for her. Maggie neglected to inform the police of certain things, but she also knew they understood she did that because of the nature of her work here. What she called her "ministry."

Maggie gave her a hug that included Sasha's backpack. "God's grace go with you."

She always said that. Sasha had never understood exactly what it meant, but she liked the words. It almost seemed like they washed over her. Made things easier to carry.

Sasha used the deer trail through the woods to the highway that ran behind Maggie's house. Sometimes new residents in more danger than usual were brought to the house by this route.

Her phone buzzed almost as soon as she got to her latest car, which she'd left somewhat hidden. She'd traded with a guy at the bar in exchange for a wad of cash. She'd been wearing a dark wig with blue streaks in the hair and colored contacts, but it was still a risk going local. Just not as much of a risk as driving around in her other car. The one that was probably on every cop's radar in town by now.

The text she'd received was from an unknown number and contained an address. She used GPS to give her directions and drove straight there.

The place where Thomas Perkins had used his phone to speak to Javier.

It was a solitary old farmhouse at the end of a cul-de-sac, set back from the rest of the houses. Upstairs was lit up. Two guys loaded stuff into the back of a pickup truck, and an SUV on the drive had the engine running.

Thomas Perkins walked out onto the front lawn and spoke to a too-skinny woman and a huge guy with her. He was giving them orders—if the finger pointed in their faces was any indication. Both nodded with every word he said.

"What are you doing?" She spoke to herself in quiet words.

Sasha took a few photos of the three of them with her phone, even though the images might not turn out enough to ID any of them. Whatever Perkins was up to, he was in a hurry and tensions were high. She saw him slap a guy on the back of the head.

The SUV was loaded up, and then it pulled out.

That left the skinny woman and big man with the pickup truck. Someone carried out a heavy bundle, wrapped in a blanket.

A whimper worked its way up Sasha's throat. "Ian."

Over the call, she'd heard him crying. Now he'd either fallen asleep, worn out from crying. Or he'd been given something so he didn't fight this. Or he was dead.

The bundle was handed to the woman who sat in the passenger seat. Relief washed over her. If he was no longer alive, they'd just throw him in the trunk and...

Sasha swallowed back bile and took more photos. The big man pulled out of the parking spot, turning around while Perkins watched from the front step. The two of them drove away with the son in their care.

"Where are you taking him?"

She was half tempted to march up to the house and start shooting until someone told her what his orders had been. Or just drive her car through the front door and demand the boy's location.

But Ian was getting farther and farther away, so there was no time to worry about the deadbeat father.

Sasha rolled down the passenger window and tossed her phone out, and then turned the car around and headed after the pickup. They drove across town to a complex of vacation homes Sasha knew was owned by a single woman in her thirties. She'd rented one of the residences a few weeks ago and questioned a guy in the garage. The owner didn't refund her security deposit.

They must've had the garage door opener with them because it rolled up as they approached. The big man pulled into the garage. Neither got out before the door descended.

Sasha stared for a second. Then she parked her car somewhere secure and walked back to the house. She set off a couple of security lights but managed to duck out of the way. She went around back and checked the windows. One was frosted, like for a bathroom. Another had curtains that had been drawn. The third, a bedroom, had blinds. One slat was broken, enough she could see through as the woman laid the boy down on a bed and stared at him for a moment. Then she rolled her eyes and walked out.

Sasha reached for the window frame, asking God—if He was up there—for it to be unlocked. She didn't want to confront the two before she got the boy out. Sure, she could find a phone somehow and call Alex, but if the cops showed up, they would find a hostage situation on their hands.

No. This was up to her.

A branch cracked. She heard a rustle in the trees and saw a flashlight. Great. This place had a security guard now.

A voice called out, "Is someone there?"

Sasha looked around. There was nowhere to go.

17

Thirty minutes after his phone buzzed with the text from Sasha they approached the house.

She'd sent him an address. She hadn't answered any of his calls since, determined not to speak to him. Just passing him intel, as she'd suggested. And after that kiss he could still feel on his cheek.

The house had been leased to a company owned by Perkins's wife, under her maiden name.

The FBI led the charge. Alex waited until they'd breached and cleared the ground level before stepping inside. Agents thundered up the stairs. He wasn't part of their team, so he had to wait since he was only representing the local police department here. This was the FBI's case and its jurisdiction. The FBI had more people and firepower. He let them do the running.

"Did you find basement access?"

"Not yet." Eric had a thunderous look on his face. He clipped his weapon to the front of his black vest to free his hands and then pulled out his phone.

"Perkins was here." Alex looked around. He wanted to know where Sasha was. Not knowing was throwing him off in such a way he didn't know where to go or what to do. How to feel about her. He wanted to rage in her defense. But how did that make him a good cop?

"That's clear." Eric nodded. "However, we still need to make sure and then we need to figure out where he's gone."

An agent pounded down the stairs and approached. "They left in a hurry."

"Same as they did with the residence." The one he and Sasha had searched.

"He's burning locations every time. We had no idea this place existed."

Eric frowned at his agent. "Now we know the lengths he'll go to in order to hide his whereabouts and that of his son. We're going to dig harder and get that boy back." He turned to Alex. "And you're going to get me Sasha."

The man had two sons of his own. It didn't surprise Alex that he'd conclude Sasha might be able to help, only that it had taken so long. Eric wouldn't want an innocent young boy to be hurt, a pawn in a war between two parents.

He was right. Alex needed to find Sasha and figure out whether or not she'd found him.

He pulled out his phone and called her number, stepping outside where it wasn't so crowded and noisy. Not because he had anything to hide. The time for doing that was over now, given they all knew he'd been in contact with her. Alex would likely get in trouble for not bringing her back in immediately to face the feds. Maybe he would even lose his job. Conroy could be pressured by the mayor into firing him, without any say in the matter.

Alex would accept whatever Conroy decided. If he was fired, he'd know it was pointless to have tried to be a cop in the first place. He wasn't good enough to do it. He'd been fooling everyone, mostly himself, all this time.

The phone rang in his ear.

A couple of rings later, he heard a tone. Far away.

Someone came out of the house behind him. He glanced

back and saw Eric. He heard it, too. Alex said, "Over there," pointing in the direction of what sounded like a ringing phone. They jogged past parked cars and the big black SUVs the HRT guys had rolled up in.

"There."

Eric fished it from the overgrown brush on the side of the street. Alex stowed his phone. "That's Sasha's phone."

"Then it's evidence." Eric tapped the screen. "She left it unlocked."

"She knew it was burned, and I'd use it to catch her or hand it to you so you could." And she'd turned the volume way up before she tossed it. "She wanted us to find the phone. She must've left something on there we should have."

"Here. In her gallery." He tilted the phone and showed the photos to Alex. "Perkins sent those two with a bundle. Looks like his son, maybe?"

Alex squinted at the screen. "The license plate."

Eric nodded. "If we can enlarge it with enough clarity, then we can run the plate number. Get an ID for these two and figure out where they would've taken him."

"What about Perkins?"

"Looks like he stayed. But an SUV also left."

"So we have a lead on Ian." Alex lifted his chin. "And Sasha gave it to us." Surely that had to count in her favor. He didn't want to demand leniency, just a good sense of what charges she faced.

"If they've ditched the pickup, or hidden it inside somewhere, we'll never find it. They could be long gone." He didn't want to voice his last thought but had to. "Perkins could have ordered them to kill the kid and dump the body somewhere."

Eric looked as sick as Alex felt about that. "Let's just follow the leads."

"And pray." If it got the kid back, he would do it.

"Why is she involved with this? Did you ask her for help?"

"She met Perkins. She knows the danger." Alex glanced at the phone. "Probably figured it's the right thing to do."

"But why? She has enough issues of her own. Why wade into this one?"

Alex just repeated the last thing he'd said. "It's the right thing to do."

Eric was about to respond when his phone rang. "Great. I thought I had more time." He swiped the screen. "Special Agent Cullings. Yes, Director. Of course."

Alex watched the tension rise in him.

"I understand that, Sir. No, there's no sign of her here." Eric moved away a couple of steps. "Yes, Sir. I—" The caller cut him off. "Understood."

And then evidently the caller hung up. Eric stared at his phone for a moment and then shook his head.

"The boss pushing pretty hard for a win from the task force?" That could be simple bureaucracy. But part of Alex didn't think so. "Or does he want a dangerous criminal off the streets?" Alex knew his sarcasm came across nice and thick.

"You don't know what she's done."

"No, I don't. Because you haven't felt the need to share that." He folded his arms. "Something that seemed strange before, but now it's more than just odd. What is she being accused of?"

Eric strode over and stared him down from his extra three inches. "Four murders that took place on a college campus in Virginia more than a decade ago. But still very fresh in the family's minds, I can assure you of that."

"You have proof?"

"She was there. That means she either killed those kids, or she knows who did."

His stomach roiled. "Anything else?" He didn't believe her capable of multiple murders, though he knew she could and had killed to defend her life before. She'd fought off all kinds of bad guys. Worked tirelessly to safeguard people she cared about.

Sasha acted out of desperation and full of emotion, even if she tried to deny it. She wasn't cold. She couldn't kill like that.

It wasn't in her. Even if she had told him about "government" work.

Alex wanted the case file notes. He needed to see for himself. "She went to school in Virginia?"

"I'm not talking about this with you. You're compromised. Given the personal connection to residents of this town like Maggie, and cops like Sergeant Donaldson, there's no way any of you could be impartial. That's why I was ordered not to tell you. Only Conroy knows the details."

"Why is your boss so hot to go after Sasha? What did she do to him?" Not to mention that Eric's wife had been Sasha's employer not too long ago.

Eric shook his head. "It's not a vendetta. Justice doesn't work like that. And it's not just those murders. There are several other cases we know she was involved with that are still open."

"So you need information from her."

"She's not getting a deal."

"The boss took that off the table? Seems strange, especially when you told him about the written statements." Alex paused. "You did tell him, right?"

Eric ignored that question. "She's giving us information on closed cases."

"Lies accepted. The wrong person jailed—or no one at all. That's not justice. Closed, or not, it seems like something that should at least be looked into."

"I have to bring her in. The person on the phone?" Eric said, "That was the Director of the FBI. This is coming from the top. No exceptions. No mistakes. No personal feelings."

"And when you wrap it all up nicely with a bow, you get a promotion. Been there." Alex shrugged. "I can tell you it turned out not to be all I thought it would be."

"I'm not having this conversation with you." Eric started to walk away.

Alex called after him. "I think Sasha's made some powerful enemies over the years. People who want her locked up, or silenced."

"Not everything is a conspiracy."

"There's a reason justice should be blind. But that doesn't mean you shouldn't ask questions." Alex's phone rang. It was the number for the office. "Lieutenant Basuto."

"It's Kaylee. There's been another envelope. Maggie brought it in a minute ago, and Sergeant Donaldson logged it into evidence. I'm sending you a photo of the paper inside. It's longer than the last one."

"Thanks." He hung up.

"What is it?"

"Do you even care?" Alex waited for Eric to answer, but he didn't. "You probably don't even believe what she's writing is true. Meanwhile, Sasha is off saving a child on her own."

"If she told us where he was, we could go get him."

"Surround the place, and demand they bring him out. That just creates a hostage situation." He sighed out his exhaustion.

"Just tell me what it is."

Alex read down the page on his phone. An account of the death of four college students in Virginia. He glanced up at Eric and told him as much.

"Just read it all."

"She saw what happened. She fought off the effects of the same drug they were dosed with and managed to pull herself out of it. They all died, except her. It's everything she remembers from what happened. Bits of things said to each other. A list of those present throughout the evening." A possible suspect list? "All so the FBI can figure out for sure who dosed and killed the rest."

Eric said nothing.

"She went to school in Virginia?"

Finally, a question Eric answered. "She worked at a hotel nearby for three years. The particular hotel she worked for was a hotbed for sex trafficking. The head of security had a block of rooms they didn't book out. His girls worked the bar downstairs and the neighborhood around it. She worked in housekeeping."

"You think she knew about the trafficking? Or those college kids did?"

"They were her friends."

Alex stared at the house. "Ian Perkins is my priority here. What you do on your end is up to you."

"But you'll freely stand in my way."

"A *child* is in danger. Same as Sasha when she was taken. She might've been older, and she was arguably in much more danger, but she was still a kid." He bellowed the words in Eric's face.

"Watch yourself, Lieutenant."

"We aren't going to agree. But isn't it obvious? Sasha got too close to someone who was hurting people. Somebody with power. He tried to kill her but it didn't work. Now he's going to get her locked up."

"She isn't a good person."

"Neither am I." He tried, but often it was like self-sabotage. He didn't believe he deserved the things others were blessed with. "Are you?"

"I'm not a criminal."

Alex sighed. He was about to repeat what he'd said about them not agreeing when an agent came running out of the house, followed by everyone who had been inside.

"Special Agent Cullings, we found basement access. There's an entire meth lab down—"

The house exploded into a fireball.

18

The explosion ripped the night sky apart with a burst of light. A boom like a crack of thunder whipped across town from the direction of the house.

Sasha used the disturbance to push off the siding and run for cover under a cluster of bushes. She ducked behind them and crouched, breathing hard and feeling the rush of adrenaline course through her. For a second, Sasha forgot all about the man and stared at the flames and smoke that curled up into the sky. The house. Thomas Perkins had blown up the house she'd directed the police and feds to.

They could be inside. Innocent lives annihilated, right along with the house.

Sasha choked back a sob and breathed through the urge to cry. If there were dead cops… She didn't know what to think, or what to do. It would be her fault. No way to prove her intent. Once again, she would be painted with the same brush as a guy like Perkins, a cop killer. A wanted man.

"I saw you creeping." The male voice belonged to a guy probably ten or so feet away, moving toward her. "I will find you. There's nowhere to run."

Cold fingers walked fear up her spine. Alternatively, a spider may have decided to take its chances searching for warmth *inside* her jacket.

Neither scenario was optimal.

If he didn't move on, she'd be forced to confront him. But Sasha didn't want to move from this spot until she accomplished what she came here to do. She needed to get Ian Perkins out of that bedroom and back in safe care—child services, or Maggie. The owner/operator of Hope Mansion was also a licensed foster parent. She could take in Ian until his mother got out of the hospital.

Sasha stayed where she was, crouched into as small of a ball as possible. Run. Hide. Stay, or go. It was always a risk, either way. That split second of indecision, while she tried to figure out which avenue of escape was best, was the worst part.

"Hey, it's me."

Sasha frowned. The guy wasn't talking to her.

"Yeah, I saw it." While he was on the phone, Sasha held still and waited to see what he would say to whoever it was he was talking to. "Yeah." He chuckled. "I guess the cops found the house already."

Sasha pursed her lips and drew in a long breath to try and settle her stomach. *Please don't be dead.* The last thing she wanted was for anyone to have been killed. Especially someone only trying to do their job. Still, all she could think of was Alex. *Please don't be dead.*

The FBI would probably think she was working with Perkins —and trying to frame him, or something like that. She needed to get that kid back to safety. And not to prove herself to them, either. Sasha didn't feel the need to do that.

Or, she hadn't.

She'd spent much too much time with Alex lately. He was rubbing off on her. Making her want to show them the truth when she'd always chosen not to care what other people thought.

"She's here. I saw her on the feeds myself." He was quiet for a few seconds. "Understood. Yes, sir."

He was talking to Perkins. Who else could it be? This guy, whoever he was, had access to the "feeds." So he was probably some kind of security guard. Which meant it was no coincidence those two inside had been ordered to bring the boy here. Perkins had places to hide—plenty of them, it seemed.

The cops hadn't known about the house. They didn't know about this place. And she'd left her phone back at the site of that still-smoldering explosion to lead them there. To lead *Alex* there. He could be dead, and she had no way of calling for the cops to come here next. Not to mention, the entire police department and the rest of the emergency services could be tied up for hours in the aftermath of that explosion.

Sasha looked back at the window where the boy slept. Exhausted, or asleep because of some more sinister reason, she didn't know. They could've drugged him. Regardless, she was glad he was resting and not currently screaming, completely traumatized.

Torn from his mother. Sent away by his father. Who knew what the child had seen his own father's men do to his mother?

She had to get him out of there.

"I'll bring her myself."

Sasha stared in the security guy's direction. Her eyes narrowed. This guy, whoever he was, thought he would subdue and bring her to Perkins? They might have figured correctly that she would come and try to rescue the boy. Or it was simply chance that this guy had seen her on his "feeds."

She heard the creak of leather. It sounded similar to a cop with a full belt of things around his waist. But this guy was no cop, and he worked for Perkins. As far as she was concerned, that meant he was fair game.

"Come out, come out, wherever you are."

Cold fingers continued their track up her spine. Sasha fought the shiver and held still. She had her stun gun. He probably held a weapon. Security guards might not always carry guns, but she figured this guy did. Whether he was the real deal, or not. This whole complex could be run by Perkins. An entire neighborhood of criminals and she'd be stuck right in the middle.

Perkins's pride had been hurt that night they met at Hope Mansion. Sure, he'd nearly bested her and had only run off when the police showed up, but he likely wanted a rematch. The chance to exercise power over her and prove to himself—and everyone he worked with—that he was still top dog.

Been there, done that.

There were now enough years that'd passed, that she finally could just about stomach thinking of the hellish ordeal she'd been through. Perkins was the same type of guy who'd abused her all those years ago. The kind who thought he could do whatever he wanted.

The difference?

She wasn't a seventeen-year-old who didn't know how to defend herself anymore.

If Perkins or any of his men came at her the way her uncle's killer had, they were going to meet a very different woman than the one who had been brutalized all those years ago.

Sasha palmed her stun gun. She probably had enough charge left for this security guard. After that, she'd have to get creative. But the government had trained her well, after a recruiter, years ago, spotted her at a dojo and looked into her. All she'd been doing was trying to learn how to not be a victim anymore. He'd done a full background and figured out what drove her.

They'd offered to train her completely, something she didn't turn down or walk away from, even when the scope of that training became clear. But by that time, she felt she owed them because Sasha had learned how to put Melina, and her trauma, in a box inside her mind.

She hadn't been driven by fear after that.

The targets they'd sent her to take care of after her training might have been bad people. Political dissidents, or enemies of freedom. Those with a terrible agenda. But it had all since been buried and nothing would ever see the light of day. Deals were all made under the table. Operations were off-book. All so no one in Washington would be the recipient of any blowback. That was why she knew the US government would never admit to knowing who she was, not even to save her life. That was just how it worked.

There was no way Perkins had *any* idea who she was.

Sasha might not have killed anyone in several years, but if it came down to her, or a man who tried to destroy his wife and thought he had absolute power to do the same with his child? Well, she was happy to make an exception. She couldn't be blamed if he pushed her to take lethal force in defense of her own life or the life of someone else.

The alternative was revenge, and that was a poor motivator. Strong emotions clouded a person's judgment. Alex and his cop friends, any number of them, might have been killed in that explosion, but she wasn't going to allow that to interfere with what was right.

Perkins needed to be stopped.

The security guard continued his search for her. She tracked his progress with the back-and-forth sweep of his flashlight beam. If he didn't find her soon, she was going to have to step out and essentially hand herself over to him. Her legs were falling asleep and would soon be worthless.

"I'm not going to kill you." He dragged the words out.

Sasha rolled her eyes. She stood up, keeping quiet. If she spoke, startling him, she could make him jump and he'd probably squeeze the trigger on that gun.

The flashlight beam settled on her. "He said he wants you alive."

"And I want that boy handed over to the police." She

pointed at the window. He would know full well who she meant. "So let's make a deal."

He started to shake his head. "No—"

"Don't bother arguing. How about you call the cops. Tell them you're the hero, the one who found that boy. After they show up here and get him back, I'll go with you to Perkins. No tricks." She held up her hands so he could see both palms open. The stun gun was tucked in the back of her belt.

"I'm supposed to believe you won't put up a fight?"

"I don't know what you've heard, but you should know all I care about is that kid in there." She motioned with one hand. "Not you. Not me, and certainly not Perkins. So long as the boy is safe, I'll do whatever you want."

His eyes flashed.

I wasn't offering that. Though, he might prove perfectly happy to take it whether she did or not.

Before that, though, he'd have to step closer to her, at which point he would find out real quick why the FBI considered her dangerous—regardless of whether she was armed or not.

She'd have to hold off killing him. If the cops had no idea he worked for Perkins, they would think she'd killed a security guard in cold blood. No one would change their mind about her after that, whether she'd want them to or not. Sasha still didn't like the idea of a potential hostage situation, but it might be unavoidable. At least someone would be working to free the boy.

If the police and feds were still alive to do it, of course. The smoke smell from the explosion lingered in the air, even here. There could have been a massacre.

Alex could be dead.

The security guard pulled out his phone with two fingers and made a call. "Yes, is this the police? I know where Ian Perkins is. I found him." He gave a street address. "The yellow house in the corner. I think it's number forty-two. It's him." He hung up. "Let's go."

"Not so fast. I said when the cops get him back. So hold your horses, because I'm not going anywhere."

"My office," he said. "We can watch from there." He motioned with the gun. "Start walking. You can hold the flashlight."

She reached for it, grabbed his wrist instead, and punched his solar plexus. He started to go down. Sasha disarmed him as he fell, but he rallied faster than she'd have thought. This guy was scrappy.

He tackled her to the ground. She landed on her back with a thud, all his weight on top of her.

He reached for her throat—the way Perkins had done. The way...

Each breath rushed in her ears as the lid she'd nailed shut on the past flung open. Melina's tragic history hurtled back to the present at full speed. But this time it would be different.

Don't kill him.

Sasha swung the butt of the gun and hit him in the head. The angle too awkward, he didn't go down. He squeezed harder. She hit him again.

Finally, he slumped on top of her. That was kind of worse.

She shoved him to the side and rolled him off her, onto the ground. Sasha kept the gun and scrambled to her feet while the rush in her ears subsided and her awareness came back.

She heard a shuffle right before a gun cocked.

Sasha froze.

19

S asha lifted the gun and pointed it at him. From a house exploding and carnage, to this? His day pretty much sucked. But considering how many cops had responded there, it had left him free to come here when the call came in.

Because he'd known it was where Sasha would be.

Alex lifted his hand. "Don't—"

Before he could finish, he felt the cold press of steel at the back of his head. He had snuck up on her, and someone else had done the same to him. If he had to guess, he'd say it was likely the big man from the photo she'd taken of the two that left with the boy.

He also needed to ask her why an unconscious man was bleeding on the grass not too far away. The man was dressed like one of those neighborhood security guys and would need medical attention. Unless it was too late and he died before they could get him some help.

"Drop your gun."

A woman's voice. So, not the big man from the photo. Alex didn't know if the woman holding a gun to his skull was talking to him or Sasha, but said anyway, "Both of you can drop your guns."

The voice behind him chuckled. "Not gonna happen."

"I'm the cop here. It's not me who is going to back off, it's the two of you."

Sasha's gaze hardened. Yes, he was lumping her in with the assailant behind him.

The woman behind him said, "Guess I'll shoot you, then."

Muzzle flash in front blinded him, and for a second Alex thought he was the one who'd been shot. Until the pressure behind him vanished, and he heard a body hit the ground.

He turned and saw the woman laying on her back, her dead eyes staring up at the sky—a bullet hole in the center of her forehead. "I'm not going to congratulate you on your marksmanship."

"How do you know I wasn't aiming for you?"

"Not funny." He shot Sasha a look. "Someone probably heard that. Let's move."

"Good." She strode toward the back of the house. "We just have to jimmy the window open and then we can get Ian."

He tugged on her elbow. "Hold up. Ian?"

"Isn't that why you're here?"

She motioned at the unconscious man. "I figured he faked that phone call, but when you showed up, I thought maybe he did follow through and call the cops. I was going to let him take me to Perkins once Ian was safe." She grabbed a phone from the ground so that she had it in one hand and the gun in the other.

"I don't suppose you're going to give me that gun."

She shook her head. "Not until Ian is safe. There's still a man in the house. A big man."

"I know. I saw your pictures."

"Good."

That was it? Just "good" and she was back to business. The last time he saw her, she'd stunned him. Literally. And even though it gave him credence with the feds where he'd been on shaky ground before, he wasn't about to thank her for leaving him unconscious on the street. Even if it did tamp down suspicion. Because he'd been incapacitated, the feds didn't jump all over him for not arresting her. But it would be a long while before he heard the end of it.

He checked to make sure the big man wasn't racing around the house to avenge the fallen woman. He'd have preferred to arrest her, but considering all the terror still coursing through him from when the gun had been pointed at the back of his head, he wasn't too cut up about the fact she was dead.

Some situations didn't have a good, or even satisfying, end. They just turned out. The woman, dead. Alex, alive. Sasha had pulled the trigger. Maybe it would hit her later that she'd taken a life, or maybe it wouldn't. He wasn't sure. Right now, it seemed like she had more important things on her mind.

"You're staring at me." She felt around the window, the cell phone stowed in her back pocket.

"How can you even tell?" He looked in both directions this time, just in case the man came creeping around the corner. "And what are you doing, anyway? You're coming with me." He reached for his cuffs.

She spun around. "First, take a look in that window and tell me that arresting me is still your first priority. Let's focus on what matters right now. After we get him out safely, I want to hear how you knew where to find me."

He peered in. On the bed lay a bundle, blonde hair peeking out the top of a gray blanket. The child shifted, and Alex saw his face. "Ian."

Mateo had been that small once. Now he was almost a man and Alex was continually proud of how his nephew navigated life with good sense—for the most part. He was a teenager, after all.

The bedroom door opened and a huge guy stepped in. Alex grabbed Sasha's arm and ducked. "Get down." He hissed the words at her.

She crouched, though not in response to what was essentially an order. "We have to get him out."

"You just killed a person." Not to mention the unconscious guy could wake up at any moment and start a ruckus.

"How did you even find me here?"

Alex had to hand it to her—She was a master of deflection. "A neighbor heard the Amber Alert we put out and saw the couple carrying in a suspicious bundle."

"Someone put all that together?"

"No one lives here, but occasionally people sleep over. Like a vacation rental, but only for a night. Always the same types—rough looking and loud—always coming and going, even into the middle of the night. That kind. Seeing a sleeping child seemed weird, though."

Alex lifted himself high enough to peer in the window. The child still slept, though the door was again shut and the man was gone. *Lord, be with him.* Ian had been terrorized, that was a given. They needed to get him out as quietly as possible. "I'll call for backup. You can stay in the car, and they'll assist. He can hand the boy over, or we can take him."

He stood, trying to figure out who was available. Everyone was at the house dealing with the aftermath of the explosion. Two FBI agents had been injured, thrown several feet through the air. They should be in the hospital by now, getting checked out. It could have been so much worse. Eric hadn't stopped saying, "Thank You, Jesus" for five straight minutes.

The fact so many of Last Chance's police force had shown up, on and off-duty cops, meant he could respond when dispatch had called about the couple and the child.

He knew it was where Sasha would be.

Sasha was now shaking her head as she also straightened up. "We don't have time for backup. You and I have to do this *now*. Perkins will know soon enough. Or something else will happen."

"You're impatient."

"If I see something I need to do, I just do it. Why wait for other problems to arise? Maybe that is impatience. Or maybe it's not letting life slip by while I sit around and do nothing about bad things happening to people. Just because someone decided to make them pawns, moving them to do their own corrupt bidding, doesn't mean we sit here and do nothing. They deserve to be safe."

Alex spotted the sheen of tears in her eyes. He closed the gap between them. "We're not going to let anyone hurt Ian. Not anymore. His days of being scared are over, okay?"

She nodded. He touched his thumb to her cheek and threaded his fingers in her thick dark hair, keeping his hold on her loose. She was like a bird. Here one second, flying away the next. Not flighty, but elusive. He wasn't sure he wanted to tie her down. A woman like Sasha might need to be free to survive.

His thumb drifted over her bottom lip.

"Are you trying to distract me so you can throw cuffs on me and get all the credit for saving the kid?"

He shot her a wry look. "Like you did when you stun-gunned me?"

"You were about to arrest me."

"So you did the reasonable thing and left me on the ground. Unconscious."

"Do you want me to apologize?"

"Would you?" He studied her, not needing her remorse. He just wanted to know how she ticked. She didn't owe him anything. Not when he knew so much of what she'd been through—and admittedly still had no clue as to most of it. That part of her was like a glacier. Plenty above the surface, but so much more below.

"Maybe."

"Wow." It slipped it out before he realized his reaction.

"I guess you don't think much of me." She turned to the window again.

"That's not it." She did what she had to. To survive. He understood that. She'd saved his life as if it was an imperative. As though she was a soldier fighting a war, even if the battle was largely within her.

How could he argue with a person's fundamental drive to remain alive? She reacted to things on a visceral level. Her code of conduct was strong, and she did what her honor demanded. Like saving the life of a child. Or having a voice in her destiny.

Sasha popped off the screen and tossed it on the ground. "Make sure the security guy doesn't wake up. He works for Perkins."

Alex spun to the unconscious man. "Uh...Sasha. He's gone. How did we not hear him get up?" He'd been distracted by her instead of doing his job. "I'm calling this in."

"Fine. While you do that, I'll get Ian." She slid up the window.

Alex moved to her as she climbed in. He should have arrested her and called in, but she did have a point that time was limited. Alex had never broken protocol before. Now, these last few days, he seemed to have blown past nearly every rule of police integrity there was.

He should quit.

But then, how would he continue to work on proving to everyone—mostly himself—that he deserved to receive good things? Even Sasha deserved the blessings of a happy life.

That was how it seemed to work for everyone else. So why wasn't it working for him?

The bedroom door flew open so hard it hit the wall and bounced back. Sasha stood in front of him, blocking the view.

"Nice try."

"You aren't taking the kid."

Two of them, facing Sasha. Both male. The big man and the security guard would be his guess, but Sasha stood in his way, determined to protect him again. The way she had when she'd taken a bullet for him.

"I'm gonna try." Confidence bled through her tone.

Real or not, he believed it. And she'd more than proven she knew what she was doing. Finding the house and following the two in the pickup here while also having the sense to leave a trail for him to find. And she'd given him photo evidence on top of that.

Her honor wasn't in question.

Alex sprinted around the house. If he could get to the front, go inside and enter the bedroom behind those two men, he could surprise them. Without backup, that was all he had.

He pulled out his phone and called dispatch, stopping at the front corner of the house to check there were no more armed men out front. It was clear.

As concisely as he could, he relayed to the new dispatcher as much as possible about Ian and the two men, as well as Sasha's presence here. The FBI would be informed. If they were done at the house, Eric would for sure be here to take custody of Sasha. Her need to save the child would be what ultimately got her arrested.

"Copy that," she responded. "A unit is on its way."

"Pull another off the explosion. Unless someone else was hurt?"

"No other reported injuries."

"Get me two cars." He needed help. "And call Conroy."

"Yes, Lieutenant."

Alex hung up. He went to the front door and kicked it in. A gunshot rang out through the house. "Sasha!" The FBI would finally get the result they were here for—all because she cared more for a child than she did her own life.

Her, in cuffs. In custody.

But Alex would know the real reason she'd been arrested.

Him.

20

The door to the interrogation room opened and Special Agent Cullings walked in.

Sasha lifted her forehead from the table. "What did the doctor say? How is the child?"

Eric stopped with one hand out and tugged the chair away from the table.

"Well?" The kid had been drugged. By the time she got to him, by first outrunning the other two men barreling toward her, she'd been unable to rouse him. She and Alex subdued the two men, and the place had flooded with police and FBI.

Now she was here. In handcuffs.

Eric sat down before answering, "He was injected with something, but they seemed to know what it was. Last I heard, he'll be fine."

Sasha let go of all the tension in a long breath. "That's good. Not being able to wake him was...scary."

"You have medical training?"

"Some field training, like for trauma care. I learned from a friend who was in the military. For a while, years ago, I thought I was going to be a nurse so I've taken some night classes." She glanced at the bland wall beside the big glass window she couldn't see through. "Didn't work out, though."

He studied her. The head of the task force that had been hunting her for weeks now. Ever since she'd shown up in Last Chance to help her friend Bridget and their boss Millie, and to catch the betrayer colleague who'd tried to kill them both—Clarke. That was when she'd landed on their radar. Eric had been shot when Clarke came for Millie. Now he was the arresting agent.

"What am I being charged with?"

He leaned back in the chair. "We're working on that. Judges around here like to take their time, you know?"

She didn't, but he likely wasn't after a response. And she was going to work to keep any conversation limited. If she mentioned anything specific, and it wasn't on his radar, she would only end up tipping her hand, and he would have even more ammunition against her. Right now, she had no idea what this was about.

And how could she? Sasha had lived so many lives. Been so many places. A lot of what she'd done was classified. He probably didn't know about that stuff. And more recently, she'd done good things. She'd even saved Alex's life just hours ago. How could the charges stem from a recent crime? She didn't think she'd done anything in the past few years to warrant an entire federal task force.

That left the past. The timespan before she started working for the government. Who knew what on earth they were thinking? Or if she would even live to see any kind of trial. It had happened to Clarke, though she knew that was Dorian. Shot on the courthouse steps minutes before his arraignment.

People like her didn't live long once they popped up in the system. A name entered triggered a search result. After that, it was only a matter of time before she would be cut down in the hall in some prison, or killed in a riot.

Not what she would have chosen, but it wasn't always possible to control the variables.

Eric opened the file in front of him. A stack of handwritten pages had been collated inside. "What's your relationship with Thomas Perkins?"

"My what?"

"Your relationship. How do you two know each other, when did you meet? That kind of thing."

"Well, let's see." She settled against the back of the hard plastic chair like she was out for coffee with a girlfriend. "He was downstairs at Hope Mansion, in the living room with four of his guys. That's the first time I've ever seen him. We exchanged words. He tried to strangle me. I think that just about covers our *relationship.*"

"The phone in your possession at the time of your arrest lists calls made to and from Perkins going back months. Text messages."

"Emails? Maybe addressed to that security guard? What with it being his phone and all."

Sasha had only grabbed his gun, which she'd discarded pretty quickly after Alex arrested both guys, and she'd tried to aid Ian. He had to have slipped it into her jacket pocket somehow. To make it look like she was the one working for Perkins.

Sasha realized what those papers were. Statements, similar to the ones she'd written for Alex. Only these were probably penned by the big guy and Perkins's security guard friend.

They were trying to set her up.

"Being belligerent isn't going to earn you any points."

Sasha said, "Then it's a good thing I don't keep score."

He said nothing.

"My phone was lost at the house." She could tell him to ask Lieutenant Basuto if he had it, which she was sure he did. Alex had seen those photos in her gallery. But that would only drag him into her issues. Like a dog with a bone, the task force would get a hankering to take down a dirty cop.

The way they'd gone after her.

And for what?

"I didn't think all this was because of Perkins."

Eric studied her, one hand on the table. Relaxed. Like he had all the time in the world. "That's a new development. I'm just trying to get the full picture."

She saw something in his gaze then. "And you think, some-how, in the time since I came to town, I've managed to get in with Perkins and whatever operation he has going on?"

Eric shrugged one shoulder. "It's certainly possible."

"But why would I do that?"

"For the money, maybe?"

He'd know she wasn't after notoriety. Instead, Sasha had lived under the radar for decades. She operated best in the shad-ows. She understood the darkness because she had been forged there, on the floor of that barn. Torn apart and left that way so that now so much scar tissue remained on her soul she didn't know how she was still alive inside.

"You think I need money? Or did you not find my Cayman's accounts yet?"

Eric glanced over his shoulder at the window. Two quiet raps responded—a light tap of acknowledgment. "Indepen-dently wealthy?"

"I earned every dollar of it just like any other working-class American."

"And you pay taxes?"

"Melina does."

He opened his mouth to say something but hesitated. The feds hadn't known about her past, and that meant neither did he. They'd been looking for Sasha. The revelation could work in her favor, or it could backfire. Depended on whether this agent would hold a grudge because she'd made him look inept in front of his subordinates.

The fact he was the husband of her former boss and friend didn't factor in. But that was good because Sasha wasn't interested in special favors. If she had broken the law, she would face the consequences just like any other criminal.

The alternative was to manipulate them. To lie and deal her way to some kind of reduced sentence. Depended on the charges, of course. Instead of thinking like a negotiator, she had a head full of questions.

Eric flipped the papers to reveal another folder underneath. He slid out a page of her writing. "Interesting tactic, delivering statements to a police lieutenant. He can't help but be sympathetic given the shared history between the two of you."

"I'm sure, to you, it would seem as though all I'm doing is playing a game. Working whatever angle I can find to get what I want."

She could see he wanted to ask her if that wasn't exactly what she was doing. Instead, he tapped the page with his index finger. "Four college kids die of a drug overdose, but you survive? It's a compelling story, but we both know you're full of crap. Not a word of this is true."

"Then tell me what happened, since apparently you know."

"Partying with your friends. You, the housekeeping girl from the hotel. Didn't one of their fathers own the building? Bunch of college guys. Of course, it got out of hand. So, you put a stop to them. The same way you put a stop to the men that hurt you."

Cullings knew about her past.

"I suppose I drugged myself in the process?" Never mind that he'd just suggested she was the one who'd killed the men in that barn, the ones who'd hurt her, when the truth was far different.

Eric shrugged one shoulder. "Probably mixed up the cups."

"And the prostitution going on in the hotel?"

"You figured out they were involved and decided to put a stop to it." Eric tipped his head to one side. "How am I doing so far?"

"It's…what did you call it? A 'compelling story.'"

"I get it. Trying to get revenge on guys who would do to women what was done to you." He paused. "I do get it."

"Mmm. So I'm a vigilante. That's it?"

"You murdered those boys in cold blood. You were young. Stands to reason you made mistakes, like getting some of the drugs in your system."

Sasha said, "Because they were behind it? A group of college boys running a prostitution ring out of an international hotel? If they had been behind it, the business would have ended after they were murdered."

"It didn't?"

"They moved it to another hotel. The head of security had a deal with someone who worked there. The girls were all moved and everything was business as usual."

"And the boys?"

"They'd gone into the hotel. As *guests*. They took pictures and talked to the girls. Trying to see if any of them would talk to the police."

"They were gathering evidence."

"Because I asked them to." Tears filled her eyes. "Because they were my friends."

The door swung open. Alex strode in first. Sasha glanced away, not wanting to meet his eyes when he would likely see plainly what was on her face. She'd given the play-by-play of what had happened to her friends in the statement. The events. Everything she'd seen and heard.

But not the "why" of it, the reason they'd been targeted by someone powerful. She couldn't prove her supposition—that it was all due to her foolish thinking that she'd be able to take down a prostitution ring back when she'd had no skills and no connections.

"I'd like to speak to my client." The voice drifted from behind Alex.

Alex said, "Her lawyer's here."

Sasha put her head down on the table. She had a screaming headache and no energy to talk to anyone else.

Eric pushed the chair back and left. She heard the lawyer walk in, and the door shut.

Sasha shook her head. "Dorian, this isn't the time. You didn't need to——" She looked up, far too much emotion at the surface.

It wasn't Dorian.

"Who are you?" She'd never seen this guy before in her life. But, in that instant, she cataloged everything she could see. Suit paid for by whoever hired him—and this guy had been paid well. He wasn't from around here, and he wasn't a thug.

He pulled out a chair and sat. "Didn't you hear? I'm your lawyer." The guy set a cell phone on the table, then placed a water bottle beside it.

There was no point asking who he was. He would only lie. "So what's the word? If you're my lawyer, then you should be giving me advice, right?"

"Right. Advice."

"Are you the one who shot at me behind the diner? You could have killed that chef guy." She wasn't about to use Stuart's name or indicate familiarity with him. That would let this guy, and whoever he worked for, know that she had vulnerabilities.

He didn't answer her question, just pushed the water bottle toward her. "This is for you. A gift."

She didn't take it. Eric had offered her coffee, but that wasn't the point. Alarm bells rang in her head.

Her "lawyer" unlocked the phone and turned it. On the screen was a picture of Millie—her former boss, and also Eric's wife—at a park with their two boys. She was only a couple of months pregnant, but the bump under her shirt was already visible.

"What is this?"

He swiped. The next photo featured Bridget. Grief rolled

through Sasha as she stared at the image and started to ascertain what this was all about. Beside the woman was her daughter, Sydney, the one Bridget had only recently met, all because of Sasha's actions—ones Bridget was never going to forgive her for.

"Drink the water, Sasha."

"What's in it?"

"Does it matter? You drink it, here and now, or I make a call and they die." He twisted the cap on the water and handed the bottle over. "It's your choice, but I'm thinking you'll make the right one."

She drew it toward her and unscrewed the cap the rest of the way. Let him think she might comply. There was poison in the water. She would have a medical emergency that led to her death, and he would feign ignorance. "Before I do, tell me who hired you. I deserve to know who wants me dead."

He tapped the phone. "I'll tell my guy to squeeze off a shot right now. He can start with the kids, so their moms can watch them die."

A fire burned in Sasha's gut. She tossed the water bottle in his face and launched herself across the table.

21

A cry that sounded like Sasha preceded a thunderous crash. Alex and Conroy had been huddled with Eric in the hall, discussing the FBI agent's conversation with Sasha before her lawyer showed up.

Alex took two steps and flung the door open. Sasha was on top of the lawyer, fist pulled back. She punched his cheekbone.

"Get her off me!" The lawyer flashed bloody teeth. "She's crazy."

Conroy pushed past him. He pulled Sasha off the lawyer while she said, "Check his phone." He heard her suck in a breath, then she yelled, "DONALDSON!"

Alex held out a hand to help the downed guy back to his feet. "What's going on?"

Sergeant Aiden Donaldson raced in to stand by Eric. "What's going on?"

Five men and one woman in an interrogation room with a table taking up most of the space made Alex's skin itch.

"Call Bridget." Sasha gasped. "There's a sniper pointed at her." Before anyone could respond, Sasha turned to Eric. "Call your wife, too. He said he would tell them to kill the kids first."

Both Aiden and Eric rushed out the door. Alex heard them

on the phone out in the hall. "Seriously?" He glanced between her and the lawyer, then back. "Snipers?"

She nodded. "Has to be more than one. Someone paid him to come here."

The lawyer was on his feet now. Alex took one wrist and turned his chest to the wall, as he grabbed out his cuffs.

Sasha shifted, and he heard the clink of hers.

"I got him." Conroy took the cuffs from Alex, leaving Sasha on her own.

He wanted to go to her but couldn't. Not if he wanted to remain impartial and above suspicion. There was enough of that from the task force already.

Alex took a step.

The lawyer lunged.

Sasha screamed, "Don't!"

He grabbed the water bottle from the floor, a small amount of liquid still inside which he tossed back into his mouth.

"No!"

She hit the bottle from his hands. Alex tried to pull her back and found his arms around her waist. It was instinct to pull her close.

Meanwhile, Conroy hauled the lawyer away by the collar of his shirt. "What..?"

The guy started to convulse.

White foam appeared around his mouth.

Another burst of instinct had him back up, Sasha with him. Her warmth against his front. He didn't hold her tightly. Not when she was cuffed, and he had a police shield on his belt. They were being watched, regardless of whether scrutiny was real right now.

Conroy had backed up to the other wall, close to the door. "Should we be worried about a contagion?"

She shook her head. "He didn't come here for murder-suicide. Just to force me to kill myself to save my friends so I don't tell the FBI anything."

"Who does he work for?"

"I asked." She shrugged. "He didn't tell me."

Conroy glanced at Alex. "Let's get his phone and see what else he has on him. But first, we need an ambulance. Maybe the medical examiner."

The guy twitched twice and stilled.

Conroy reached down and touched two fingers to his neck. "He's dead."

"We need to make sure there's no failsafe." Sasha didn't move from his hold on her. "Could be he's supposed to check in or whoever is in charge gives the green light to the snipers."

Conroy glanced at him. Alex nodded. "Let's go."

He led Sasha around the far side of the table and out into the hall.

"My office."

Alex nodded to his boss. "Copy that."

"Okay, good." Eric held his phone to his ear as he paced the hall. "No, sit tight. There's a detail on the way." The fed glanced at Sasha as they passed, as though he wanted to say something but didn't know what.

Alex could think of a few things. But voicing them likely wasn't a stellar idea. His personal feelings were beginning to override the professional side he tried to have out front at all times. He was the lieutenant, after all. Except right now he had Sasha with him, and she'd nearly died. He wasn't feeling super professional.

Alex led her to Conroy's office and shut the door. He wanted to tell her to sit but couldn't get the words out. "I can't believe he nearly killed you." Threatening the kids?

"You guys don't vet the people you let in here?"

"Drugged water. Snipers." Alex ran his hands down his face. It had to be the middle of the night by now and none of them had slept. Yet Sasha looked like she was well rested. Unruffled. "He tried to kill you!"

Her blank expression softened a bit. "He didn't. And the kids are fine, right?"

He nodded. Anything otherwise, and he'd have heard. "I can't believe you jumped across the table at him."

Sasha lifted her chin. "Is whatever I say here going to be part of my official statement regarding what happened? Because I might need that lawyer after all. At least, one that isn't trying to kill me."

"You aren't bothered by this?"

She just stood there, stoic.

"I know you've been through a lot in your life, so your tolerance might be a little higher—"

She shook her head. "That's not it. You're expecting me to be overcome with some emotional reaction. Adrenaline and shock."

"Honestly, yeah." Because even he was having trouble controlling the urge to throw something across the room, just for the satisfaction of hearing it shatter.

"My emotions are the *only* thing that I have control over. Especially when I'm victimized or made a target. Or people I care about are at the receiving end of sniper scopes. If you think I'm not going to freak out later when I'm alone—if I even get that chance—you'd be wrong. But the feelings I have aren't for public display."

"Because you think you have to hide from me?"

"In the chief's office, in a police station, surrounded by cops and feds. All of whom are mad at me even though I had nothing to do with the house exploding. Yes, I have to hide." She paused a second. "But not from you."

He let out a breath, more relieved than he should've been. But he liked that she didn't feel like she had to pretend.

"Even though you arrested me."

His brows rose. "I didn't slap cuffs on you."

She shot him a look and settled in a chair. Alex leaned on the cabinet, his hips on the counter. The last thing he wanted was to get into that conversation. At least right now. He needed her focused, so he could get her initial impressions. "Did you know that guy?"

"Never seen him before. I actually thought he was Dorian at first, just coming to check on me." She studied her fingers, laced together on her lap. Cuffs on her wrists. "Until I realized he wasn't. That's when he told me to drink the water—"

Alex held himself still. If he blew up, angry at the dead guy, she could shut down. As it was, it felt like he had to draw her out. She lived behind a series of battlements she'd erected to keep herself safe from fear and pain.

He understood it. He just didn't like that she felt as though she had to do it. Alex wanted to keep her safe. Then she'd know she could let go a little bit.

"—and that if I didn't, then my friends and their children would die." A shiver moved through her. That was the only concession she gave her body as to what had happened. That tiny bleed away of the stress.

"Someone hired him. Sent him here to silence you."

"Because they couldn't wait."

He nodded. "You were in custody, and he was hoping to get to you before you could say anything to the feds."

"There's no guarantee I already didn't. It was a risky move to expose himself like that, trapped in a room with me. No way to get out of the police station after I did die. Unless he planned to say I asked for him to bring the bottle to do it to myself." She sighed. "There's probably an email from one of my accounts to him. A fake one, planted there to make it look like my death was my idea."

"You think I'd have believed that?"

She studied him for a second. The way she tended to do.

"You don't believe me, or you're just surprised?"

She said, "You realize no one has ever taken my side on anything. Not ever, my whole life."

He'd remembered a few things she'd told him about her

mother, years ago. Some of it came back. "Not even Bridget, or Millie?"

"Bridget walked away when she thought I planned to kill Clarke. At no point did she come here and speak on my behalf, and given the fact her husband is your sergeant, I didn't expect her to. She has enough going on in her life to worry about me."

"And Millie?"

"She's Eric's wife. She can't get in the middle of his task force case. Maybe she doesn't even know they're looking for me."

"So you expect nothing from people who are supposed to be your friends. Least of all that they would turn out to support you." Alex pushed off the cabinet and crouched in front of her.

She shrugged one shoulder, probably pretending it didn't bother her when he could see it did. Though, she valiantly tried to hide it. "People have their own lives."

"And you've learned to fight your battles alone because no one shows up to stand with you."

She swallowed.

"Those boys' deaths weren't your fault."

"Someone gave them tainted drugs so they could get rid of the threat we presented and keep operating in the hotel."

"But you survived."

She winced. "I was a mess. By the time I recovered, the operation was long gone. The girls…" A tear rolled down her cheek.

Alex wanted to swipe it away with his thumb, but she beat him to it. "None of that was your fault."

"I tried to stop it. When I told the boys—my friends—about what was happening, they agreed to go to the hotel and make contact. Ask the girls if they wanted to get out. Tell them that we'd help them." Another tear fell. "A few of them were in their teens. I know some people do that stuff…willingly. These girls weren't there by choice. I could tell."

He touched her cheek then. "I'm sorry you couldn't help them. Melina would be proud of you for trying."

Perhaps it was strange, considering she *was* Melina. But given the softening of her lips, he figured she understood.

"She would." Sasha shook her head. "But even with everything I've done, it never seems like enough."

The words rocked Alex. *It never seems like enough.* He straightened, absorbing the words like a punch to the sternum that sent him reeling. All he'd tried to do. The way he strove to earn the things everyone else was blessed with.

Never enough.

Someone tapped on the door. He turned to see Bridget walk in, hesitation in her steps. She glanced between them. "Can I... talk to Sasha?"

Alex nodded. He strode out without looking back at her. Sasha was chipping away at everything he'd built, determined to break through what he shored up every day when he came to work. He did the right thing. He said the right thing. He believed in the right things.

She could make it all come crumbling down.

If he let her.

22

S asha watched him leave. It felt like someone had cut off part of her, taking it with them as they left. Stolen. Lost. Bereft.

"Are you okay?" Bridget crossed from the door and sat in a chair close to her. "You seem…" She shook her head.

Sasha didn't want to talk about herself. "Is Sydney okay?"

"Because of you. Again. That's what you want me to say?" Bridget had withstood some crazy storms in her life. Not the same as Sasha, but the younger woman had been scarred nonetheless. Sasha had seen sort of a little sister in her. She'd taken Bridget under her wing. Taught her how to pick a lock and trained her with every weapon Sasha could think of.

The pattern wasn't lost on her.

She found people who needed protection, usually women, and tried to save them. Or taught them how to save themselves.

The past few weeks at Hope Mansion—until Emily Perkins —she hadn't come across anyone who needed her help. It left her devoid and wondering what to do with her life.

A shrink would probably have a field day with her, which was why Sasha had never stuck with one. She was scared to tell anyone everything. Even the smallest thing and people turned their backs on her. Why would a therapist be any different?

No one even got close to understanding, until Alex. And yet, what had Alex done when she'd explained how not one single person in her life had ever stood with her or truly had her back? Not even Zander, who'd been her husband, had supported her when it counted. What did Alex do when she finally peeled away that layer? He'd walked out.

He thought the same as everyone else. That either she could take care of herself and didn't need him, or she wasn't worth the time. Too bad—that mindset of her not being worth the time had birthed in her a need to prove to everyone that she could take care of things herself. This only made them believe that she didn't need anyone. But of course, that wasn't true.

She'd wanted Alex to believe her and believe *in* her. She wanted just one person on her side when it felt like the whole world was against her.

"Do you want to tell me what's going on?"

Sasha looked at her friend. Freshly styled hair, a ring on her finger. A child, another on the way, soon enough, and a police sergeant husband. Yet, she knew that under the surface lived a much different story. Maybe the *whole* world wasn't against her.

Sasha shifted and the cuffs on her hands clinked.

Bridget turned to the door where Aiden stood listening. "Can we take those off?"

He shook his head. "Sorry."

"It's fine." Sasha hardly cared. She'd suffered far worse indignity than a pair of handcuffs. If they were removed, she would only give in to the urge to run. Flee. Get as far away from all this as possible, and that was about the worst thing she could do right now. The cops and feds here would tackle her to the floor and put them back on.

"And I'm fine."

"You expect me to believe that?" Bridget paused. "You forget I know you."

Sasha narrowed her eyes.

Bridget smiled. "I'm not lying. I can see right through you, but only sometimes. Maybe you're just out of practice since you've been on vacation for a couple of months."

"You think I'm rusty?"

"I've had time to think. To recall you, and the things you said. How you said them. I've come to some conclusions."

"Are you gunning for a position as my priest or my therapist?"

"Considering you need both, and that person would get to help you, I'd consider that a compliment."

Sasha sighed. "It's late. I'm sure you want to get home to Sydney—"

"Don't." Bridget shook her head. "Don't bring her into this. She's not a tool to be used to manipulate me. That part of our relationship is over now."

Sasha said nothing.

"You told me my baby was dead. Doing that saved her life. It saved mine too, and not just back then. You did it again a few months ago. Now we're together and Sydney has her whole life ahead of her."

"So go live it."

"Do you want me to look you in the eye and tell you I can't love you because of what you did?"

Sasha looked at the desk. It was the coward's way, but she didn't have the strength right now. She could handle hate. Anger. She had plenty of shields to defend against those attacks. What she couldn't handle were the good emotions Bridget wanted to hand over. Kindness, compassion, and love—from the right person—got under her foundations and wormed its way in regardless.

Even with all she gained, it would be a net loss.

Bridget wanted to give it to Sasha because it was who she was. But that wasn't what Sasha needed.

"That's not how this works."

Sasha said, "I know you think that. I know you go to church now, and you're all about forgiveness and love."

"But…"

Sasha shrugged. What more was there to say?

"Aiden told me a lot. About the written statements you've been making, and Melina." She choked over the name. "It makes sense now. You make sense."

"Don't be crazy."

Bridget grinned. "Okay, so not completely. But I get you a lot more now than I did before. The way you are, and how you feel you need to be. To survive."

Sasha was glad for her. It was nice that Bridget understood. That would help her live with her peace as she raised the daughter she'd only just met. She would think of Sasha along with her other memories. The life she used to have. And not be filled with rage and bitterness over Sasha's actions.

"I still think you should meet her."

Sasha shook her head. "No."

"You're scared of her." Bridget leaned back in her chair, a grin on her face. "You're scared of a first grader."

"I am not."

"Then meet her."

"No."

"Why not?"

"I just don't want to."

"Yeah," Bridget said. "Because you're a big scaredy pants. Sure, you can take on gunmen, bunches of them, without batting an eyelash. You get shot and keep trucking. Doesn't matter what life throws at you, you just keep rolling. Until you're faced with a little girl, her red hair and pigtails. Then you run away scared."

"I've been arrested. I can hardly meet her in cuffs."

"Sure. That's the reason."

Sasha pressed her lips together.

"Told you."

She grunted her frustration.

"I know the FBI is all hot to cart you off for a trial, or what-ever, but we'll figure it out. Get you a great lawyer."

"Don't get involved."

Over at the door, Aiden relaxed. She hadn't realized until now that he'd been so tense. The amount he'd visibly deflated when she'd told Bridget she shouldn't get involved made it clear. He gave her a tiny nod.

Bridget had to know there was nothing she could do to help that wouldn't backfire and make her life worse. Her husband was a cop. People would ask how they knew each other, who this woman was who was helping Sasha. They'd discover that they both used to work for the same company and figure out the clandestine private service they had provided to burned spies, former special forces, and anyone else whose life would be in danger at home. All their hard work, exposed.

"Bridget, you have a life here. A child and a husband. You don't need to worry about me."

"You can say that as many times as you want, but I won't believe you mean it."

"I don't need you." Sasha didn't need anyone.

She might never know who'd sent the lawyer, but it didn't matter. They were just one on a whole list of people who had it out for her.

She couldn't have a nice, safe life. Not like Bridget. Sasha was too far gone.

Her plan was still good, even if there was someone out there trying to circumvent it. She could tell her last story and get the truth out there. After that, Sasha would go out on her terms. No trial. No lengthy prison sentence. No "accident" in the yard that landed her in a coffin.

Probably no one would come to her funeral. Not for a friend who had been convicted of so many crimes—whatever they would turn out to be. Her mother would go on TV and tell the world that she'd always known her daughter would turn out like this.

Bridget was just about to say something when Conroy strode in. "We went through the phone your lawyer brought with him." He sat at his desk and slid his chair in. "Not your lawyer. You know what I mean."

Sasha nodded.

He frowned. "It doesn't look good."

Bridget said, "How not good?"

"Should you even be telling me?" Sasha asked. After all, who cared what was on the phone?

"Probably not. Neither should I be running my own investigation into you and your life, concurrently, with the FBI. However—" He shrugged. "—I'm the Chief of Police, and several things don't add up."

"Doesn't matter."

No one said anything. Or argued with her statement. Maybe she did want to know what was on the phone, but it really wouldn't make much of a difference. How it implicated her and what it implicated her in. Either way, she wouldn't be alive much longer, so it didn't matter.

She shrugged. "Whoever sent him is hedging their bets. Killing me outside the diner didn't work. He waited, but I gave him no opening. So, he hears I've been arrested and scrambles for an idea. He targets Sydney, as well as Eric and Millie's boys. That doesn't work. So the fallback is on his phone."

Conroy nodded.

Sasha stood. "I'd like to be escorted to holding."

"Can't say I've ever had a suspect ask to be put in jail before." He glanced at Aiden. "Escort her please, Sergeant."

"Yes, Sir." He took Sasha's elbow and led her through the main bullpen toward a door in the corner. The room was silent. Everyone there watching, saying nothing.

"You saved Ian Perkins tonight." Aiden tugged her along. "Then you go and save my daughter and the Cullings' kids."

"All part of the service."

"And then you do that. You push everyone away so you don't have to deal with them being close to you."

"It's too risky. I'm like a time bomb and you know Bridget is better off with me out of her life."

He stopped at the door. "I'm beginning to wonder if that's true."

Sasha rolled her eyes. "Whatever."

She was seriously tired if she was acting like this, but it usually worked. Especially with men. He'd write her off as "drama" and go on with his life accompanied by zero worries or regret concerning her.

"You know, she did the same thing. Even after finding out Sydney was alive after all, she kept Sydney out of her life until the danger was over, despite how much she wanted to finally meet her daughter."

"So?"

"I'm guessing she got that from you."

As if she and Bridget were anything alike. They were night and day, the only thing they had in common was the training they'd shared. Missions. Dinners spent planning. Rescues. Escapes. Sasha much preferred to work alone.

That's why it was best that Alex left her. Because he couldn't —or wouldn't—support her. She would rather know now that he wasn't going to stay, and not get in any deeper with him, only to just lose him later.

When it would hurt much worse.

"As much as you say you don't want her help, you're not going to be happy alone."

"It's for the best." Always had been. Always would be.

He led her to a cell, and she walked inside. Aiden started to say something behind her, but she cut him off. "I need paper and a pencil."

"I'll talk to Cullings." He removed her cuffs and left.

Sasha breathed out a long exhale. Alone was better. For the best. A tear rolled down her cheek, but she swiped it away.

She had another statement to write.

23

"**D**id you get some sleep?"

Alex shut the door to Conroy's office just after nine the next morning. "Does it matter? How is she?"

Never mind that he'd spent the whole night tossing and turning. He'd never see her again. Alex would have to watch her walk away, taken by the FBI so she could stand trial for whatever charges they could come up with. No way would they spend this much in resources for a small charge with only a minimal sentence.

They were going for a big fish, and they thought Sasha was it.

Someone had to be pulling their strings. He'd said as much to his boss last night, and even now it seemed like Conroy had been working for a while already this morning. How early did he get in?

"I want to help her." Alex didn't like exposing the truth of his feelings like this. But the chief didn't seem surprised. Or perturbed.

"She's about to be transported out of here by the FBI task force."

"This morning?" That gave them almost no time to figure something out.

"They're wrapping up breakfast, and then they'll be on their way over here." Conroy leaned back in his chair. "Go talk to her."

Alex wanted to pace, but he held himself still. "There's nothing I can do. All we have are suspicions, right? So far nothing close to pushing for a deal for her, let alone immunity based on her testifying. We don't know who the lawyer worked for, or why they're targeting her. She knows too much."

He wanted to tell her he was trying to help, but that would only give her false hope which was the last thing she needed. What if it went nowhere? What if nothing could be done?

He leaned both palms on the edge of Conroy's cabinet and hung his head. The idea of failing when he'd spent his entire career pushing to be the best didn't sit well. Especially when it could negatively affect Sasha. The one person who didn't need any more bad in her life.

Though, even if he didn't get her hopes up, maybe he could try. What would it hurt to just see if he could find *something* that might help her?

Her participation in so many cases over the years meant he had no idea what specific event would tip the balance in her favor. The justice system was structured how it was structured, and that meant deals could be made. Sometimes awful people went free or were put in witness protection in exchange for helping the government take down a bigger fish.

"She's been writing another statement for the last three hours. Maybe this will be it."

Alex strode out, across the bullpen, to the door that led to the holding cells in the basement. Someone spoke to him. Alex ignored them, even when they called his rank. He waved a hand over his shoulder. Nothing could make him stop. This could be the last time he ever saw her.

It wasn't even about the statement. He just wanted to spend time with her before she was shipped off to stand trial while he had to live the rest of his life with the regret of not being good enough.

She was sitting on the cot, the papers on her knee. "I'm almost done."

He watched her, marveling again at her capacity to withstand what would break most people. She was stronger than anyone he'd ever met. Not just in the face of her past and the horrible experiences she'd been through, but also when an assassin had directly attacked her. A man who had ended his own life rather than face the consequences from the police or his boss. That put this in the "seriously serious" category. Whoever was behind the attempt—or both attempts—on her life had power and influence. Or a lot of money.

Someone with the clout to push the FBI into targeting her with an investigation.

Though, all that had been to simply locate her. Once the feds found her, a man was sent to Last Chance to kill her.

Now that the assassin was dead, whoever wanted to shut her up forever wasn't likely going to stop.

She looked up. "Oh, hey. I didn't know it was you."

He couldn't help softening toward her. The same way that helping her was now imperative.

Alex motioned to the paper. "Tell me what it says."

He needed as much information as possible. Delaying the feds wasn't possible with what they had. She'd have to be fast.

Sasha tri-folded the papers. "I need to make a phone call." There was more than one sheet, and she left the pen on the bed as she stood. This wasn't normal operating procedure for someone in holding, having access to something that could be used as a weapon. The fact she had it and was being monitored by Conroy meant his boss also thought there was more to this than any of them knew.

"Tell me, and I'll get you a phone."

Sasha approached the bars. "I was contracted to kill a man,

supposedly some high-clearance-guy-turned-enemy-of-the-state." She spoke about it like she was describing a boring day for the stock market.

Alex didn't know if he would ever get used to that.

She continued, "As I always do, I looked into him. Not just what my handler sent me. I had Dorian do a deep dive. What he found was…" She shook her head. "Anyway, I didn't kill him. I paid a visit to all his former colleagues at the lab where he worked. Found out he'd created some schematic for a new weapons system. Something that wouldn't show up on any of our radar or satellite systems. It was brand new technology, way ahead of anything the military uses currently."

"And someone wanted him dead?"

"Far as I could tell, it was a rival business run by his old partner. That guy—his name and all the information are in the statement—is BFFs with a senator on the Armed Services Committee. They wanted to steal his schematics, kill him, and then present the technology themselves. It was all outlined on their server. An entire presentation for when they were going to take it up the chain to get funding.

"By the time they sent me, he'd already taken the information and fled. He was long gone and on the run. When I caught up to him, we had a chat about what they wanted me to do to him. He agreed to give me the flash drive in exchange for his life. I would fake his death and say the job was done, but that I never found the information. No one is looking for him anymore. No one knows I have it."

"And the statement?"

"I don't have a whole lot of cards to play in this scenario, but the location of that flash drive is one of them. I'm holding onto it. But I have a signed contract and the paper trail, which the FBI should be able to salvage something from. If he was willing to kill a man just to get ahead in business, then who knows what else he's done?"

She handed the papers through the bars.

"I'll make sure justice is done." He couldn't help but wonder if either this business partner or the senator were the ones behind the attacks on her life. Or someone else from her past entirely. "Thank you for trusting me with this information."

Truth was, Sasha had trusted him with a whole lot more than that. Not just her future and her freedom, but she'd asked him to take care of his nephew's friend, Jonah. Given his age, he had a hunch as to who he was and what he meant to her—how he'd come to be her son. He didn't want to think about what'd happened to her anymore, but he had to—there were a limited number of conclusions he could draw.

"What?"

He had to ask her. "Is Jonah..." How did he even ask?

"My son?"

He nodded.

Her answering nod was barely discernable, but he caught her wink. "I'm not sure how that's any of your business." She was playing for the security cameras. In the end, she added a huff and turned away from the bars.

"Fine. Keep your secrets." He'd garnered plenty of information. Whether it would be enough was in question. He might have to figure that out after she was gone. "I'm only trying to help you." Alex added a smidge of attitude to his tone.

She swung around, her hair flying, and planted a hand on her hip. It was the most un-Sasha-like thing he'd ever seen her do. "Help? Ha. As if a cop could, or would, help me. Besides, my life is a federal matter now. I'll never get out of prison once they're done bringing the hammer down. So what's a local yokel-beat cop *lieutenant* going to do anyway?"

Gees, she was laying it on thick. Alex decided to hand it right back to her in kind. "Seems like you thought I could do plenty for you. Or was it all a lie? Everything we shared."

Her eyes flared. He'd surprised her, insinuating that. She said, "You think I cared about you? You were nothing but a means to an end."

"And what did you gain? The chance to save a kid so you could pretend to be a hero? Use that to convince the feds you're a good person, maybe?" He stepped close to the bars, nearly touching it with his nose. "We all know the truth."

She closed in as well, that trifold paper in her hand. She had the pen again now. The drama of her pacing across the holding cell had been to retrieve it. He'd been so focused on her that he hadn't even noticed her swipe it off the bed.

She was good. Real good.

"Doesn't matter." She shook her head, all her attention on him even while the pen moved in her hand as she scrawled something on the paper. "None of this matters, because I'm blowing this backward burg and I'll never be back."

"Because you'll be doing life in prison."

"Nah, we both know I'm not gonna last that long. I'll be dead before I hit gen pop."

She thought she would be murdered in prison? Alex's stomach roiled. He gripped the bars on either side of her face. "I won't let that happen."

"There you go again, trying to be the hero. It doesn't suit you."

She was wrong about that. He might be trying to prove something to the world, but he could be the hero any time and every time he wanted. Something she was going to have to learn soon enough.

"Lieutenant Basuto."

He stared at Sasha for another second before he glanced at the Special Agent in the hall. "Yes?"

"It's time for her to go."

She pressed the papers against his chest. "My phone call."

His fingers touched hers for a second while intercepting the paper, but with an audience and cameras everywhere, it just wasn't the time. He stepped back, slipped the paper into the inside breast pocket of his suit jacket. "I'll get the duty officer to open up for you."

"Thanks."

Alex strode past him, out the door. She was escorted into the bullpen a minute later. Handcuffed again.

The task force agents stood around her as the special agent led her to a phone.

Alex strode over. "She can use mine."

He handed over his police department cell phone.

She dialed a number and listened to it ring. "It's me. Liquidate my assets, I want to make a withdrawal."

Eric snatched the phone from her hand. "Who is this?" He shifted the phone. "They hung up."

Alex retrieved the phone. They could trace the call, but he doubted anything would come of it. It was too brief. Then he looked down at the paper she'd given him.

On the side she'd written the first line of an address—the bank in town if he wasn't mistaken. Under it was a number.

Below that it said, *Maggie has the key.*

A safety deposit box.

She'd given him the weapon specs?

24

Eric led her to the black SUV waiting outside. Behind it was a matching vehicle that also had government plates.

Sasha's steps faltered as she stepped outside and the door to the police department closed behind her. Alex hadn't come out. Sure, she'd given him the information so he could get into Melina's safety deposit box. She still figured he could've come and said goodbye to her.

She hardly counted a fake argument in holding as being any kind of last words to each other.

A honk overhead jogged her from her thoughts. Up in the overcast sky, a flock of Canadian Geese flew by.

"Okay?"

She didn't look at Eric. Was she *okay*? No, she wasn't. She'd just jumped at a flock of birds. And he should know she wasn't all right, considering he was arresting her for whoever knew what. Conspiracy something. She hadn't even understood what they said with the noise rushing in her ears at the time. It was just a formality, though. They would dig even deeper into her life now that they knew she was Melina. Everything she'd ever done would be exposed. Probably even the classified stuff. If who she thought was behind this really was pulling their strings, this was about keeping her from telling anyone what she knew—especially the FBI.

Killing her because she presented some kind of threat.

Revenge.

There were limited reasons anyone would go to this length to get rid of her.

She half expected to be shot before her head was guided into the car. "Bulletproof vest would've been nice."

She climbed in. It had only been a bunch of geese, not an actual threat. And yet everything in her wanted to shake from the adrenaline. Her emotions were too close to the surface after seeing Alex. Telling that last story. Thinking about Melina again.

The life she might've had if everything hadn't been torn apart. Would she have fallen for Alex, married, and made a family with him? Mateo would be her nephew. His mother would be her *Mama*. Life would've been good instead of the disaster it was now.

A familiar face sat in the backseat. Sasha took a seat on the other end of the third row. Eric sat in one of the captain's chairs in the middle. Three more agents got in, and the driver got on his radio.

"Millie." This couldn't have been authorized by the FBI director. Millie was her former boss and Eric's wife. Her presence here wasn't a coincidence.

"Sasha." She matched the tone Sasha had used.

"Come here often?"

Millie pushed out a quiet laugh. "We don't have much time." She shifted in the seat and rubbed a hand on the side of her belly. Child number three, a surprise to Eric. She had to be three-plus months now, her pregnancy visible earlier than the last time. Something Sasha had seen in that photo the "lawyer" had shown her.

"Another boy?" She couldn't help but think of Jonah. Yet more emotion welled up until tears blurred her vision. Sasha wanted to groan. Millie would see through all of it, as she usually did.

"Tell me about your college friends. The ones who were murdered. OD'd."

Sasha shifted in the chair. She closed her eyes, head leaned back on the headrest. It was pretty uncomfortable, but it was all the rest she'd have. Given she was in a convoy of federal vehicles and surrounded by agents, she figured she was pretty safe. And Eric wouldn't have let his wife come here to talk to her if he thought there was legitimate danger.

"Why?" She didn't open her eyes.

"Because something funny is going on. The task force can't give anyone an indication they aren't doing anything but their jobs. If someone is in the shadows out there targeting you, they aren't going to catch the person by pushing back. We lull them into a false sense of security, and then we pounce."

Sasha looked at her friend then. "Pounce?"

"I have two boys. You're lucky I don't refer to you as 'bro.'"

She laughed. It sort of sounded like crying, though, which made it even sadder.

"I have a top candidate right now as to who is behind this."

"Alex has one, too," Sasha said. "I gave him another statement. That may be what the candidate is after. Though, when that guy tried to poison me, he didn't ask where the flash drive was."

Eric twisted in his seat. "Flash drive?"

Millie waved him off. "We can get to that. I want to know about the boys, though."

Eric had filled her in. Because he doubted what he was asked by his boss to do? Millie had always been the kind of woman who thought outside the box. She'd been a CIA agent and knew Sasha would do what it took to get the job done— because she was the same.

"Don't worry about it." There wasn't time for any of them

to figure out who was behind it and stop them. It didn't matter anyway.

"Really? Cause your first statement implicated the Mayor of Richmond, Virginia as the mastermind behind a murder-suicide. He's gone unchecked for *years* because no one could substantiate their theories. So guess who was the father of one of your friends who was murdered? Because if you don't say, 'the Mayor of Richmond, Virginia' you'd be wrong."

Sasha turned so she could say something, but Millie continued, "And if you were wondering who the head of security was at the time you worked in housekeeping? The guy with the funky scar on his eyebrow? Dark hair?"

Sasha didn't know if she was supposed to nod, but Mille was right, so she did. It seemed like her boss didn't need the confirmation.

She kept talking. "*That* guy? He's the Mayor's cousin. He's laid low for years, keeping his nose clean. But now he works on the Mayor's staff. So, of course, I called a friend of mine in Richmond. She's headed over to talk to some of the mayor's female staff. Find out if anything's going on that the FBI might want to know about."

"If he was behind it, why kill his son?"

"We'll find out."

"Why not just take my statement and go arrest them?"

"Something about needing corroborating evidence?" Millie half-smiled.

Sasha wanted to share it but couldn't quite manage. "Weird."

"Right?" Millie chuckled.

Eric did not seem amused.

Sasha said, "Thank you."

She didn't say for what, and she didn't have to. Millie knew. Her friend had done a lot of work. As much as she'd bemoaned the fact no one had ever stood with her, the truth was that the evidence right in front of her proved her wrong now. Millie was a wife and mom. Her only interest in getting involved with this whole thing was for Sasha. To help her.

The way Bridget seemed to want to help despite the fact Sasha had lied to her in one of the most grievous of ways.

She didn't know if Bridget forgave her. Some people liked to say they did and then bring it back up later. Use the forgiveness they'd granted as a weapon to manipulate. To garner favors.

Meanwhile, Millie probably didn't want anything. That she knew of.

For all Sasha knew, her former boss was about to ask her to kill someone as "payment" for helping her now.

The question was whether Millie intended to help Sasha go free, or if she just wanted to take someone else down while Sasha went to prison for what was probably going to be a legitimate crime. God knew she'd done some horrible things in her life, and trauma wasn't an excuse that covered every conceivable action. At least, she figured He knew that considering every time she thought about Him, all she could think about were all the horrible things she'd done.

The others in her life who had been "saved," as they called it, mustn't have done anything like what she had, or they would experience the same shame and guilt. It didn't exactly make her want to pursue a relationship with Him in the limited time she had left. Once this was over, she and God could figure out what happened to her next. Without her final days being earmarked by remorse.

"So I'm working on this mayor angle," Millie said, "and you don't need to worry. If it's him, I'll figure this out."

Sasha nodded. "I'm not worried."

Millie frowned. Sasha pretended like she hadn't seen it. The dance was one she knew well. What to reveal, what to conceal. How much to say. What she could give away through body language. Every nuance of her life had been controlled for years. She could have, one day, shaken it off and found some semblance of a normal life, but that wasn't going to happen now.

"What does Alex have?"

The way Millie said his name was a question all on its own. Sasha ignored that as well. "A missing man. I helped fake his death and, in exchange for a new life, I have what he was hiding from everyone. I told him I'd keep it safe."

"He didn't keep...whatever it was?"

Sasha shook her head. "Too tempting to take the schematic and build it. He wanted a clean slate, not even a shadow of what he'd been before in his old life. Pretty sure he's running a dive bar somewhere now. Living in flip flops with a permanent tan and a wardrobe of Hawaiian shirts."

"And people think you don't care. That you feel nothing."

Sasha didn't need to get into that. "Doesn't matter."

"You said that before. What do you mean by that?"

She was aware, too aware of all the FBI agents in the vehicle listening to their conversation. They were on the highway now and headed out of town, probably to the airport. If she told Millie about Dorian, they would invade his life.

He might have killed Clarke for her. As if she'd asked him to do it when she very much had not. But she still needed him. Still counted him as a friend.

Zander hadn't liked him. As if that meant anything.

Sasha shrugged off all of it. The questions. The theories. Millie and Eric, and whatever they'd discussed that had him breaking protocol and bringing his wife on a prisoner transfer. "I made a call."

Millie stared hard at her. "Eric, did she make a withdrawal?"

He said, "Liquidate everything."

"Sasha."

"It's done. No taking it back now." She was going out on her terms. And she would repeat that mantra until it happened, all the while trying to remind herself that it was the right thing to do.

For everyone.

They had lives and families. She would find her peace.

What else was there to do?

"Someone like me doesn't get rescued. No one is going to be able to prove my innocence, because I'm not innocent." Sasha was nothing but a stain on this world. One that needed to be erased, not cleaned up in an attempt to make her appear good like everyone else. "Don't bother trying to help me. Just do the right thing because that's what people like you do."

"Sash—"

"You aren't going to change my mind. And there's no point in it since it's already done." Dorian would go dark until it was done. There was no stopping him. After all, that was the plan they'd put in place.

"What's this?" The driver muttered the words. Up ahead was a pair of flashing hazard lights and a bunch of orange cones.

The front seat passenger said, "Roadblock, or an accident." He unbuckled his seatbelt. "I'll go find out how long it's going to take them to clear."

Eric said, "I'll radio behind and let them know."

The car rolled to a stop and the passenger opened his door to get out.

Multiple men poured from the cars stopped up ahead, each one armed with an assault rifle and a bulletproof vest. Radios. Sunglasses. Earpieces. They were pros.

As a unit, they opened fire on the SUVs.

Sasha hit the button for her seatbelt and lunged toward Millie. "Get down!"

25

"And you just let her leave?"

Alex lowered his coffee mug. "Mama, it's not like that."

"Then tell me what it is like because I'm afraid I don't understand why you let that girl get taken away."

"She was arrested. By the FBI."

His mom made a face like that wasn't such a big deal.

"There's nothing I can do about a federal investigation." When her expression didn't change, he continued, "I'm a local cop. I have nothing to do with the FBI. I can't interfere or I risk my job. Conroy might understand, but the mayor won't and I'd probably wind up getting fired if I made waves."

She made a "hmph" noise and took a sip of tea.

They were waiting for Mateo, who was supposed to be coming over for lunch as well. All Alex wanted to do was hit the gym and pound on a heavy bag until he could no longer lift his arms. Maybe not the best workout tactic, but it might make him feel better to get out some frustration. This feeling of powerlessness wasn't something he enjoyed. Especially when he knew what he wanted deep down and that it went against everything he was supposed to do as a cop.

Alex was beyond frustrated that there was such a difference between his duty and his desire.

He'd never had a problem being a cop before. Following the rules and working to keep everyone who worked for the Last Chance Police Department safe so they could help in the community—protecting and serving—was something that had always come naturally to him.

Who was going to do that for Sasha?

She'd already had a lawyer show up to try and kill her. The friends she'd had weren't more than burned bridges at this point, albeit ones that seemed willing to work to repair the friendship. And then there was the mysterious "Dorian" who was more than likely a wanted man himself. Sasha had told him that her friend killed Clarke for her. She should've written him that statement as well, so he could pass it on to the FBI.

Instead, he had a piece of scratch paper in his pocket. Her statement had been entered into evidence. And he had an appointment with the bank, later, after he went to see Maggie and picked up the key.

Alex let out a long sigh.

She was gone, and all he had was her safety deposit box. That was the last thing he wanted. Some flash drive—a weapon schematic. But she'd trusted him with it, so he would honor that trust and make sure it never landed in the wrong hands.

More cases to be investigated. Sasha's life was like a catalog of crimes she'd been involved in from the periphery. Things she'd seen, places she'd gone. Death. Pain. He wanted to help her, but she seemed so content to go her way. Make her own plan. After she'd had her own will stripped from her so thoroughly, he didn't begrudge her the need to control her fate. To find peace the way she needed to.

"I don't like talking about your father, but maybe it's time I did. Seems like you ended up with the wrong idea about some things."

Alex's dad had passed away after a heart attack six years

ago. Alejandro Senior had been big and imposing, a man whose presence was all he needed to run a tight ship. After years in the Navy, he'd been a pro at motivating those around him. Whether they wanted to be managed or not.

"What about him?"

Mama set her mug down. "He rewarded you for doing the right thing. After that man was killed…"

He knew she was talking about Sasha's uncle. They'd seen him laid out on his dining table, cut open. The man who'd killed him, the guy the drugs had belonged to, had been fishing baggies from the dead man's abdomen.

And that was before the man had taken Sasha with him as he left, leaving Alex alone and practically catatonic with the dead man. Her parting screams of anger and grief haunted his dreams for years.

It all washed over him. Like a king tide, Alex was swept back into that nightmare with no way to fight it.

"*Mijo.*"

He blinked to find his mom beside him, her hand on his knee. "Tell me about dad." That would be better than thinking about what'd happened.

"He came down hard on you after you saw that. 'What did you do?' As if you had any involvement, or caused it somehow. As if it was in some way your fault for being there at precisely that time." She shook her head, settled now back into her chair.

Alex hadn't even noticed that she'd moved to him and then returned to her seat. Years later, and he was still losing time because of what'd happened. He should be over it by now. And then, there was Sasha. She'd been there. She'd suffered much worse after seeing her uncle splayed out like that on the kitchen table, not to mention the trauma of what'd happened afterward. Did she freak out, shut down, block stuff out? No, she didn't. She'd dealt with it her way, and seemingly without the weaknesses he did.

"He was just trying to wrap his mind around what

happened. He didn't mean it was at all your fault. But you took on board that you must've done something wrong, or failed somehow. He taught you that perfection was rewarded. That only good people get good things, and *Mijo* that just isn't true."

Alex took a sip of coffee while she continued, "Javier didn't care. He walked away from your father's expectations a long time ago. But you didn't. After that trauma, you absorbed all of it, and I'm sorry I didn't know what to say to change your way of thinking. You stayed away from anything bad. You were a wonderful boy, but you weren't okay. You felt you had to be good all the time. But life isn't black and white. There's a whole lot of gray in the world, and if you think this woman is worth fighting for, then you owe it to yourself to ignore what you 'should' do and follow what God has put in your heart."

"Even if I get fired in the process?" He didn't want to lose his job. It had been his identity for so long. But was that worth Sasha's freedom?

"The two of you are connected. You always have been."

Alex didn't know what to say to that. Maybe she was reading too much sentimentality into him. Yes, Sasha was...captivating. She'd brightened his life in the short time she'd been back, even if he'd been actively hunting her. They'd saved a child together. Shared several moments.

And then he'd watched her walk away.

"It's been a long time." Maybe it was too late.

Mama stared him down. "You didn't feel it? When you were with her?"

How did she...ah, he'd brought Sasha here after she was shot saving his life. Alex didn't lie to his mother. "I felt it."

"I know." She took a sip of tea, a smile on her lips. "Mamas always know."

He chuckled as the door opened. But it wasn't Mateo, it was Jonah. And he looked like he'd been roughed up.

Alex pushed his chair back. "Hey, are you—"

"Lieutenant Basuto." His breath came hard, little-boy fear

on his teenage face. "They took Mateo."

Alex led him to a chair. "Tell me what happened."

Mama offered him water. Jonah just shook his head of dark hair, the too-long strands falling over his forehead. Up close, Alex could see Sasha in his features. Genetic markers she'd handed down to him. She'd given him to the pastor and his wife and left town. He didn't blame her one bit after what'd happened to her. The boy was healthy and safe.

Or, he had been.

"Jonah." Alex prompted him.

The kid's lip quivered, but he held it together. "There were four of them. Leather jackets and jeans. Tattoos."

"Seen them before ever?"

He shook his head.

Alex thought of the man who'd roughed up Javier and grazed Sasha. Don Evers was in jail now. It couldn't be him, but it could be the same crew. Guys who were muscle for Thomas Perkins.

"Mateo said he was supposed to have lunch. I was gonna come with him. They shoved me against the wall, and they took Mateo. Stuffed him in their truck and drove off." Jonah sniffed. "I hit my head so it took me some time to shake it off. I came right here."

Alex pulled out a chair and sat. "Did you hear them say anything?"

He had to wonder at the timing. Surely this wasn't about Javier. At least, that wouldn't make much sense. Perkins's son and wife were both safe. Was he more concerned about recompense for his debts than keeping his family? Back to business as usual in some other house, given the previous one had exploded.

Alex was the one who'd asked Javier to get Perkins's address. Could be it was on him that Mateo had been snatched. Yet another person he'd failed because he'd tried to do the right thing and it backfired.

"They said to tell you."

Alex got up. "Let's go to the police station. I need to get your statement and check in with the chief."

Tell *him*. Not Javier.

That was what they'd said when they took his nephew. What did that mean?

As Jonah stood, Alex called his brother. No answer.

After they hit the police station, he could get the search started. He needed a license plate, maybe from a security camera. Along with Jonah's statement, it would help form a full picture of who took Mateo.

Whatever it took to get him back.

He drove the kid—more a man at this point, but still very much a boy right now—to the station. As they pulled up, Alex said, "Do you want me to call your folks, have them come down here?"

Jonah shook his head. "Maybe later."

They climbed out. "You have problems with them?" Alex knew Jonah was aware of his adoption. Not like the pastor and his wife boasted about it, but they shared the information freely.

"Nah. They just don't get it, you know? Why I'm friends with Mateo."

"Ah."

"Doesn't matter." Jonah shrugged. "We look out for each other, and that's just the way it is."

He was a good kid. Did Sasha know she'd passed on that ingrained sense of honor? The same need to help someone in trouble she cared about. Sure, it had to be partly the way he was raised. But she had that loyalty in her and he could see it even now, mirrored in the baby she'd given birth to.

The weight of knowing this settled on him. Jonah might never know his birth mother, let alone that she'd been here in town.

Alex clapped him on the shoulder and squeezed. "Let's go figure this out."

Inside, Kaylee was behind the desk. She buzzed them in

188 | LISA PHILLIPS

while Alex called his brother again. Still no answer. She asked, "What happened?"

"Mateo was snatched off the street."

She gasped and put a hand over her mouth, then recovered quickly to take Jonah's arm and lead him in. "Let's get you some paper. We need you to write everything down."

Alex contacted Savannah since Detective Wilcox had no pressing cases right now. She replied seconds later that she was on her way and so was her husband, local PI Tate Hudson. Conroy showed up as well, during Alex's next attempt at calling his brother.

Voicemail picked up, but the mailbox was full.

He lowered the phone.

"Easy." Conroy gave him a steady look. "Don't throw your phone. That won't help."

Alex ran his hands down his face instead, then scrubbed them through his hair. He wanted to go out with his gun and shake people down until someone told him where his nephew was.

"Sergeant Donaldson is on the street. So is Officer Ridgeman. Everyone else is either on their way or didn't call in yet. We'll find him." Conroy strode to Jonah and took a thorough statement faster than Alex had ever seen.

"I need to go to my brother's house." Tate and Savannah had already hit the streets.

Conroy nodded. "Yes, you do."

Jonah jumped up from the chair. "I'm coming too."

Phones buzzed around the room. The desk phone rang. Conroy's phone chimed its ringtone. In his pocket, Alex's phone buzzed.

Kaylee crossed to the desk to answer hers.

Conroy beat him to his. "Chief Barnes." He listened for a second, paled, and said, "Understood."

He hung up the phone.

"The task force convoy was hit."

26

M illie lay on the floor under Sasha, covered by her friend's body. Sasha had made sure the baby she carried in her abdomen was safe, all the while, windows shattered and bullets hammered the sides of the SUV.

It felt like they'd been firing for an hour, though it couldn't have been that long.

She shifted to look at Eric. He'd shoved open his door and now returned fire from behind that small amount of cover.

They weren't going to last much longer.

Millie grunted under her. "Give me a gun at least. I'm not too pregnant to shoot somebody."

"No way," Sasha said. "You can stay down. And besides, I don't even have a gun. I'm still handcuffed. Now shush."

Sasha could hardly hear her over the steady rapport of gunfire. So far as she could tell, no one had the upper hand. Through the windshield, she spotted a gunman fall backward, felled by a bullet fired by one of the three agents. The car behind had joined in. They were still overwhelmed.

Soon enough, a gunman would get too close and paint the inside of the SUV with Sasha's blood. After all, that was the plan. Right? Kill her so she couldn't talk and was no longer able to tell the FBI what she'd seen.

Whatever it was she wasn't supposed to know.

The driver was dead. The front passenger continued to fire. The other middle row guy, on the opposite side of Eric, was out of the car, sheltered behind his door.

"We need to get out of here."

Sasha looked down at Millie. "Sit tight."

Before Millie could say anything, Sasha clambered carefully over the pregnant woman and squeezed between the middle seats.

"Hey. What are you doing?" The guy to her left took his attention from the gunmen and put it on her.

She started to raise her hands. Started to tell him she had a plan.

A bullet slammed into his forehead, and he fell to the ground.

Sasha heard the whimper but didn't realize she had been the one to make that noise. She scrambled over a backpack. The guy in the driver's seat stared at her with dead eyes. Keeping her head down, she leaned over and pulled the door handle. It took a second to get it to swing open, but she used the guy's body weight to help. He fell out of the door. She had to get his lower half out, too.

Sasha felt the trickle of tears roll down her face.

Why? Why was she reacting like this now, of all times? All she'd had for years was a stone-cold sense of right and wrong— according to her. Some people called it situational ethics. She called it survival.

Now it seemed like she had an emotion about everything.

She couldn't just fight for her life or the others' lives. She had to feel it too. The weight of responsibility. The fear for Millie's baby.

Sasha snaked her way into the driver's seat. The engine was still running. "Get in."

"What?" The guy to her right, out the passenger side door, glanced at her.

"Pay attention to the gunmen!" He would get killed like his colleague if he wasn't careful.

But he was careful, keeping one eye on the advancing men and one on her as it were. A bullet tore through his arm. He yelped and fell onto the seat, shifting his gun to the other hand so he could continue to fire.

"Get in." She needed Eric on board as well. "Cullings!"

"Go!"

Sasha didn't waste a beat before she put the SUV in drive and hit the gas. Eric fired three shots as she blew toward the barricade in front of them.

Two cars had stopped, nose to nose. The federal car behind would catch on and follow. She hoped. Sasha just wanted to get Millie out of the line of fire.

The front passenger door slammed shut.

She didn't waste any time. As soon as Eric's door also slammed shut, she hit the gas, barreling into the front bumper of one car, her foot down on the gas. Bullets peppered the side of the SUV. Glass shattered.

They jolted, the wheels spun, and she managed to get the other car pushed out of the way. The engine roared. Sasha gripped the wheel as they hurtled down the highway. "Is everyone good?"

The passenger seat agent gaped at her. "Did you just save our lives?"

Before she could answer, Eric said, "I'll call the other car. Make sure they're coming with."

She didn't like that they'd left those agents behind. They could be executed by the gunmen because of what she'd done.

"Uh-oh." That was Millie.

Sasha glanced in the rearview. "Get your head down!"

Eric spoke on his phone. Millie tucked herself out of sight.

Out the back window, Sasha spotted a vehicle belonging to the gunmen barreling after them. "We've got company."

She could use some assistance right now. Zander and his team of private security experts, currently gallivanting halfway across the world. *Don't worry about me. I don't need your help, remember?* She shoved aside those unhelpful, grudging thoughts.

Millie had shown up to help, and now look at what happened.

Sasha would always be better off on her own.

A gunman leaned out a window behind them and opened fire.

"These guys are relentless."

The passenger agent grunted. He eyed her cuffs, seemingly a bit confused about this turn of events.

"Why don't you lean out the window and return the favor?"

He shifted. "I'm bleeding like a stuck pig. I can't believe those guys killed half our team." His voice sounded hollow. "We have to go back and help the others."

"They're good," Eric said. "They headed in the opposite direction to split the focus. Said there's a car in pursuit of them, too."

"Great." Sasha gripped the wheel. "I should just keep driving?"

A bullet hit the back corner. The SUV swerved and her stomach churned. Now wasn't a good time to throw up.

"Call the Last Chance PD or something!"

Eric said, "I already sent the notification in. We have procedures for this."

"Great, because I have no idea where I'm going, and your pregnant wife is in the back row."

"Don't drag me into your argument." Millie sounded irritated. Not that she didn't like being pregnant. Probably more that she wanted to be in the thick of the action. Any action. Millie might have been sidelined a lot lately, but it seemed to Sasha that she and Eric were closer than ever. Taking a back seat—in this case, literally *and* figuratively—had probably been good for Millie and Eric.

Sasha fought for control as the highway rounded several switchbacks in a row. She didn't want to slow down, but it was that or sail over the edge into the canyon below. Or whatever was down there. At least the winter snow had melted. The last thing she needed right now was to hit a patch of ice.

"Just keep going."

Sasha nodded. She might be the one driving, but she was also handcuffed still. The FBI was in charge.

"And put your seatbelt on," Eric ordered. "Everyone belt up. We don't know how long this will last."

There was an edge to his tone she couldn't decipher. Sasha couldn't glance back to figure out where his head was at. There was no time, anyway. The injured passenger reached around to grab Sasha's seatbelt and clicked it into place.

"Thanks," Sasha said. It wasn't like she could have put her own seatbelt on while handcuffed. She inherently knew their orders were to keep the prisoner safe no matter what, but a small part of her thought maybe Eric cared a little about his wife's friend.

Another bullet hit them, shattering the back window.

"Millie, you good?"

"Yeah, Sasha," she sounded exasperated. "I'm fine."

The car didn't seem too bad yet. If they could just—

A tire exploded. The car swerved. Sasha bit back a scream and held on for control. An indiscernible prayer burst in her mind, but her lips couldn't make the words. Everything in her was eclipsed by fear.

The car started to spin.

They smashed through the barrier and the world tipped as they flew, front end first, down the canyon. Below, an icy river raged.

The car bumped and bounced.

They hit a boulder.

Sasha tried to steer. The SUV didn't respond.

"Millie!" Eric yelled. "Jesus, help us!"

They hit another boulder and the car dumped over onto its side, the engine still screaming. Sasha blinked. Her arm was pinned underneath her and smashed against the window below her. The agent who had been to her right now dangled above her. Unconscious with a giant knot on his head.

"Millie." She heard Eric move.

Sasha lifted her hands and nearly screamed. One wrist felt like someone had stuck it through with a hot poker. She hissed out a breath through clenched teeth and tried to figure out what'd just happened.

The engine ticked over. Steam flooded the cab. Something was on fire. The window beside her face was cracked. Water started to trickle in. Ice-cold snow runoff. She recoiled from it, even as a shiver moved through her.

Sasha used her elbow to unlatch her seatbelt and clambered upright, not even moving her painful wrist a tiny bit. It was hard, and there were a couple of sharp stabbing pains. She ignored them and got to where she could see out the front window.

The passenger agent was still out.

She yelled back to Eric, "How's Millie?"

"She's good. You see anything?"

"I can see some of the road from here, but I don't see our tail." That didn't mean those men weren't on their way down the canyon now to finish the job.

"Help is headed to us. It won't be long before Chief Barnes and his people show up. Then we can get out of here."

She kept her eyes peeled, then glanced back for a second. If she had to defend them, she'd need a weapon. Not that any fed would give her one. She was a wanted criminal. They wouldn't trust her. But something about the way Eric looked at her now made her think he might—if it saved his wife's life.

She returned her attention to the outside while another

shiver juddered her body. She wasn't able to stop the quiver of her lips. Cold settled inside her. The water made the temperature in the SUV drop. It was barely forty-five outside. Spring temperatures around here, but it could still become a problem.

"Make sure Millie is out of the water." She didn't turn, just kept scanning around them. "It's freezing."

"Copy that." His voice was quiet when he added, "You saved us."

"I saved myself. You just happened to be in the car." Her voice shook the lie with each shiver. She clenched all her muscles. It wouldn't be comfortable for long, but she needed to try and hold herself together.

She held her wrist against her stomach with her other hand, the cuffs clinking.

"Here." Eric climbed to her. He held a key in his hand and unlocked the handcuffs for her. He winced. "Your wrist."

"Don't worry about it." She turned back to the window. "I don't want to be caught unawares again." There was no one outside. No one was coming.

"Good. You should make a run for it. Leave us here and go." He shifted and handed over a phone. "I've got people headed here for us. Take Millie's phone and call Lieutenant Basuto. Have him pick you up. I'll tell everyone you escaped in the chaos. If you lay low, it'll give me time to figure out what's going on."

She stared at him. "You're setting me free?"

"As I said, you escaped. Understand?"

She would be on the run. Still a fugitive. For as long as it would be before someone figured out who had her in their sights. And that might never happen.

"Now go."

27

P lenty of cops had gone to the scene. What they'd find was an armed, fully-trained group of feds.

Alex took Jonah to Javier's house because they were the only ones now looking for Mateo except Tate and Savannah, and he hadn't heard from the detective and her PI husband.

His chest squeezed. Sasha was in trouble. He wanted to be there to save her, but that wasn't what he needed to be doing right now.

Jonah glanced over as they made their way to the trailer's front door.

This was where he should be. Taking care of his family. Letting everyone else do their jobs and help the task force while he and Jonah tried to figure out how to find Mateo. "You said those guys told you to tell me, right?"

Jonah nodded. He bent and found the hidden key, which Alex used to let them inside.

"Whoa." Jonah had lifted up to see over Alex's shoulder as he surveyed the room.

"Yeah." Alex stepped in and immediately felt something under his shoe. "Someone trashed the place."

Everything Mateo and Javier owned had been tossed on the

floor. Cushions were torn open. Furniture smashed. The TV, his brother's prized possession, lay on its face. Smashed as well, probably.

"This seems like rage. Not like they were looking for something."

Jonah was quiet for a second. "Is there a difference?"

"Yes." Alex glanced at him. He was worried, scared for his friend. If Jonah had known who Sasha was, and what was currently happening across town, he'd be worried for her too.

The timing seriously sucked.

Maybe being out of the loop was what made him bothered that he couldn't be there. He sent a text to Conroy and asked for an update. Not just for Jonah, but for himself. Which meant, when the chief replied and asked how the search for Mateo was going, Alex needed something to tell him. "Javier!"

"Is he even here?"

"Look around. Maybe he's out back." There was a patio area and a patch of fake grass often used at kids' play areas and on golf courses where the real stuff didn't grow. He could be out there.

"Unless he got taken like Mateo."

Alex couldn't argue about that possibility. He didn't want Jonah to be the one to find him if the worst had happened, but the kid was determined to be here. He'd argued to come with Alex, saying it would save time. Alex could ask questions while they looked. Jonah could help him figure it out.

Staring at a near replica of Sasha's eyes while the kid argued to help save his friend? Alex couldn't deny him. Maybe it was guilt at not rolling out to where the task force had been hit. Feeling inept because he couldn't be in two places at once. Raging against an ambush, or whatever had happened, at the same time his nephew went missing. Torn between the two.

Whatever the reason, he was glad now that Jonah was here. That Mateo had a friend willing to risk himself to find him. The way Alex did.

No matter what Javier had Mateo wrapped up in, Alex would protect Jonah while they got the kid back. He could do at least that much.

For Sasha.

Because she was the one who would want him here. Not there, helping her. She counted Jonah's life above her own. The boys needed more help right now than she did.

The screen door snapped back against the frame and Jonah stepped back inside. "He's not out there."

They shared a look. Like deep down they both had been hoping this was just like any other day. Javier could be passed out like usual on the plastic patio furniture, an empty beer bottle in his hand. Several more empties on the concrete slab under his chair. The fact he hadn't answered his phone and wasn't out in the back alarmed them both.

Jonah's face paled. "Do you think he's dead?"

"Depends who those guys worked for. The ones who took Mateo." He figured Perkins was involved but had to wonder why the guy was worried about his brother and nephew when he should be hiding from the cops. "Bottom line? My brother is a grown man I expect to be able to take care of himself. Our priority here is Mateo."

"Okay." The kid looked like he was about to cry.

Alex felt his pain. Though his fear morphed into more of a frustration that quickly translated into anger he had to check or he'd wind up doing or saying something he shouldn't. "Can you tell me anything else about what Javier was into with Perkins?"

Something shifted in Jonah's expression.

"It wasn't just Javier," Alex said.

Jonah looked relieved at his speculation and, at the same time, still afraid.

"What were you guys doing?"

"Odd jobs, mostly." Jonah shifted. He leaned against the wall, both for support and to instinctively brace for Alex's reaction to what he said next.

Alex did all he could to keep his emotions in check. He needed to know everything, without freaking Jonah out so much he shut down.

"We cleaned out a house he just bought. Tossed everything in the Dumpster out front and then repainted before his carpet guys came in." Jonah scratched the side of his head, then rubbed his palm above his ear in frustration. "A couple of times we delivered——" He swallowed. "—stuff."

Ah, *stuff.* "Drugs? Money?"

Jonah's eyes filled with tears. "Just packages. A backpack, or a duffel. He told us not to look inside, so we didn't. I think that's why he kept hiring us."

"Perkins?"

Jonah shook his head. "A guy who works for him."

Alex opened his mouth to ask who the guy was when his phone rang. The name on the screen was *Cullings.* Eric probably didn't know Alex was trying to locate his missing nephew. He swiped to answer. "I'm busy."

Silence greeted him. Then a familiar voice. "I n-need help."

"Sasha?" She sounded...he didn't even know how she sounded. "What's going on?"

"F-fell in." Her voice quavered on every consonant. "It's cold."

"Where are you?"

"Alex-x." She dragged out the last letter of his name, her voice subdued in a way that seriously worried him.

"You have Eric's phone."

"Told me... Go."

The special agent had given her his phone and told her to go? That made no sense.

"Said." She paused. "Call you." It sounded like each word was difficult.

"You need to look at the phone. Listen to me, Sasha. Can you listen?"

"Yes."

"Find the maps app and share your location with me. Can you do that?"

"Think s-so."

"Just focus. You can do this." He stared at his brother's trailer and the mess that surrounded him while he listed to her shuffle and rustle against the microphone. Long enough he prompted her. "Sasha?"

"I did it."

His phone buzzed, confirming what she'd said. "We're coming to you."

"Just you. No one...else."

"It's Jonah. He's with me right now. We're coming to you, okay?" Silence greeted him. "Sasha."

Nothing.

The call never ended. Alex left the line open. "Come on."

"What are we doing?"

"Finding a friend of mine." They raced down the front steps.

"Does the friend know where Mateo is?" Jonah opened the passenger door.

Across the roof, Alex said, "She'll want to help if she can, but right now it sounds like she's in trouble. Once we get her settled, we'll be back looking for Mateo, okay?" When Jonah nodded, he said, "Get in. You can tell me more in the car."

As he pulled out, Alex continued, "We will figure this out. But you need to tell me everything."

Jonah nodded. "Mateo didn't want you to know, or you'd hate him like you hate his dad."

"I don't hate Javier." Though, he could see how two teen boys might think that. "I just can't help him until he wants to help himself. And until then, there's nothing I can do."

"The guy who gives us the jobs is at the gas station. He's the night manager. Steph."

"Okay. That's good." Alex would go talk to him, just as soon as the GPS led him right to where Sasha was.

The signal was coming from a spot two miles from the highway. He parked his car off the shoulder and grabbed a blanket from the trunk. The sky was gray, but it hadn't started raining. If it did, and Sasha was already wet and cold, she was going to have a miserable time until he got her somewhere dry.

They took a trail that snaked up the mountain, then forked off onto another one. Jonah kept pace with him the whole time. Both he and Mateo ran track and were on the basketball team together.

"Who is she?"

Alex couldn't get into the fact Sasha was Jonah's actual birth mother. *Lord, is this Your plan?* There wasn't even time for that, though. "A friend of mine, like I said."

"And she's in trouble?"

He checked the phone, then kept going in the right direction. "I'm sorry we aren't finding Mateo right now—"

Jonah cut him off. "She's in trouble, right?"

Alex nodded.

"She's the one I saw? She got shot."

"Right." It seemed like that hadn't even slowed her down. So much had happened since then, he wondered what state he would find her in.

"There!"

Alex's eyes followed where Jonah pointed, and he saw her. He pocketed the phone and ran with the blanket to crouch beside her body. She was laying on the grass and halfway propped up against a rock. "She's out cold." And her skin was freezing. "Help me get the blanket around her."

Jonah did as he was asked, and Alex gathered her into his arms. The phone lay on the grass. Jonah moved to pick it up.

"Leave that here." Eric was going to have to get a new phone. He didn't want anyone tracking Sasha while she wasn't able to speak for herself.

Jonah didn't argue. Alex carried Sasha back to the car, laid

202 | LISA PHILLIPS

her on the backseat, and got in. When he drove past the hospital, Jonah said, "I thought we were stopping there."

Alex pulled up at a stoplight, tempted to put his lights and sirens on. He glanced back at Sasha and saw her cheeks already had color back in them. "Not the hospital."

Jonah glanced at him but, again, didn't argue.

Alex pulled into Mama's driveway, and Jonah held the door while he carried her inside. "Mom!"

"It must be bad if you're calling me—" She came into view in the hall and saw Sasha in her arms. "Again?"

"She's just cold and passed out."

"Use the guest bedroom. Maybe she'll stay long enough for tea this time." She turned and headed there, tugging the blanket and sheets back on the bed. "I'll get my heated blanket."

"Don't warm her up too fast. And if you need help, call Dean."

She muttered on her way out the door, which made Jonah smile. Until it morphed back to a frown. "Will she be okay?"

"I hope so. Because we need to go see the night manager and find out where Perkins has Mateo." Fear rippled through him, causing a shudder he didn't bother to hold back. It was okay if Jonah knew he was scared. That only meant it was all right for the kid to show the same emotion.

Mama came back in.

"Keep an eye on her. Please?" He added, "And call me when she wakes up."

Her brows lifted.

"Please. I have to do something important. Jonah is going to stay here with you." The kid started to object, so Alex shook his head. "Watch out for her." In exchange, Jonah knew he would find Mateo.

"Mama, have you heard from Javier?"

She shook her head. "Not for a week at least. He dropped Mateo off yesterday, but didn't stay." It registered in her expression before she said, "Where is Mateo?"

"I'm going to figure that out. When I know something, I'll let you know."

"Bring me my grandson, Alejandro."

He nodded, glancing once at Sasha. Still unconscious. Then he walked out the door. "Yes, ma'am."

28

S asha smelled lavender. She blinked. It was still light out, so not that much time had passed. Or was it the next day? The water.

"Whoa." A man's face swam into view. "Easy there."

Her heart stuttered. "Jonah?"

The teen boy blinked. "Uh, how do you know my name?"

Sasha had to recover fast. Too bad her body was warm enough she wasn't sure she had the energy to move, and her brain wasn't going much quicker than that. She started to shake her head, then realized that would be redundant. She had to remember his friend's name, the other teen boy, Alex's nephew.

Instead, Jonah took a step toward her. "I'm Mateo's friend. You know Lieutenant Basuto, right? He acted like he knew you."

"Right. Thanks." She touched the side of her head with the palm of her hand. "Not quite firing on all cylinders yet."

"Seems like you had an ordeal."

Sasha didn't want to get into that. This was terrible. Why did he have to be here? "You should go. It's not safe to be around me."

He watched her cautiously, as though he'd been told to stick around no matter what. "Seems to me the only person who gets hurt is you."

"What?"

"That guy shot you, right? And now this…whatever it is."

Sasha had no idea how to respond to that. It was kind of true. "Where am I?"

"Abuela—oh. Uh, Mateo's grandma? The lieutenant's mom. We're at her house."

"Okay. He brought me here before." Sasha studied him. Beyond the fact he shouldn't be around her, everything in her wanted to just…absorb all that he was. Close up.

Her son.

"Are you okay?" He pulled up a chair and sat. "What happened to you?"

He didn't know she was a fugitive, or that the FBI agent who led the task force had allowed her to escape. For the first time in her life, she cared whether someone thought bad of her or not. Maybe for the second time, actually, considering the way she felt about Alex. But with Jonah? Way different.

She didn't want to lie, but she also didn't want him to know the truth.

Sasha said, "Where is Alex?"

"Finding Mateo." Fear washed over his face.

She pushed at the blankets and nearly screamed. Her wrist was bound with a bandage. How had she not remembered that? Just more confirmation that her brain was not firing on all cylinders.

"Are you going to puke? I could get a bucket or something."

His words broke through the fog of pain. Sasha managed to laugh, though it sounded pathetic. "What am I wearing?"

"Oh, well." His cheeks pinked.

Terror rolled through her. "Did you—"

"No!" He yelled, "No way. That's so creepy." He looked like

he wanted to be the one to throw up now. "Abuela took off your wet clothes. She said some parts were frozen solid." He motioned to the shirt she wore. "That's Mateo's T-shirt."

"Oh."

"She had me wrap your hand, though. I've done it a lot."

"On yourself?"

He shook his head. "My mom sprained her wrist one time, so I helped her."

Sasha was pretty sure she'd broken hers. Time would tell. Still, hearing him talk about his mother was enough to make her want to…do something other than lay here. He'd chalk her discomfort up to their conversation and what she'd been through. He wouldn't have any idea she was thinking about the features he had that looked so much like her own.

Nothing had been passed down from her relatives, genetically speaking, that she'd ever been able to appreciate.

She'd imagined the moment she would meet Jonah. She never thought it would happen, but she had played out the scene in her mind plenty of times. She'd thought seeing Jonah would make her mind want to go back to those few days she'd been held after her uncle's death. Each of the potential sperm donors she'd been forced to… Well, her mind didn't even shy away from it. The whole thing was simply…years ago.

Looking at Jonah, though, it was like none of it even mattered. He was here. How that had come to be, she didn't care. For the first time in her life, she thought that maybe she had finally moved on far enough to find some semblance of freedom from the hold it'd had over her ever since.

She wanted to fiddle with the blanket but the pain in her wrist was about to make her pass out. "Tell me about Mateo?"

There had to be a seriously good reason Alex wasn't here, asking what had happened to her. He'd left her son, of all people, to stay with her. There had to be something going on.

He settled into an older-looking armchair. The majority of

the room was decorated in florals, but with a Hispanic twist. There was a gorgeous, red-painted pot on the dresser Sasha wanted a closer look at.

"A bunch of guys jumped out of a van. They shoved us against this wall, took Mateo, and told me to tell the lieutenant what'd happened."

"They work for Perkins?"

He frowned for a second, then nodded.

"Alex has gone to find him?"

"I think he's talking to this one guy." He shifted, nervous now. "We do jobs for him sometimes."

She nodded, trying to look like she didn't care. Jonah didn't need to get involved with someone like Perkins or the people who worked for him. Where were his parents in this? They should've stopped him. Given him a bigger allowance. Something parents did—something she had no idea about because she'd never raised a child.

She was the one who had given him away.

Now he was practically a grown man, worried about his friend. Looking out for her. The kind of kid who wrapped his mom's wrist because she'd sprained it.

Sasha wondered how he was with his father. Did they have a good relationship? She'd never had a healthy one with anyone who should've been able to take care of her. Then there were her romantic relationships. Disasters, each and every one. At least she and Zander could still be friends. That was the one shining light in her life—the fact she hadn't completely burned that bridge.

How did she think anything could come of her and Alex? She was still a fugitive. He was a cop. This wasn't some epic love-conquered-all story. It was her life, and she'd never had a good thing come her way the whole time she'd lived it. Things would hardly take a whole new turn all of a sudden with no warning.

Just because she'd woken up to her first conversation with Jonah, and been given a chance to meet him, didn't mean anything. It wasn't a portent of things to come. Just Alex, doing what he could.

"Why do you keep looking at me like that?"

"Like what?" She blanked her expression. "I don't know what you mean."

He shook his head. Like he knew she was humoring him.

Sasha said, "Why don't you tell me what you *didn't* tell Alex about what happened to Mateo?"

He swallowed. "How'd you know?"

"Call it intuition." She'd like to say it was their genetic connection, but the truth was she'd interrogated a lot of people in her life.

"When they took Mateo—" His voice broke. "He didn't just say, 'tell Alex.' And I'm not talking about the fact he punched me in the face as well." Jonah pointed to his cheekbone. It was turning purple. "He also said, 'Tell Alex that Perkins wants the woman to bring him his son. That's the only way he gets his nephew back.' I have no idea what that means."

"That must have been pretty scary for you. Watching them take your friend and being threatened."

Jonah glanced out the window, probably to hide the sheen of tears he didn't want her to see. "No scarier than it is for Mateo right now. If he's even still alive."

"I want to sugarcoat this for you, but the truth is, if they kill him, they have nothing to bargain with. They need Alex to get me and have me bring in Ian, right?"

Jonah shrugged. "That's the kid?"

She nodded. "If Mateo is dead, they have no exchange." She swallowed back some emotion of her own. All because he was afraid for his friend, and she was absorbing it. Feelings right now? They were awful and inconvenient. She had to be the hardened criminal on the run, and instead she was in a fluffy bed, snuggled up and talking to the son she'd given away.

What she didn't need right now was to feel this connection with him. The pull that drew her to ask more questions. Get to know him.

That was *seriously* the last thing she needed to be doing.

Sasha used her healthy hand to push back the edge of the covers. It was past time to go. The longer she stayed, the more she wanted to be part of these peoples' lives. They were like a dog allergy. The longer you were around the animal, the more you were able to ignore the symptoms. Or blame them on something else entirely. All the while, getting sicker and sicker every day.

"Do you need help?" He strode to the door and called out into the hallway, "Abuela!"

Sasha winced. "I don't need help. I just need a phone."

Her feet were freezing. She lifted her good hand and ran it down her hair. Great, it probably looked like a rat's nest, and she had nothing to fix it with—which would take two hands anyway. Only one seemed to want to cooperate. The other was like being stuck with a hot poker.

The older woman came bustling in. "What is it, *mi hija*?"

She'd called Sasha, "my daughter." That wasn't good at all.

"I need a phone." The faster she could get out of there, the better. This was getting worse and worse. "And some shoes." No, that wouldn't work. Unless she could get to Hope Mansion and the rest of her stuff Maggie kept there. Even a police search wouldn't find that.

"Here. You can use mine." Jonah held out a phone, already unlocked.

She dialed Dorian's number. He was the fastest way to get transportation out of town. It wasn't like she could call up a rideshare.

He didn't answer.

Sasha lowered the phone.

"They didn't answer?"

She wasn't going to explain to Jonah or Alex's mother. Why

on earth would Alex bring her here again? He shouldn't trust someone like her with people he cared about. The man was delusional if he thought her being here was a good idea.

Dorian had never not picked up.

She gasped.

Jonah crouched in front of her. "What is it?"

"Nothing. I just remembered why he couldn't pick up." Why he wouldn't answer, now of all times. She'd called him from the police station.

Liquidate all my assets.

Radio silence until the job was done.

Sasha got up, careful not to knock Jonah over. She moved to the window and tugged the curtains closed. It wasn't safe.

Alex's mama turned the light on. "What is it?"

Sasha fought back the tears. "I need my things!"

Jonah flinched at her outburst. Alex's mom didn't even react. She just said, "The dryer won't be done for twenty minutes. Get back in bed, Sasha."

She knew. Of course, Alex's mom knew *precisely* who she was. Probably also that she was wanted by the FBI. And why wouldn't she know everything? Alex would confide in her. She would keep the confidence.

Meanwhile, Sasha had to fight to not throw the lamp across the room. Why did everyone have to *know*? All she wanted was to be someone else, some*where* else.

The phone rang in her hand.

On screen, it said, *Lieutenant Basuto.* Alex. She swiped her thumb and put it to her ear. The words she wanted to say would make both of them—these people who were here to take care of her—upset. She had to check it. She might want to walk away, but burning the bridge Alex wanted built wasn't the answer to venting her frustration.

Instead, she said, "Did you find him?" Maybe she could help get Mateo back before Dorian finished his job. Then again,

Perkins was expecting her and his son, Ian. Two birds? "Because I can figure out a deal. Get Mateo back for you."

Just so long as Dorian was done before Perkins got his hands on her.

History was *not* going to repeat itself.

29

Alex waited while Sasha came down the stairs, standing in the same spot where she'd run away from him after Perkins had ambushed his wife at Hope Mansion.

"You gave me orders, and then you hung up on me." And yet, despite the fact his words held a slightly accusatory tone, he couldn't help but stare at her.

She'd been in an FBI ambush, nearly caught hypothermia, and she looked this good? It occurred to him that his perspective contained some bias. He liked her. He didn't like that she was on the opposite side of the law, but the attraction couldn't be denied. And the second she'd found out about Mateo, she'd jumped on board to save his nephew.

Which was exactly what he should be doing right now.

"I found the house."

She stepped off the last stair and stood eye-to-eye with him. Black boots, jeans, and a gray sweater.

"How do you look this good?"

Her cheeks pinked. She touched her unbandaged hand to one cheek. "I'm seriously blushing right now?" She shook her head. "Let's just go before this gets worse."

"Thanks."

Before he could say more, Maggie appeared with a sling. "Here." She tugged it over Sasha's shoulder so her bandaged wrist could lay snug inside.

Sasha blew out a breath, relief washing over her face. "Thank you. That's *way* better."

"Are you sure you want to help me?"

"Are you kidding?" She put her good hand on her hip. "He's a kid, so let's go. We don't have time for ridiculous questions."

She strode to the front door.

Maggie chuckled. Alex spun to her. She blanked her expression and said, "You should probably go save Mateo."

"That's what I *was* doing." He trailed after her. "Before she called me and ordered me here to come get her."

He heard Maggie laugh again as he stepped outside. Sasha was beside his car already. His personal car, given he was no longer on duty, and he didn't want to show up in a police car. Too big of a giveaway that he was a cop. Perkins might be anticipating a rescue attempt, or he might not, but busting in there would give everything away.

Alex knew he was going to get into trouble at work. Conroy couldn't allow his missteps to go on much longer. He was operating outside the bounds of procedure. That was why he'd emailed Conroy and explained everything. They might need backup, or someone might call 911 because they saw or heard something. It was only right for the department to have a heads up.

Yes, that meant he could go in tomorrow and find himself under suspension. He was fully expecting it to happen, given everything with Sasha, and this on top of it.

However, it was the right thing to do.

Like having her help.

She faced the car door, ready to get in as soon as he beeped the locks.

"Hey."

She spun as he approached, a little too fast.

"Sorry. I didn't mean to startle you." He tried to make out her expression in the dim light of the parking lot. Maggie had switched off the security lights for their departure. Otherwise, they'd have been blinded by the white lights. Lit up like a stadium.

"Let's just go."

Before he clicked the locks, Alex touched the side of her face. She flinched, so he hesitated, but then she stepped in and touched her cheek to his hand, instead of him making the connection. Alex said, "Are you okay?"

"I don't like it that Mateo is in danger. He seems like a good kid."

"He is."

"But even if he wasn't, I would still want to help retrieve him."

"I know."

To Sasha, people who couldn't defend themselves should be saved. It was ingrained in her, a result of her experiences. He felt the same way and would jump in, even if it wasn't his nephew they were helping.

He just wanted to know one thing. "How would you feel if someone wanted to save you?"

"I don't need that." She bristled. "Not anymore." He couldn't help the fact his feelings were hurt. Alex started to pull away from her, but she wrapped her fingers around his forearm, his palm still against her cheek. "But that doesn't mean I don't appreciate it."

Alex leaned in and touched his lips to hers. "Thank you for coming with me. I'm glad you're okay. Or at least feeling good enough for this."

One of her eyebrows rose. "Uh, sure. I feel great."

He kissed her again, knowing full well she had every intention of being here with him no matter how awful she felt. "Like I said, thank you."

"I needed the distraction. Who knows what will happen with

the FBI? I may as well do something worthwhile if I'm not going to be around much longer."

He flinched so hard his thumb beeped the locks on the car. "Sasha—"

She sprang out of his arms. "Come on."

She climbed in, and he drove them to the address the has station guy—the one who worked for Perkins—had given him.

"A used car lot?" She glanced over. "Are they serious?"

Alex parked the car and shrugged. "I guess Perkins likes to diversify. He's got fingers in pies all over town."

"Conroy needs to take him down."

"He's working on getting both the security guard and the big guy who had Ian to testify against him. But he's been a *little* busy with the whole FBI taskforce thing."

Sasha winced. "I hate that."

"It's how police work goes. Always plenty to do." He squeezed her knee. "You didn't ask someone to target you, waste the FBI's time, and try to kill you."

"Those agents are dead. Shot in front of me." Her voice sounded hollow. She gasped. "Millie! Is she okay?"

"Eric has her at the hospital. Conroy said the doctor wants to keep her overnight just to be safe, but she and the baby are stable."

Sasha let out a long sigh. "Thank You, God."

"You pray a lot?"

"I know Millie and Eric believe, so I figure He was looking out for them."

"And you?"

She glanced out the side window. "Why would He watch out for someone like me? If He is, He's doing a terrible job." Before he could respond to that, she said, "Let's just find Mateo."

"Eric is working from the hospital. Looking deeper into your case and who was behind the initial interest in you."

"Doesn't matter. Jonah is scared, and I don't like it. That's all that matters right now."

"He's a good kid," Alex said, more as a prompt for her to talk about her son than for any other reason. *Her son.*

But all she did was nod. "Let's go."

As they circled the forecourt, headed for the main building, she spoke again, "We should take separate entrances."

"Nope." Alex pulled his personal gun from the holster on the back of his belt. Then he got another weapon, also registered to him, and handed it to her. "We aren't splitting up."

The last time he'd watched her walk away from him, she'd nearly frozen to death. After nearly being shot by gunmen. He wasn't sure his heart could take much more.

"I'm fine."

"You have to know there's no way I'm going to believe that."

"That's why I like you." She leaned close. "You're a smart guy."

Alex chuckled.

"So let's go, smart guy." She pulled open the back door and listened for a second through a crack a couple of inches wide. Then she stepped in.

Alex kept her in front of him. As they crept down a back hall, checking every door as they went, he prayed at each one that they would find Mateo. He didn't like the idea of his brother missing, and his nephew in the hands of a man who'd beat his wife and terrorized his son. A guy who sold drugs and extorted people…and who knew what else.

Watching her work, he could see why Bridget spoke so highly of her operational skills. Alex had to not get distracted by her. They were here for one thing.

Inside was a maze. The showroom glistened, a sports car rotating on a platform, even though no one was in attendance. It was after-hours, so why had the guy sent Alex here?

"Could be a trap?"

Sasha surveyed the showroom without turning. "Traps have to be sprung."

And yet, it was obvious that there was no one here.

He spotted something under the back of the sports car and headed for it while she watched his back. Alex stepped onto the platform and crouched at the back bumper. He reached for it, registering fast enough to pull back. "I've got blood. We need to figure out how to open—"

She reached into the open driver's side window and the trunk clicked. The lid opened four inches or so, but didn't lift all the way.

It could be Mateo.

He stared at the open trunk lid. The blood on the carpet pooled to such a degree it had seeped through and was now dripping down beneath the car and onto the platform.

She came to stand beside him. "We need to know."

Alex flipped the lid.

Javier lay inside. Pale skin. His body curled awkwardly, obviously stuffed inside. Shot in the chest first.

Alex stumbled off the platform and set his hands on his knees, bending to suck in deep breaths. *Javier.* That meant Mateo was fatherless—if he was even still alive. Mama was going to be devastated.

"This guy hates you."

Alex felt the tickle of tears on his cheeks. He swiped them away with the heel of his hand. "What are you talking about?"

"Jonah said he mentioned me." She glanced around. "This seems more like it's a personal vendetta —against you. I think Perkins hates you."

"I have to call this in." Before he could pull out his phone, a door closed somewhere in the building. The clang of metal rang through the whole cavernous space.

He spun around. Sasha did as well. But when he looked to find her, she was gone.

Perkins hates you.

He had Mateo. He'd killed Javier. But why, and why now? Alex was the one who drove Emily Perkins and her son, Ian, to Hope Mansion in the first place. If she was right, Perkins must have a serious grudge against him over that. Perkins might have had his own dealings with Javier, which led to his brother owing the guy money, but now Javier could never pay.

Not a stellar business plan.

So he'd done it for another reason. To get back at Alex? Taking the hit, just to make a point.

Footfalls echoed down the hallway. Alex found some cover. Two men, tough guys in jeans and boots. T-shirts. One had a chain hanging from his belt, probably clipped to his wallet and tucked into his back pocket.

He thought this was partially about Sasha and their altercation at Hope Mansion. Still, Perkins didn't know who she was. Right?

The trap was about to snap shut and both of them would be inside.

Alex led with his weapon. "Last Chance Police! Hands up!"

Both drew guns and opened fire. Alex dove to the side and crouched behind the cover of the sports car currently rotating on the platform. This was not a good hiding spot. He needed to move before it turned a full rotation, and he ended up a sitting duck.

As it turned and brought him into full view of the two gunmen, Alex could only think one thing.

Perkins had set them up.

And it was Mateo who would pay the price.

"Give me my friend back!"

Alex whipped around so fast he almost fell back. Jonah stood at the far end of the showroom, waving a gun with one shaky hand at the two men.

"No!" Sasha screamed.

A gun went off, and Jonah fell.

30

Something inside Sasha tore open. She watched Jonah fall backward, blood everywhere. He landed. Still. No groan. No movement. The shot still echoed in her ears. "No!"

It was like being cut in two with a sword—or so she imagined. Her being, sliced right down the middle. Never to be put back together again.

The world tunneled into a single image. Jonah bleeding on the ground.

"Alex!" She didn't know why she called his name then, only that it felt like she was frozen and had no clue what to do.

He was already moving. He raced to the supine boy. He was so still. Dead. Alive. She didn't know.

Sasha turned and her gaze solidified on the two men. The shooter, his gun still raised. The other man with him, standing in front.

She raced at the shooter, past the second man.

She slammed into his middle and knocked him back. Pain tore through her forearm, still in the sling. They hit the floor, sliding several feet across the slippery tile at the force of her impact.

He grunted. She grabbed for his gun and realized she held one of her own. In the shock, she'd forgotten that.

Sasha brought her arm up as fast and as hard as possible and clipped his chin with it. Her mind threatened to blank again, thinking only of Jonah. She couldn't let that happen.

He tried to shove her off. He rolled her onto her side. She scrambled back.

The other guy laughed. "She tackled you."

In a flash, Sasha lifted her gun and fired at him.

He yelped, thrown back two paces and clutched his arm.

Satisfaction rolled through her as she screamed at him, like a wild thing. That slice to her being had probably snapped her hold on sanity. It didn't matter what was done to her, or how badly her wrist hurt right now. Shoot someone she cared about? Someone she'd gone to such lengths to protect? No. Just, no.

The shooter shifted. She swung the gun again, but her arm slammed into his, and she dropped it.

He grabbed her hand, twisted her on the floor, and put a knee in her back. Pain tore through her wrist. Sasha screamed, flailing. The sling was long gone now.

"Quiet down."

She didn't.

"The cops are on their way," Alex yelled across the room. "So either lay down your weapons, or you'll have to face the Last Chance police when they show up in minutes. And if you get in the way of EMTs seeing to this boy, I'll shoot you both myself."

The shooter hauled her to her feet, one giant hand holding both of hers behind her back. Tears rolled down her face. She leaned to the side and vomited everything in her stomach. Her wrist hurt so bad, and he was twisting it still. She wanted to lay down and cry in defeat. Cry for her boy laying too still across the room from her.

The shooter cursed and shifted her away from him. "I didn't sign up for this."

"You killed him!" She looked at Alex, but they all knew who she was talking to. The guy didn't let go of her hands. Her head swam. "I'm going to throw up again."

He didn't adjust his grip. Just kept squeezing.

"Let her go."

The shooter lifted his gun with his free hand and trained it on Alex. His friend did the same. "She comes with us."

"I don't think so." Alex faced off with them.

Sirens could be heard in the distance.

"As I said, don't keep the EMTs from helping this boy. If you do, I'm coming after you with a murder charge."

The shooter started moving, walking her in front of him. She stumbled. They were headed for a side door. She glanced at Alex. "Help Jonah."

He stared at her. The look in his eyes was one she couldn't take on. It was too much. The pain, the desperation. He mouthed something. She couldn't make out the words.

Pressure on her wrists increased. Sasha twisted around so she didn't fall and let out a cry of frustration.

"Sasha!" Finally, Alex called after her.

The sound of his voice cut her even more than seeing Jonah fall.

There was nothing Alex could do for her, and she didn't want him to help her when he needed to help Jonah. Plus, if he did manage to subdue these two, that would mean she'd still be here when the police showed up. An escapee, a wanted fugitive.

That wouldn't go down well.

She would probably be blamed for the deaths of those couple of FBI agents who were gunned down. As if making someone hate you meant you could be forced to take responsibility for their actions. She didn't even know who was pulling their strings—or why.

What had she done to them?

The shooter led her down the hall, laughing. "He was hoping you'd come."

Perkins. That was the only person her tired brain could come up with. He'd targeted Alex, asked for her, killed Javier. He was responsible for Jonah being shot.

God, please don't let him be dead.

Jonah was a pastor's kid. That should mean God would listen to her about him, right? After all, He took care of His people. They prayed, and He helped them.

Sasha had given up asking for good things. They would never come for someone like her. So she prayed for Jonah. God could hear, and He might help her son when she couldn't because He and Jonah had that connection.

One she didn't have because she'd given him away.

The second shooter shoved the door open ahead of them. "Come on."

They were fast-walking now. Outside to a truck.

For a split second, she expected a bullet to slam into her skull. She would fall to the floor, and it would all be over. Finally, she would have her peace.

Instead, nothing happened.

Dorian wasn't here.

The shooter shoved her onto the backseat and finally let go of her hands. She brought them to the front, so she could push up with her good hand. Roll over. Kick him, and then dive out the door.

Too bad her body didn't function as fast as her mind. Before she could do anything, the door shut behind her, jamming one booted foot between the seat and the door.

They both got in front, the shooter in the passenger seat where he could hold that gun on her. The one he'd used to shoot Jonah.

That boy was my son.

She couldn't scream it at them the way she wanted to. If either one told Perkins, he would hold it over her as leverage. That is, if he was still alive.

"Shame we can't take a detour," the driver said. "Have some fun."

The shooter looked down her body, then back up. "Maybe after Perkins has her for a while, he'll share."

There was no more vomit in her, otherwise she'd have deposited more on the floor of the truck.

Sasha's entire body was numb. She almost felt as though she was floating, unable to move any of her limbs. What was the point of trying when there was nothing left in her life? Alex was with Jonah and would take care of him. She was alone, the way she had always been.

If she tried to take out Perkins, they'd probably kill her.

She was thinking that would be the best scenario. Especially if Dorian didn't catch up in time. Maybe he wasn't even in town yet, though she had no idea what was taking so long. He'd promised to do this for her.

And then there was Mateo.

Javier had been back at the dealership, in the trunk of that car. Where had Perkins taken his son? Was Mateo dead, or alive?

She needed to know that before she killed Perkins.

Which she had every intention of doing, and not just if he or any of his people planned to touch her without her consent.

Sasha forced her brain to catalog the situation. Her goals were to find Mateo and kill Perkins. Maybe not in exactly that order. She could have one of Perkins's men find him or tell her where he was.

That might work.

The door opened. One of the two men slid her out and dumped her onto his shoulder. Her stomach ached and her head swam. Both hands dangled so that every few steps her broken wrist bumped the back of his leg. The whole cycle repeated over again each time, the ache followed by the head swim, followed by the bump.

They were inside. Tile hallway. Oak baseboards. Modern,

but not mass produced. This was a house that screamed, "money."

Everything flipped upside down. She realized it was her and not the world around her when her backside hit the chair, and she slumped into the chair unaided.

Pretending she was less than physically and mentally present was an excellent tactic. Too bad it wasn't exactly an act. She was likely going to have to fake her way into convincing Perkins—currently sitting across an ornate heavy wood desk from her—she was in a better state.

Sasha flipped her hair back with her good hand. "Was that entirely necessary?" She tried to make the words sound strong but wasn't sure she succeeded.

Thomas Perkins studied her with the eye of a man assessing a side of beef. "We'll have to get you cleaned up."

She glanced around, giving his office the same assessing look. As much as she could muster into pulling it off. This was a gorgeous office. "Who knew a small-town guy like you could have a place like this."

"You know nothing about me. The reach I have. The influence I command."

"So tell me." The time he spent talking would give her time to think. To compose herself, and get her brain to spin back up to regular operating speeds. Her wrist was killing her, but the rest she was pretty sure she could ignore now that her stomach was empty.

"I have a better idea." Perkins stood. "I'll have someone escort you to your room. They'll bring you a meal, and you can get cleaned up. There's something for you to wear in the closet."

As if she was going to go along with all that. Be the docile woman he'd wanted in his wife, a woman who would stick around long enough to give him a son. She had no intention of doing that. *Been there.* She already had the nightmares that went along with it.

"Where is Mateo Basuto?"

"Stand up."

"Tell me where he is. I take him and go, and you don't find out exactly what avalanche you just brought down on yourself by dragging me here in this state. Shooting a boy and kidnapping another."

Something flickered in his gaze. "I knew from the first day I met you this was going to be worth it. Threats won't work, but they are amusing."

"You have no idea what you just invited in." After all, he had no idea who she was. Sasha was just angry enough to lose her cool, and she was prepared to drag out every ugly secret just so he knew she had plenty of imagination when it came to bringing pain to a man who thought he could keep a woman captive for his amusement.

"No idea? I think you're mistaken on that." He leaned forward a fraction. "Melina."

"Melina is dead." Sasha stared up at him. "You're a local wannabe crime lord with no clue who I am."

Red and blue flashing lights appeared through the window, shining on the far wall and onto a painting she suspected was a knock-off. Perkins grabbed her arm and dragged her to her feet, then to the hall. The front door. One of his men swung it open.

He held a gun to her head, behind the door where no one could see, and faced off with three police cars and double that number of officers.

Through the crack by the hinges, she spied Conroy as he called out from behind his car door, "You're harboring a wanted fugitive. Send her out, and we'll be on our way. If you don't, we'll be forced to enter the premises and search for her ourselves."

Her lips curled into a smile. Until Perkins shifted and spoke to one of his men.

"You know what to do."

31

"Care to explain this?"

Alex didn't look at his boss. He kept his eyes on the front door of this ridiculously expensive-looking house. He'd never even been up this way, not until an officer spotted the truck those two guys had been driving and called in to report that he'd seen Sasha's kidnappers.

The door slammed shut. A commotion kicked off inside. "We have to get in there."

He looked at his boss and saw Conroy's expression.

Did the chief want him to say, "please?"

Alex had been forced to watch someone take Sasha from him again. So much like the day she'd been seventeen and he barely fifteen. Dragged away against her will.

He'd seen the look on her face. Fear. These days it was over-laid with the strength she had. The knowledge of what might happen, and the fact she could have to relive it. But still, at the core, was the fear.

Hurt. Captured.

"Let's go." Conroy turned to the group. "Move in!" His voice rang out. He didn't give Alex any more of his time or attention.

That was for the best, even if it disappointed him. Alex didn't want to get yelled at for being involved when this was a personal case. His emotions were compromised, but there was no way he wouldn't participate when both Mateo and Sasha were in that house.

He was sure of it.

He would be part of the takedown. Perkins was going to be arrested. He would get his family back, and he'd be able to tell Sasha that, the last time he'd seen Jonah, he'd been alive. Fighting for his life and probably headed to surgery even now. But he'd been breathing. Heart beating. Torn apart by that bullet, one that had embedded itself into his chest, but alive. Alex didn't know if he would make it, but he *could*, and that would give her hope.

She needed to know.

Alex trailed behind the chief to the front door, where Conroy had one of the officers kick the door in. He headed inside, and they worked room by room through the ground floor of the house.

Perkins's people scattered. The cops ran down each one and cuffs were slapped on.

"Where is he?"

"Lieutenant."

Alex backed out of the face of one of Perkins's men and looked at the chief.

"Check the garage," Conroy ordered.

Alex spun and made his way there, heading in the general direction of the exterior garage door. This place was a maze of opulent rooms. Thick rugs. Dark wood. He didn't want to know how many people's lives had been ruined for Thomas Perkins to be able to afford this place.

The garage had three bays—two SUVs, and a sports car at the end. Officer Frees had followed him. Alex figured Conroy ordered him to babysit so Alex didn't do something they would all regret.

One of the garage doors rolled up. The middle one.

Alex raced to the hood of the SUV between the other two vehicles and lifted his gun, aiming it square at the man in the driver's seat as he moved quickly to the door. He held aim and reached for the door handle, yanking on it. "Get out."

Perkins lifted both hands. "I guess you caught me."

Alex tugged on his arm to assist the man in getting out. He figured he was about to be suspended anyway...

No, doing whatever he wanted to Perkins wouldn't be professional. He shouldn't cross even more lines than he had to.

He shoved Perkins against the side of the SUV. Frees held his gun on Perkins while Alex cuffed his hands behind his back.

"No weapons? Nothing else on him?"

Alex shook his head. A pat down had revealed nothing, not even a wallet. "He was going to run. Probably planning on starting a new life elsewhere. Florida, maybe. Kick it with the big-time drug lords where it's warm all the time."

After Frees did a quick once-over through the vehicle's interior for anyone else, Alex tugged Perkins away so he could lead the guy back through the house.

"I don't like hurricanes," Frees said. "I'd never live there."

Perkins said, "Neither of you is going to ask me about your nephew?"

"He's either here or not, alive or—" Alex hated it, but his voice broke. "—not. What you say won't make much difference." Even if Alex did want to wail on the guy until gave up information about Mateo and Sasha. Getting him into custody was the ultimate priority, and then he'd have the bandwidth to worry about finding Mateo and Sasha.

Wherever they were, he prayed they were okay.

The frustration of not knowing was enough he practically shoved Perkins at Conroy. "Ask him where they are."

Conroy lifted a brow. "Mr. Perkins, where is Mateo Basuto?"

Perkins only smirked. Alex wanted to punch that look off his face.

"Where is Sasha Camilero?"

"Who?"

Alex turned away. Conroy continued their conversation in a low, deadly voice, while Alex moved to the wall and slammed a fist into it. He busted a hole through the drywall and set a cloud of dust poofing into the air.

He spun back. "Where are they?"

Conroy winced.

"Lieutenant."

He whirled around to find Donaldson down the hall. The sergeant said, "Come with me," and then disappeared.

Alex sprinted. He pulled back on his pace and forced himself to jog to where Sergeant Donaldson stood by a door. Frees was right behind him again. Babysitting.

Alex clenched his back teeth. Before he could ask the question, Donaldson said, "Down here."

The set of stairs led to a basement hallway. Doors lined the wall, all open except one. Sasha stood in front of it, looking frustrated. Beyond her, a man—one of Perkins's guys—lay unconscious, or dead, on the floor.

"Ms. Camilero is helping us." Donaldson said, "I'm also hesitant to cuff her since it's clear she has a broken wrist."

Alex pulled her close and held her tight against him, his face in her hair. "Mateo." It wasn't a question. More of a heart's cry, now that he had her back, to know if his nephew was okay.

Her stiffness dissipated, and she wrapped her arms around him. "He's inside, but I can't get the door open."

"Frees." Alex didn't need to add instructions.

"On it," the officer said.

He needed to ask her another question before they got Mateo out. "Did Perkins..?" He couldn't even say it.

She stared up at him.

"Did he hurt you?"

Sasha shook her head. "He didn't touch me. Not like that."

Alex shifted her and turned to the door, more relieved than

he wanted to admit. No way should Sasha have to go through that again.

The hall closed in. They needed to get out of here.

He could talk with Conroy and get things settled when this was all done. Right now, there were more pressing priorities.

Frees braced, then kicked it in.

"Oh."

He gave Sasha a squeeze. Beyond the door, a young man had been tied to a chair, his face completely obscured by bruises and swelling. "Mateo."

She stepped out of his arms, signaling that he should go to his nephew. They had found Mateo. Not that he was taking credit for discovering the location Mateo had been held captive. It had been discovered because he followed Perkins's men after they took Sasha. All he felt right now was relief that he had his nephew back with him.

And the question of how he would tell Mateo that his father was dead.

"Hey." Alex touched his shoulder, more to reassure himself that the kid was alive.

Frees used his multitool to cut Mateo free, leaving the kid's arms loose. One hung at a funny angle.

He glanced over his shoulder at the sergeant. "Ambulance?"

Donaldson nodded. "On its way."

Sasha stood beside the sergeant, who eyed her. He wanted to arrest her and didn't plan to let her out of his sight. But so far, she wasn't presenting a problem.

"Mateo, can you hear me?" Alex didn't want to pat his cheek. It was swollen, one eye nearly completely closed. Bruises everywhere. The shoulder was dislocated.

Mateo moaned. One eye opened, glassy, but Alex saw the moment he registered who was there. "No." A cut on his lip was split open and blood trickled down.

"Don't try to talk. We're getting you some help, okay? Then it won't hurt as much." That wasn't true, though. Was it? Mateo had lost his father. Alex was going to have to help him through that kind of hurt.

Mateo moaned again. "Perkins."

"We got him." Alex held the side of his nephew's head, the way he'd cuffed the kid gently so many times to chastise him. Tease him. Friendly, family stuff that didn't seem like much at the time, but now it seemed like everything. "He's going to jail."

Mateo started to shake his head. "Not done. Hates you."

"It is done. You don't need to worry about him anymore. Conroy took him to a car. He's been arrested." Alex turned to the others. "Let's get him out of here."

Donaldson winced. "We should wait for the EMTs. They can carry him upstairs."

"No." Mateo moaned the word.

"I agree with him. We're going now."

Mateo exhaled, the sound of it full of relief. He wanted out of here. That meant Alex wasn't going to hang around. Not when the quicker they could get him out of this house, the faster Mateo could go to the hospital and Alex could have his conversation with Conroy. He could get on with his life.

He hauled Mateo's good arm over his shoulder. The other dangled. "Brace, yeah? Cause this is gonna hurt."

To his credit, the kid didn't make much noise. "You're doing great." He started to walk. It was rocky, even with the others helping.

The hallway was empty. If there had been an unconscious man here before, and he hadn't just imagined it. The guy must've woken up and run off. While they were all in the room? Donaldson had to have been so focused on Sasha that he hadn't noticed.

They got Mateo to the bottom of the stairs that led up to the ground floor, and Alex pushed thoughts of the other guy from his mind. That would be a worry for later.

He stared up at the stairway. It was too narrow. Alex was going to have to carry Mateo himself.

"Ready?"

"Did...disarm."

There was no good in waiting, especially right now, but Alex had to ask. "What?"

Mateo fought to get the words out. "Perkins. Blow up."

"Let's get out of here." He started up the stairs. Whatever Mateo was trying to tell him, it didn't sound good and only added to Alex's drive to get up there and outside. Clear of whatever Mateo had figured out. Whatever Perkins had going on.

Two steps up, a boom shook the house.

Heat and debris came at them in a rush, like slamming a fast-moving car into a brick wall. The weight of it flung them back so that Alex fell back, Mateo in his arms.

Into the depths.

32

Her arm hurt so badly Sasha wanted to tear it off. She tried to take a breath but got a lungful of dust and smoke. Coughing wasn't much more pleasant than trying to move. Not that she had any interest in moving her arm, or anything else, for that matter.

Even if she could. She squinted to clear the grit from her eyes.

It was dark. She could hear movement. The house settling or someone else down here, she didn't know.

Her mind raced, bringing to the surface the seconds before and after the upstairs had exploded. The labored steps she'd taken up the first few stairs. The fireball that followed the deafening boom. Alex had fallen, Mateo still in his arms. The rest of them had been thrown back at the same time.

Sasha tried to look around. It was pretty dark, except for the glow from the corner to her left.

"Is anyone there!" The voice had a low tone. One of the cops, maybe. She was the only woman down here.

Sasha tried to reply. Nothing came out of her throat, and she had to cough.

He spoke again, "Hello?" So much fear.

She thought of Jonah, and a tear rolled down her face.

She heard whoever it was mumble, then nothing.

Her chest spasmed. She tried to roll over, one arm clutched against her chest. Everything flipped upside down in a freaky way, and she didn't know which way was up or which was down. Her stomach rolled. Her head spun. She managed to moan, and it didn't sound good at all.

She pushed off the floor with her functioning hand. Sasha managed to lift to a sitting position and looked around. The house above them had to have exploded, but thankfully not down here. The ceiling appeared to be intact. The stairwell Alex had been about to go up was now blocked with drywall and debris from two-by-four planks, the shredded edges nothing but shards of wood.

Donaldson—her friend's husband—lay against one wall, unconscious. Sergeant stripes on his sleeves.

Sasha lifted the edge of a shard of drywall. It fell apart in her hands. She tucked her legs closer to her body, ignoring the sting of scratches and the spots where she was bruised.

The stairs—what was left of them, anyway—weren't a viable exit anymore.

The other side of the hall had a kind of window—not much bigger than a mail slot. Through the frosted glass, with decorative wires crisscrossing it, she could see an orange glow.

Was the house on fire?

She sniffed and looked for smoke but didn't see any. Maybe they were protected down here.

A laugh bubbled up. Protected? That was a joke, considering the house had come down on top of them.

And yet, she hadn't died.

Sasha had contracted a friend to do her the ultimate favor—end her life. The fact he hadn't done it thus far meant Dorian hadn't had the chance. He would never deny her request. Instead, he'd wait for the perfect opportunity no matter how long it took. His skills meant that it wouldn't take long.

But she was still here.

An explosion—not Dorian's work. She'd been specific about there being no collateral damage. The house above them had seriously *exploded*. She blew out a choppy breath that broke a couple of times, and then she crawled to Donaldson.

She was alive.

Sasha had to stop. Hang her head, and let it just wash over her. *She was alive.* After everything she'd been through. All the times she'd thought the end was upon her. And now, she had finally contracted someone to do the job for her and put her out of her misery... on her terms. Her choice of what her destiny would be. But no, it still hadn't worked. She'd been in a house explosion, and she still wasn't even dead. It was like a cruel joke.

Tears dripped from her face. *Please don't save me if you're going to let any of them die.* Her body bucked and a sob worked its way up. She let it out since there was no point bottling it up anymore. Would God do that to her? Allow her to live and let one of the others die. That made no sense whatsoever. She didn't deserve that. Neither did they.

People like Alex. Mateo. Bridget's husband, Aiden. The other cop, the big one. She was the one who should be dead right now, not any one of them. And not Jonah. He might have been a product of what had been done to her, but that didn't mean he deserved to be tarred with the same brush. Stained for the rest of his life for something that was in no way his fault. He deserved peace.

The peace she'd been trying to find this whole time. The peace she'd thought was on the other side.

Only, it seemed like she wasn't going to be allowed to find this peace in whatever life happened after death. She'd planned to take her chances. It had to be better than what she'd gone through in her life on earth, and she was done allowing other people to have power over her. Their selfish actions. Their agendas. Revenge. Hatred. Anger and frustration.

Then Alex had come along.

Or maybe he'd always been there. His presence like bookends in her life—the presence that held everything together.

He'd been there before she was taken.

He was here now, at the end.

Maybe it was poetry. Or some gift she didn't deserve being handed to her—a recompense for what she'd been through. A little goodness in the pain.

Was that You, God? Could he have given that to her? She wanted to know why, and what she was supposed to do with it. Everything in her bristled against expectations. She'd had so much demanded of her that being able to make her own decisions and choices meant everything to her. Take away that, and she may as well not be here. Death was better than being trapped.

Red and blue flashing lights illuminated a portion of the ceiling through that mail slot window.

"Help." That one word was a whisper from her lips.

Sasha got her feet under her but had no strength to push up to standing. She collapsed back down and crawled to Donaldson. Two fingers against his chin told her he was still alive.

She dug in his pocket and pulled out a cell phone. His thumbprint unlocked it. Sasha took it with her as she moved to the others. She needed to know—though she dreaded the answer—and so she had to check.

Mateo was first. Two fingers, faint pulse.

Alex… She reached for him and stopped. Did she even want to know if he was dead or alive?

His body moved. Breath filled his lungs and he exhaled, parting his lips.

"Alex." Her voice was hoarse and barely audible, while inside her head she was screaming.

He moaned. Blinked.

"Alex." She cleared her throat, trying to swallow around the soreness. "Alex, wake up." She wanted to see his face. And why not? He'd been a solid fixture in her life. Lately, he was the one she looked to. Her friend. Not to mention the attraction. Add that in, and she didn't know what it would be like without him.

When he didn't stir more than just that, she figured he was out enough that it was safe to admit how she felt. No witnesses. No expectations.

"I shouldn't love you, but I do."

It was the last thing he needed to hear right now. Precisely why this was the best time to say it.

Sasha sat and looked at the phone. It was locked again. She'd waited too long, and it had timed out. Exhaustion weighed on her. Donaldson was several feet away. She would have to crawl back over there.

The phone illuminated, then began to vibrate.

Bridget.

Sasha swiped the screen and put it to her ear. "H-hey." She could hardly speak.

"Sash? Is that you? Oh, I'm so glad you're okay. I love you, and I want to know who's down there and all the details. But where's Aiden? Why didn't he answer his phone?"

Bridget had been separated from him for years—because of Sasha's actions. Sasha didn't blame her now for wanting to know if her husband was all right.

Sasha said, "He's alive. And Mateo and Alex." She couldn't get out the words. *Help her understand that I'm sorry.*

If God was as inclined to give her things for no reason as He seemed to be—right now, at least—maybe He would do this.

"Okay. That's good. *Alive.* Okay." Relief rolled through Bridget's tone.

"I don't know where the big one is." Sasha tried to explain. To say more. "Sorry."

She was so sorry. For everything. She'd kept Bridget from her daughter and the man she'd made her with. It had worked out for the best. At the time she had been convinced she was doing the right thing—and even now she was sure of her actions. Still, she'd caused her friend pain. Sasha felt so ashamed.

She felt darkness close in, unconsciousness threatening to take over. "Help."

The phone tumbled onto her lap, and her world swallowed up into nothing.

In what seemed like mere seconds, but was no doubt at least a few hours, Sasha surfaced in a bright place, lights shining in her face.

"She's coming around."

The light shifted. People spoke to one another, but she couldn't make out the words. The more she tried, the farther away she drifted, until the world tumbled down again.

It felt like being sucked under a wave.

She surfaced again to muted light and the quiet of an empty room. Her wrist was bandaged, laying across her stomach. Blankets tucked around her. Skin gritty. Hair on her cheek. She batted it away.

Or tried to.

Her good hand was cuffed to the bed rail.

Whoever got her out of that basement had told the hospital exactly who she was. She would be treated like a criminal. Tiptoed around. Booked. Transported to jail or federal prison.

"Good. You're awake." A figure in dark clothing turned from the window. "I didn't want to do this without talking to you. Not after everything that happened."

For a moment she thought the man was Alex. Everything in her swelled, reaching for him. The cuff clinked. She couldn't go to him.

But it wasn't Alex.

He'd been down in that basement. He would be in a bed like this one, or with his nephew. After they'd found his brother in the trunk of that car, he would want to be with family, not here with her. Alex and Sasha. The cop and the criminal once again.

The man stepped closer.

"Dorian." The word was a barely audible whisper.

He stood beside her bed. "I hardly know where to begin." He looked angry. "I saw you with him. Heard you call for him."

Alex. Ah...he knew she cared for him. Why would that affect what she'd asked him to do? Unless he thought he should offer for her to change her mind. To decide she wanted to live after all.

"We were supposed to be together. You and I. Then you find him and profess your love for him. But you still want to die?" He shook his head, fury tightening his features. "Because you don't want to be with me."

What was he talking about?

"It's for the best if you think about it. And I'm happy to assist." He didn't seem pleased. Under the anger, there was a layer of grief.

"Dorian." She wanted to tell him no. That she might've changed her mind and needed more time to think it over, but she couldn't form the words. She had no strength. No way to formulate what she wanted to say. All Sasha could make her mouth speak was one word. "No."

She didn't understand the look on his face.

"It's not your decision anymore. We were a team, you and I. I thought it would be just us forever, the way it should be."

He...what? She blinked and stared at him.

"You made your choice, and it wasn't to be with me. I won't live in a world where you delude yourself into believing there's more for you than me. There won't be. There won't *ever* be."

Dorian pulled a needle from his pocket.

"No."

"It's not your choice anymore." He uncapped the needle.

33

"Near as we can tell, Perkins had the place wired. He got you in, and after he was walked out, it blew up." Conroy shook his head. "He watched from the back of a squad car."

"That house?" Alex could hardly believe any of it. He shot his boss a look and shook his head as he pulled on his shirt and started to fasten the buttons. "Not sure I'd blow up a house like that."

"It was a rental."

Alex felt his eyebrows rise. He stopped buttoning. "Seriously? With basement holding cells?"

"They were supposed to be for storage." Conroy continued, "It was all done under another name, so we never found him—until you followed Sasha from the dealership and our officer spotted the truck."

Alex gave himself a second. Sure, he was getting dressed so he could leave, but that didn't mean he felt a hundred percent.

"You don't want to stay overnight? Let the doctors make sure you're okay?"

He shook his head carefully. "Mateo—"

"Has your mother with him."

"Jonah—"

"Is out of surgery. His parents are here for when he wakes up."

"What about Frees? Donaldson?"

"Beat up, but the prognosis is good on the sergeant. They're running more tests on Frees, and as soon as I know anything, I'll let you know."

"Then I guess that leaves Sasha."

"She's in police custody upstairs."

Alex stared at his feet while he tried to figure out where he was going to get the energy to put on his shoes. Maybe he could ask his mom to do it.

After years of relying on his own strength to prove he was good enough to get the things he wanted, he couldn't even bend over and do up his laces if he wanted to. There was an unfortunate kind of irony to it.

No matter what he'd done, or all he'd tried to achieve, he'd gotten nowhere. *Is that just how it's going to be, Lord?*

"I want her out from under this." Finally, he admitted it out loud to Conroy.

No matter that they'd already discussed her case several times, he'd been hesitant to let his boss know how much he cared for her and wanted to help her. In turn, Conroy hadn't committed to helping her the way he might with another innocent person. Too risky for a police chief to align himself against the FBI. The mayor wouldn't look too favorably on that.

"I don't blame you," Conroy said carefully. "I find myself wanting to do the same. Not because she's a woman in trouble. Even if she did do some of the things the FBI says she did, that doesn't mean we can't give her the benefit of the doubt. Innocent until proven guilty. Something the FBI has yet to do."

"Okay." He wanted to ask, "Now what?" but kept his mouth shut instead.

"I imagine Eric will want to speak with Sasha. As for you, I'm putting you on a two-week suspension. The mayor argued for a month, but we're a small department so our numbers will suffer. The sergeant is recovering as well. Still, he won't be back to the office right away. I can't have all my supervisors out of commission at the same time. When you come back to work, I have you booked in for a training seminar with the state police about operating with professionalism and respect within the community."

"Understood." Alex didn't care what the punishment was. He'd crossed a line getting personal with Sasha. Helping her. If she was convicted and sent to federal prison, it would look even worse on him. There could be accessory charges, considering he'd aided her escape. Alternatively, Eric could get her some kind of deal, and she could go free.

Alex wanted to see her. "I should tell her Jonah is going to be okay."

Conroy nodded. "Then you can find something to do with your two-week vacation. Though, you might want to think about taking a nap. I know what it feels like to get blown up."

Alex didn't laugh. He went back to something Conroy had said a second ago. "Eric wants to speak with her?"

"He's waiting for her to wake up."

For a moment, he considered being there with her when she did. Eric would come in and tell her he had authorization for an immunity deal. That the person who'd used the FBI to target her had been uncovered.

Conroy kicked over Alex's shoes. "Put those on before you go walking around the hospital."

Alex shoved his feet into his beat-up running shoes—the ones he always toed off. The backs caved in, but he wiggled his foot until it fixed itself. He needed new ones anyway.

Conroy eyed him as he stood. Alex said, "I'm good."

"Mmm. I might be inclined to believe that if you weren't so pale."

"Great, I look sickly. I've got two weeks to nap, as you said." He was feeling energized now. Alex wanted to fight for what he wanted. Not to prove he was good enough. He had plenty of limitations, and though he hadn't done the right thing every time lately, the choices were ones he could live with. Yes, he wanted to fight for Sasha.

He was trying, despite his human nature, to be a man he could be proud of. The kind of man Mateo would need in his life now that the vacuum of his father's death needed to be filled.

He took the elevator upstairs and spoke with the nurse behind the desk. She pointed him to where a uniformed Last Chance officer stood outside.

Jessica.

"Hey."

She straightened. "Lieutenant Basuto."

"Take your detective's exam yet?"

"I'm this close." She held her thumb and first finger half an inch apart. "But a lot scared. What if I don't pass?"

He wanted to stay and reassure her, but he also wanted to get in and see Sasha. "Just take the test, or you'll never know."

"Right." She nodded. "Thanks, Lieutenant."

Alex opened the door.

"I can't believe you guys got blown up. That's *crazy*. And I know crazy."

Alex turned back to her, his shoulder propping the door open. "Is Donaldson all right?" They were friends. Maybe she was scared for him. "You could go see him. I'll hang out here until you get back."

"Okay. That would be good. Thanks."

He heard a shuffle in the room. Sasha had to be awake. As Jess headed for the elevator, Alex stepped inside.

There was a man by the bed that could be a nurse or doctor, though he wasn't wearing scrubs. But something didn't seem right. His eyes narrowed in on the needle. The man tossed it on the floor.

Sasha's eyes rolled back in her bed, and she started to seize.

Alex slammed his hand into the emergency button on the

wall. The man rounded the bed. "Not so fast." Alex had no gun, but there was no way he would let this guy leave. Not when he'd just injected something into Sasha.

Alarms blared. From the bed and a speaker in the ceiling.

Alex cut the man off from his escape. "You're under arrest, and you're going to tell me exactly what that was."

If they knew the substance, the doctor could reverse it.

Rubber-soled shoes pounded the floor into the room. "What happened?"

He didn't need to answer before they surrounded the bed, one issuing orders of stuff he didn't understand and the rest rushing to do the doctor's bidding.

Alex faced off with the man. He had a square jaw and looked younger than he probably was, but his eyes were dead. *Dorian.* This was the man Sasha had asked to take care of her— finish her off. End her life. Kill her.

"You shouldn't have done that."

"It's over. I did both her and I a favor." His expression didn't change one bit. "Now, only I have to live with it."

"You can think about it in prison. You'll have plenty of time to do that. A whole life sentence." Alex watched him intently while he spoke, waiting for Dorian to make even a slight move. Rush him. Shoot him with some concealed gun before he raced for the door and tried to get away with this.

Alex didn't want to distract any of the medical personnel, but he needed help. "Call security."

"We're losing her. Push epi." Those were the words he understood, though what she'd said was much more complicated.

"It's too late." Dorian's blank expression shifted and something like satisfaction crossed his face.

Alex shoved him against the wall. "You're under arrest."

Dorian shoved back.

Alex stumbled against the end of the bed.

"Get out of here! Both of you!"

He grabbed Dorian's jacket and dragged him to the door, then shoved him into the hallway. "I need security!"

A nurse ran to the desk phone.

"Doesn't matter." Dorian sneered. "It's already done."

Alex felt the burn of tears in his eyes. His vision blurred.

"And *that* is why." Dorian pointed a finger at his face. "Because she doesn't want you?"

Dorian smirked. "Now she won't have anyone."

"So you murdered her?"

"Hands up." It was Conroy.

Alex backed up. "He injected her with something. He killed her." His breath came fast, making the words hard to get out. "She's dead. He killed her."

"I said, 'hands up.'" Conroy held out cuffs. "Lieutenant."

Alex shoved away the urge to pass out, took the handcuffs, and spun Dorian to face the wall. Dorian's elbow came back and slammed into Alex's face. His nose erupted with sharp pain.

He landed smack on his tailbone against the floor. Hearing footsteps, he turned to see Conroy racing after Dorian. At the end of the hall, Special Agent Cullings turned the corner. He stuck out his foot and sent the fleeing man sliding across the floor.

Dorian cried out in frustration.

Eric stooped down, cuffed Dorian, and lifted him to his feet. "This one yours?"

Conroy said, "Attempted murder. Could be murder one if the doctor calls it." He glanced at Alex. "If Sasha Camilero dies."

Alex didn't want to hear the rest of the conversation. It was too hard to strain to hear from this far away in a busy hospital. And they weren't words he wanted to hear, anyway. He scrambled to the room where they were still working on Sasha.

The doctor gaped. "Your nose."

He could feel the warm trickle down over his lips. Alex lifted his shirt to press against the flow of blood. All that did was reveal the bandage over the giant bruise on his side where his rib had been cracked.

She started to say something. Alex cut her off.

"Is she…" He couldn't finish.

"We gave her an antidote to the medicine he administered."

"How did you know what it was?"

She motioned to the needle. "Do you want me to explain the intricacies, or should I continue to work on stabilizing my patient?"

Alex motioned to Sasha with his chin.

"Good answer." She peered closely at Sasha's eyes, shining a light directly into her pupil. "Keep an eye on her blood pressure."

The nurse said, "Yes, doctor."

"She's alive." Alex let out a long exhale.

The doctor rolled her eyes. "Of course. I don't lose people if I can help it. But it was your quick thinking to sound the alarm that saved her."

Alex felt someone enter the room behind him.

"She's alive." It was Eric.

The doctor rolled her eyes again. "I don't lose people, and I *don't* repeat myself."

Eric clapped a hand on Alex's shoulder. His knees crumpled, and his backside hit the floor, his fingers bumping his shirt into his nose.

"Whoa, dude. Sorry." Eric crouched.

Alex's eyes watered. He squeezed them shut.

"Let's get you some help." The nurse helped him stand. She started to escort him out, but Alex shook his head.

"Nope. I'm not leaving." It sounded funny, talking through a broken nose. And it seriously hurt. But he walked—more like stomped, but whatever—to a chair and sat in it. "Look at me here, but I'm not going anywhere."

"Good call." Eric leaned against the wall, arms folded. "Me, too." As though it was an everyday occurrence, a perfectly natural thing to do.

The doctor strode around the bed. "Keep me posted if anything changes."

"Yes, doctor."

She walked out. Jessica appeared in the doorway, her face bright red above her police uniform collar. "Someone tried to kill her!"

Alex leaned his head back against the wall. "I didn't know he would be in here."

Eric said, "You didn't see him come in?"

Jess shook her head. "No one came in since I took my post on the door. He must've been hiding in here. This is unbelievable." She strode into the room. "I miss *everything* good."

Eric started to laugh.

Alex had to fight the urge. "My nose hurts."

34

"You're here."

Alex shut the door behind him as he said, "Sorry to leave you for a few minutes. I had something to take care of." He turned to the bed, and she got a good look at him.

"Oh. Ouch." Sasha winced. His nose was a mess, a white bandage taped over the bridge. Already bruising made its way across his cheeks.

"Yeah." He lifted a hand and let it fall back to his side. "I want to scratch it, but I have a feeling that would be a really bad idea."

She grinned, tucked in the hospital bed. After she'd nearly died, Conroy agreed to have the cuffs removed. He'd also posted an officer inside and outside the room, just to make sure she was safe. That meant the smirking, blonde Officer Ridgeman—soon to be a detective, according to the constant reel of stories she'd told since Sasha woke up—could hear every word they said.

Alex glanced over his shoulder. "You wanna get lost?"

Jess, as she'd told Sasha to call her said, "Nope. The last time I left, she nearly died."

"I told you that wasn't your fault."

Sasha stared at him. Did he think it was his? As it was, it'd been nearly a day since she'd practically flatlined and the doctor had to quickly counteract the substance Dorian injected into her. Now her former friend was in police custody, along with Thomas Perkins.

She should be safe. In theory.

One thing Sasha had learned through the trials in her life, was to never take safety for granted. However many days she had left, she would always be looking for the threat. But she planned also to be talking to God about that, and everything else, as well. After all, He was the reason she was still here.

She just hadn't had the chance to process what to do about it.

Alex sighed and settled on the edge of the bed. He hesitated to take her hand. She reached out and slid her hand in his.

"Hey."

The corners of his mouth curled up. It was inviting, but given their audience, she wasn't about to do anything. "Hey."

"You guys are *so* cute."

Alex shot the cop a look. Sasha couldn't help but giggle. The movement jogged her arm, and she moaned. He said, "See! Get lost, Ridgeman."

"Fine." The cop rolled her eyes. "None of you ever let me in on the good stuff."

"I will throw a pillow at you."

"Fine." She lifted a hand and let the door shut behind her.

"That's better."

Before Sasha could agree, Alex leaned forward to touch his lips to hers. He hesitated right before he made contact. "Now that I think about it, bumping my nose on your cheek might not feel so good." He lifted her hand, still clasped in his, and touched his lips gently to the back of her hand.

"Wow."

"What?"

"I didn't know that could feel so..."

He kissed her again.

"Yeah, that."

Alex smiled against her skin, then lowered her hand. "I'm glad you're all right."

"I can't believe you took down Dorian." She shook her head. "I thought I was a goner, and the moment I realized it, I also realized I…" How was she supposed to say this without sounding hokey? She'd already told him how she felt, never mind that he'd been unconscious at the time so hadn't heard it.

"You what?"

"I didn't want to leave."

"I'm glad."

"That doesn't mean it might not happen. I could still get transported out by the FBI."

Alex shook his head. "We'll deal with that. Can you stick with me right now? Be here with me in this moment and don't worry about what happens next."

"That's usually what I do. But right now, it's hard not worrying about what might happen, or if I'll ever be out from under suspicion." Or even if she would ever manage to walk free again in her life. She could spend the rest of her years in federal prison, and there would be nothing either of them could do about that.

The last thing Sasha wanted was for Alex's career to suffer because of his relationship with her. A cop couldn't be connected like that with a convicted criminal. Even now, as merely a suspect, she gave him problems.

He started to argue.

"Don't." She shook her head, tucking her broken wrist more securely against her front. It was a defensive move, but she wanted to shore up those walls right now. The alternative was too painful. "You've been suspended. I'd still be in handcuffs if Dorian hadn't come here to kill me."

Before he could say anything, a short knock sounded on the door. It opened right after. Someone whose sense of their authority meant they could enter when they wanted because they had a right to be there. That, or they cared for her safety. Or Alex's. Or both.

Special Agent Eric Cullings entered. "This a good time?"

Alex shot him a look that made Sasha want to laugh.

"Well, anyway. I have a few things I need to go over and I have a meeting in an hour, so it's either now or Sasha waits not knowing for hours."

"Tell me. Please."

Alex squeezed her hand. She was glad he was on board, considering she would likely need his support with this.

Eric studied the two of them. "Okay, we're in the nascency with this. Nothing is set in stone yet, and I need to do a whole lot of corroboration and evidence gathering. I've got people on it, but we have to be very careful not to tip off the wrong person. So far, whoever is behind this has been aware of every move my team and I have made."

Alex said simply, "Who?"

"The Mayor of Richmond."

They both looked at her.

"Am I wrong?"

Eric said, "What makes you think that?"

"The first attempt on my life came following the statement I made to Alex about the murder-suicide. The one I know he was responsible for. After that, I told you about the hotel business and how my friends—including his son—were killed."

Eric nodded.

"He tried to kill me too, back then. As soon as he found me here, he sent someone to kill me. When that didn't work, he sent a team. Your agents died."

Eric nodded. "Millie didn't lose the baby, thankfully, but yes. Lives were lost. Men serving this country."

"Because of me."

"No." Alex shook his head, giving her good hand another squeeze.

"He's right," Eric said. "The one at fault here is the mayor. That is if this all checks out."

"I just can't figure out why now? I mean, it's not like I resurfaced suddenly. Though, he could've heard my name come up after what had happened with Aiden and Bridget." They'd gone up against a cartel and an old coworker of Bridget and Sasha's —one who had shot Eric. "But it was like, all of a sudden the FBI was after me as this big-time criminal."

"I'm only going to say this once, and not as an FBI agent." He tossed his badge on the bedside table. "But I'm sorry. For everything. Millie has been reading me the riot act for weeks about going after you."

"She knows I was never a good person."

"She would disagree. As far as I can see, you protect the people you care about. And you have serious skills to do that because you've had to learn how to survive through *anything.*"

Sasha didn't want to talk about this. She had a lot of moving on to do if she wanted to get a handle on her past, but with an FBI agent who had recently targeted her? It was Sasha's turn to squeeze Alex's hand. She hoped he got the message.

He didn't look at her, but asked Eric, "Why do you think the Mayor chose now?"

Eric stowed the wallet containing his FBI badge back in his jacket. "Because he's running for the Senate. He needs you to be implicated in the death of his son so he can look like a sympathetic, grieving father and a guy who advocates for justice at the same time."

Sasha felt her eyebrows rise.

"Can't jeopardize a chance at a lifetime of money for a whole lot of arguing and not getting much done." Eric grinned. "At least, that's what I figure they do in Washington. Our friend, the Mayor, needs his closet cleaned out so there's not even a whiff of a scandal. And now we know there's not just one skeleton in there, but several."

"He wants me dead so I can't talk."

Alex shifted. "Witness protection?"

"That's up to the judge," Eric said. "But I'm not sure he can argue with the present threat when we have agents dead."

Sasha bit the inside of her lip. *Witness protection?* The last thing she wanted was to have to start a new life all over again. She liked the one she had. Changing everything and going somewhere no one knew who she was didn't sound like her idea of safe. She wouldn't have any of her loved ones around her. Sure, that meant no one she cared about would be in the line of fire either, but she'd finally met Jonah. She wanted to watch him play football. See him graduate high school in a few months.

"We're going to figure all this out." Eric pinned her with a steady look that she had to admit did make her feel better. "One step at a time. One hurdle at a time. But I have to ask now, will you testify against him if that becomes necessary?"

Do the right thing?

"Yes."

Alex lifted her hand and kissed the back. Not like before. This time it wasn't so intimate. More like reassuring.

Still, it didn't settle her. Witness protection and testifying meant a new life in a new city. No contact with anyone from her old life.

Alex shifted, putting his body ever so slightly in front of her. Defending her the way no one ever had before. And that only made it worse.

"Sasha's had a rough few days. Maybe you could continue this later."

Eric nodded to her. "I have what I need for now. I'll go talk to the judge and see what I can do."

"And in the meantime?" She had to know, even though her voice sounded strained. "Am I still under arrest?"

"I spoke with Conroy. You'll be under protective custody in a safe house here in Last Chance. I'll work as quickly as I can, though. Okay?"

She nodded. The longer it took, the more time she'd have to spend with Alex. If Conroy let them see each other.

Eric strode out.

"Sorry." Alex turned to her. "He can be pretty pushy, and he didn't need to put all of that on you at once."

"It's okay. I needed to know."

"You're going to be okay. We'll keep you safe, and this mayor guy won't be able to get to you."

"That's not the problem." He really didn't know?

"Tell me. Trust me with it."

"You're not like any man I've ever met." And yes, she included Zander in that. He was a good guy, but not like Alex. "And now Eric is talking about witness protection. What do I do with that?" She would have to leave. He'd never see her again.

Jonah.

Mateo and Alex. His mom.

Her friends, Bridget and Millie.

"You have a life. Understandably, you don't want to lose it." He touched her cheek, stroking a thumb over her cheekbone. "But testifying is the right thing. If it's the only way to get a conviction."

He was so good. So much better than her. Always doing the right thing, and then saving her when she'd never done anything to deserve it. She couldn't ask him to leave his whole family. The life he knew.

Kind of like what God had done.

Not only had He kept her alive when she should have died many times before, God had also given her hope. This tiny slice of the life she could have. With Alex, and his family. His town.

Another shot at Last Chance.

Too bad it wasn't meant to be.

35

He knew she was scared, even if she wasn't going to admit it. Alex paced across the hall and turned to rest against the wall. He leaned his head back and closed his eyes for a moment while everything from the last few days came crashing down. There was zero point denying everything that'd happened. That would only lead to him losing it because he hadn't fully processed things.

A few minutes later, someone called out down the hall. "Basuto."

He opened his eyes and saw Conroy headed his way. "Chief."

Conroy looked like he wanted to make a joke, but he didn't. "What is it?"

"They just compiled the results of Frees's testing."

Officer Frees had been down in the basement when the house above them had exploded. He'd been pinned under a section of the frame, something Alex hadn't known because he was unconscious. By the time they dug them all out and got them transported to the hospital, Frees had sustained serious damage. Alex had been more focused on Mateo and Sasha.

"And?" This didn't sound like it was going to be good.

"He's paralyzed."

Alex sagged against the wall.

"He's not taking it too well, and he kicked me out. He won't talk to anyone."

"I should try." Alex might be able to order Frees to let him in. The guy was a former Marine and now a cop, and Alex was his lieutenant. The reflex for Frees to obey a command from a superior might get him in the door at least. After that, it depended.

Conroy tipped his head to the side. "Maybe after he's absorbed it all." The grief on his face was genuine. "And I'll have to look at hiring another officer or two. The gap Frees will leave in the department is not insignificant. I'm thinking…" His voice trailed off.

"You want a K9 officer?" Donaldson had been bugging them about the idea for weeks now.

"Let's just say I'm considering it."

Alex would've grinned at any other time. But right now, when he'd just sat through that conversation between Eric and Sasha, he couldn't quite manage it. He was still trying to wrap his mind over them wanting her to testify and how they planned to put her in witness protection to keep her safe while she did it —and maybe forever if the threat continued.

He would lose her.

"Sasha good?"

Alex nodded even though he wasn't sure if that was true. His phone buzzed, preventing him from saying more. He checked it and told Conroy, "I need to go see Mama. She and Mateo are headed to visit Jonah. Ridgeman is with Sasha again."

Conroy nodded.

Alex headed for the elevator, grateful for all the support he had and wondering what his life would be like if he wasn't surrounded by them. That's what witness protection would be like. Solitude. Only a US Marshal for a handler, and no friends. No family. No support system. He wouldn't be able to be a cop. His life would look entirely different.

Two floors up in ICU, Jonah was recovering from his surgery. In the hall it wasn't Mama and Mateo that he found, but the kid's parents. The couple Sasha had given her baby to. He wanted to hear the whole story, but only if she wanted to tell it to him.

"Lieutenant Basuto." Timothy Daniels, the church pastor, stuck his hand out.

Alex shook. "How is he?"

The wife, whose name Alex couldn't remember right now, flushed. "Frustrated. In pain. But the doctors tell us that's a good sign. It means he's rallying, and he's willing to fight to get stronger."

Alex nodded.

"Your mother and Mateo are inside with him. That should help." The wife smiled, but it faltered. "And…she's here, isn't she? Sasha Camilero. That's what Maggie told me her name is now."

Alex didn't know what to say to that either, so he let the wife continue while Pastor Daniels watched carefully.

"Jonah has been asking after her."

Alex felt his brows rise. "He knows?"

The pastor said, "We've never hidden from him that he was a gift given to us by God. But his birth mother asked for no contact, and we've advised him to respect her wishes. Still, he's curious, as you can imagine."

"I'm sure." Alex felt the need to reassure them. "I know she didn't tell him anything."

"I think when he met her, he figured it out." The pastor continued with a gleam in his eye, "My son is a smart boy."

One who was almost fully grown, as far as Alex could see.

"He's also a good man. Willing to step into danger to protect his friend." It might have been foolhardy for Jonah to show up at the car dealership, but it was also noble. He'd had good intentions, and he would heal from being shot.

The wife nodded. "Oh, we know."

They looked exhausted, but not unhappy.

Before any of them could say more, Mama and Mateo stepped out. "Sasha?"

Alex blinked at Mateo's abrupt question. His nephew looked exhausted and extremely brokenhearted, as well as carrying several injuries. His arm was in a sling and he wore the deep grief of a kid who'd lost a father that had never been what he'd needed him to be in the first place.

Alex said, "She likely won't be here for long, but I'll get word to her that he asked to see her."

"Thank you." The wife squeezed his arm and the two of them headed into their son's room.

"How is he?" Alex figured Mateo's take would be different than the parents'.

"Pissed."

Mama whirled around. "Excuse me?"

"Sorry." Mateo blushed. "He's uh…super mad. He has to have help just to pee."

Mama's eyes narrowed.

"But considering he got shot in the chest, I guess he's gonna be okay if he doesn't get murdered by the doctors first for being so annoying. And he wants to see Sasha." Mateo paused. "Is she really his birth mom?"

Alex nodded.

"Whoa. And you like *know* her." Mateo's eyes widened. "Crazy. Are you guys like…having a *thing*?"

"Yes."

"Awesome."

Alex shook his head, smiling. "Are you doing okay?" He

studied his nephew. It had been a few days and he was still focused on his friend, but, in reality, Mateo had lost his father.

"Every single day, I hung out with *Abuela* all the time until dad made me come home. Now that he's gone, I'm hanging out all the time with *Abuela*." Mateo shrugged, but Alex could see the grief in his eyes. Even if the day-to-day idea of a father wasn't any different for Mateo, the idea of what could have been had to feel heavy. Even if Mateo wasn't ready to admit it.

Mama hugged him.

Alex squeezed his uninjured shoulder. "Okay."

Things might change, and probably would as he processed his grief, but for now he was all right. Alex's mom was taking good care of him.

He kissed her on the cheek.

She patted his, giving him that knowing look mothers got when they figured out all your secrets. She knew he might not be here forever. And yet, how could he even think about leaving his family? Never seeing Mateo again. Leaving the department. For a woman one could say he hardly knew? That was crazy.

He said his goodbyes and went back downstairs, contemplating the alternative. Letting Sasha go and watching her walk away.

Losing her forever.

There was so much promise in what they'd share so far. Like a gift, dangling in front of him. Would he accept it, or allow the timing to cause him to lose the gift? He didn't like the idea of missing out.

Aiden and Bridget stood outside her room, about to go in, when Donaldson spotted him.

"Hey." He put out his hand and they shook.

Aiden said, "How are you—"

"I want to know what your intentions are."

Both of them turned to Bridget.

She folded her arms. "Well? It's a valid question, isn't it?"

Aiden ducked his head and squeezed the back of his neck.

Alex caught the edge of a smile. But apparently, his friend was going to do nothing to stop his wife from pinning Alex down about his "intentions."

"I care a lot about Sasha. I always have." He had a life here. It wasn't like they'd officially committed to each other, right?

Aiden glanced at his wife. "Told you."

She didn't look pleased.

"Whatever happens is between Sasha and me."

"Not good enough." Bridget folded her arms over her chest. "She and I have been friends for a long time."

"And when you found out she lied to you, you cut her off."

"It's not like I knew what was going on with her. I mean… Zander? What is that about? I had no idea she'd been married before. She told me nothing about her life."

"But you claim you guys are friends."

"Excuse me?"

Aiden shifted, ready to defend his wife.

As if Alex was going to let this go any further south. "What happens between Sasha and me, she can tell you herself."

"She doesn't need to be hurt anymore. If you—"

"Bridget." Alex cut her off. "She'll tell you herself." When she geared up to say more, he spoke again. "I know more about her than you think. I know exactly what she's been through. Things aren't going to be perfect, but I'm not going to hurt her."

She made a face because she knew he was telling the truth. "I'm gonna go talk to her before she's released."

"Good, you should." Alex nodded.

The door swung shut behind her.

He turned to his sergeant. "Is it me, or is she probably going to tell Sasha I'm not worth it, and she shouldn't have anything to do with me?"

Aiden smirked. "She's just looking out for her friend."

"I wasn't lying. I have no intention of hurting her."

"Sometimes we do it even when we don't intend to. It's just

life, and we have to figure out how to move on from the pain. Or live with it."

"Sasha has lived with enough already. More than one person should ever have had to go through."

Aiden studied him for a second. "Okay." He nodded. "And if she goes into witness protection?"

"I only just heard about that. We don't know what's going to happen."

"So you have no idea what to do." Aiden paused a second, then said, "And you're scared."

Alex started to argue. He realized there was nothing he could say that would be true. No question, he was willing to sacrifice to explore what was there between the two of them. But the price for that might be higher than he could pay and actually live with.

Jess came out of the room and Aiden went to talk to her. Alex reeled from the idea that he might be reacting based on fear.

It wasn't fear to not want to leave Mateo and never see him.

And yet, the truth was that he would be staying because he was scared to take the risk. For years, he'd tried to live a good life so that he deserved good things. Deep down he was still that fifteen-year-old experiencing something so gruesome his mind couldn't process it. A scared boy who reacted by controlling the world around him, refusing to remember how bad it had been.

As if he could play it safe and that would guarantee nothing like that ever happened again.

Instead, the formula hadn't worked. He didn't get good things because he tried to be a good person. God had given him something unexpected that he didn't deserve at a time when his control had slipped. He'd been the worst version of himself lately, going against his oath and reacting on emotion. But it wasn't about a reward, it was about grace.

Alex didn't want to play it safe because he was afraid of what might happen. The reward of taking the risk could be

262 | LISA PHILLIPS

everything he'd ever wanted. A relationship. A family of his own, and a life of blessing he didn't deserve. *Thank You, Lord.*

If he wanted that, then he needed to stand up and be brave. Tell her how he felt. Take the risk, no matter how afraid he was.

Like Sasha had done.

36

"Don't worry about me. Just work on getting yourself better. You're going to be just fine." Sasha smiled, even though she didn't entirely believe her own words, and squeezed Jonah's hand the way Alex had done with her. "Then I'll be able to come and see you play football."

Jonah's skin was pale and clammy, and he was fading fast. The infection that arose post-surgery flared in him. She was worried and probably doing a poor job of hiding it.

Jonah's lips parted. "I missed you." His voice was barely audible.

She leaned close and touched his cheek. "I know, baby. I missed you, too."

Her mind went to that tiny boy Maggie had wrapped up in a blanket. She stared at his face. The tiny baby had grown up. A tear rolled down her cheek as she worked to memorize every inch of his face. She would probably never get the chance again to stare at him. If he was awake, it would be awkward. Only if it was safe, could they ever could see each other again. If. If.

She had no idea what the coming weeks would bring. Sasha was about to be taken into protective custody by the police. If she didn't distance herself from him, Jonah could be put in danger and then she really might never see him again.

Sasha laid a kiss on his cheek and left his room.

Alex immediately took her hand, and they walked together to the elevator—complete with police escort. Parking garage. Unmarked car. Another vehicle behind it, also unmarked. She sat in the passenger seat while Alex drove.

"How is your wrist doing?"

She stared out the window and shrugged one shoulder. "When the swelling goes down, I'll get a cast."

He pulled onto the street.

Fear rolled through her unbidden. Thomas Perkins was in prison, and so was Dorian. The only threat that remained was the mayor of Richmond, and Eric was taking care of that.

People were dead. Others in the hospital. All because of the things she'd seen and done, and the fact she didn't want to end her life without speaking the truth.

Plenty of people in the world made themselves targets for evil because they chose to tell the truth.

Sasha didn't feel good, or noble enough, to be included with them. But she could pray. Bridget had given her a Bible. Sasha was starting to read the gospel of John. She had a long way to go, and it was a good place to start.

The car was way too quiet, so she asked, "How about you? No lingering effects from being blown up?"

She heard a small exhale of breath from his nose. He thought she was funny—something that pleased her. "Ouch."

Sasha hadn't had a whole lot of laughter in her life. And if she got put in witness protection, she would be too lonely for fun, or joy. "Sorry about your nose."

"I'm good, Sash. Don't worry about me."

"What about Mateo?"

"He seems to be good, too. I mean, he lost his father and that can't be easy. But the truth is, Javier wasn't much of a dad. I hate to say it, but he is better off with Mama."

"And you. He'll always have you."

"Mmm." The sound was pretty noncommittal. "Yeah, he will."

She didn't know what to infer by that. He was suggesting something to her, but there was no way she could figure out what it was right now. Her brain was too full of everything that had happened and what could happen next.

"What about Aiden and Bridget? They're good."

"Seems like it." He reached over and squeezed her knee. "Savannah thinks Bridget's pregnant, but she's only told the half of the department that can keep a secret because neither Aiden nor Bridget has made any kind of announcement. And both Savannah and Tate were the ones who helped pull us all out of the rubble of that house."

Sasha smiled to herself. "I'm glad." Her friend was happy. It was great to be able to hear about it firsthand instead of hearing about it through the grapevine. "What about Frees? I heard he isn't okay."

"The damage meant he completely lost feeling in both legs. He isn't okay."

"I'm sure it feels like the end of the world, even though it certainly isn't."

"I know." Another knee squeeze. "It's a tough thing to go through. Losing everything you've worked for in your career and having to suddenly figure out what to do next with the rest of your life."

There was a tone in his voice. Some unspoken thing that told her he'd been forced to consider new paths his life could take. Ones he'd never thought he'd ever be on.

He was thinking about being with her?

It sure sounded like that's what he was saying. Or, at least he was considering it.

But he must not have decided yet, or he'd have told her. Sasha didn't have all that much time. How long would this take? She wanted to have this thing between them—whatever it might be—settled before the FBI handed her over to the marshals and she was gone forever.

Alex pulled into the driveway and kept going through the open gate to stop in the RV parking space. A nondescript house in a nondescript neighborhood she would never have noticed otherwise, which she figured was entirely by design. The Last Chance Police Department wasn't taking any risks keeping her safe. And even Alex, technically suspended for the next few weeks, was planning to hang there with her.

He'd explained to her how coming and going increased the risk, and he would sleep in the guest room while the officers on duty were outside doing regular sweeps of the perimeter. She'd heard Zander recite the spiel more than once, but with Alex it was so much more meaningful.

He was staying to protect her, yes, but also to spend time with her while they waited to find out what was next.

The officer on duty stepped out of the side door. She stayed put while Alex rounded the car and held the door for her. Sasha wasn't supposed to move until they gave her the okay. It was almost amusing, considering how trained she was in protecting herself. But the fact someone else was taking care of her? She rested in that feeling.

Safe. Protected. Cared for. Maybe even loved.

Not the officers. This was a job to them, even though they knew she meant something personally to Alex. And Aiden, because of Bridget.

It meant more because it was Alex.

But that didn't mean it wasn't awkward being alone with him. Nothing to talk about because they had no new information. No danger to run from. No gunmen chasing them, trying to kill one—or both—of them.

Being safe was...unnatural.

"Tea? Coffee?"

She turned to see him head for the kitchen. Sasha followed and watched him move around in the small space, getting down two mugs and filling the electric kettle. She'd told him how she drank instant coffee—though, only the good stuff—and he'd had them get her some. She hadn't admitted her addiction to bananas yet, though there were some in the fruit bowl on the end of the counter.

Beside a huge vase of flowers.

"What..?"

"Oh, yeah. Those came for you." He sounded mad.

She opened the card wedged between two giant daisy blooms and read the note. It was signed, "Z." Above which he'd had the flower shop write, "Glad you're safe and sound."

Sasha chuckled, shaking her head.

"Zander?"

"Does he not know the threat is still real? Why else would I be in protective custody?" The note made no sense.

"Maybe he just wanted to cheer you up?" Alex still sounded mad. Probably jealous.

It was kind of cute.

"Sending flowers to make me feel better?" She shook her head. "Nope. Not his style at all. Any message he sends is a *message*. And he's *really* good at that."

"Should I have understood that?"

She grinned and waved the card. "Glad you're safe and sound? That means something. We just don't know what it is yet."

He handed her a steaming mug of milky, caffeinated good-ness. She lifted it to her nose and inhaled, closing her eyes. "Mmm."

When she opened them, he was still standing close and staring at her now. "What?"

"You're incredibly cute. Quiet, and content." He leaned close and softly touched his lips to hers. "When bad guys aren't hunting you down."

She shivered. Then the lingering question made it to her lips. "I'm just a normal, everyday girl...."

"I'm not sure you'll ever be normal." A smile curled his lips.

"...What if 'normal' me is boring? I mean, what do I do? Get a *job*?" She shivered.

He let out a burst of laughter. "You'll never be boring."

"Oh." Phew.

Alex laughed harder. He took her mug from her.

"Hey, I was drinking that."

He slid his arms around her. Her arm—the broken one—was in a sling against her front, but she slid her other one up and held onto the back of his neck. Alex drew her close for a kiss. Not too close or she'd have squished her arm, and she was thankful for his consideration.

When he leaned back a fraction she said, "Thank you for being here with me."

"Of course." He was about to say more when a commotion from the hall caught their attention.

"Are we interrupting?" Eric strode in, a completely unrepentant look on his face. "So sorry about that."

"Right." Alex didn't let go of her. He settled his hips on the edge of the dining table and held her close to his front.

Behind Eric, Millie came in. Sasha hugged her boss without Alex letting go. Because he didn't, and she didn't want him to either.

"How are you?" Sasha motioned to the rounded stomach under Millie's shirt.

She beamed. "We're good." Millie wound her arm through Eric's and he gave her an indulgent smile. Three kids and they were still in love. Maybe more so now, after all they'd been through.

But Sasha couldn't get caught up in those thoughts. She said, "If you're here—" She motioned between them. "—then does that mean..."

Millie nodded, her smile wide.

"The threat is over." Alex squeezed her middle.

Eric frowned. "Hey, I was supposed to be the one to share the good news."

"What happened?" Sasha was scared to hope. She wanted this too badly. "Tell us."

Alex leaned his chin on her shoulder.

Eric said, "An arrest warrant was served to the residence of the Mayor of Richmond, Virginia just after eight-thirty this morning. The mayor had called in sick, so agents went inside and spoke with the housekeeper. When they entered the mayor's home office, where the housekeeper indicated he would be even though he felt ill, they discovered him dead in his extremely nice leather chair. Seriously, more than one person called me about the chair. They're all requisitioning one for their desks as we speak, even though there's no way that's gonna fly."

"He's dead."

Millie grinned. "He's dead."

"How?" Alex asked.

"It would appear he shot himself. All the physical evidence indicates as such, and so that's the way we're sure the medical examiner will go when she completes the paperwork later today." Eric grinned for the first time since entering. "And all the evidence was there on his computer." He shrugged. "I guess he just felt so guilty he didn't want to live with what he'd done anymore."

Millie said, "Because he was too much of a coward to face it."

Eric glanced at her. "True. But the fact is, it's done. The threat is over. You're safe now, Sasha. And there's going to be a whole lot of paperwork, but that's the worst of what you'll have to face."

She didn't know what to say.

"I still want statements from you and more detail about everything. I'd like to be as thorough as possible."

She nodded. Millie gave her another hug, and Eric shook Alex's hand. The two of them left.

Alex turned her in his arms.

She started to speak, then stopped.

"Don't know what to say?"

She shook her head. "I'm really...free?"

Alex grinned and pulled her in for another kiss, this time a celebration—and this time her hand got a tiny bit squished. "I know it's early, but I'm falling for you."

She bit her lip and nodded.

"Since I saw you again, I've been...captivated. I don't even know how to describe it. You're everything I'm not, and everything I want to be. Strong. Resilient. And yet I want to wrap you up in yards of cotton wool so that nothing ever happens to you."

She kissed him then.

When she pulled back, Sasha held onto him. "You've been part of my life forever, in a way no one else has ever been. I don't want that to change. I love how close you are to your family, and I want to be part of it. Your roots are in this town. I want mine here, too. With you."

"I like the sound of that."

They kissed for a while longer. Until the police detail came in and told them they were headed out.

Sasha borrowed Alex's phone and sent Zander a text. Two simple words.

Thank you.

I HOPE you enjoyed *Expired Betrayal*, please consider leaving a review, it really helps others find their next read!

Turn the page for the first 2 chapters of the 9th story in the Last Chance County series: *Expired Flight*

U.S.A. TODAY BESTSELLING AUTHOR
LISA PHILLIPS PRESENTS

EXPIRED
FLIGHT

LAST CHANCE COUNTY BOOK NINE

Publisher: Lisa Phillips

Cover design: Ryan Schwarz

Edited by: Jen Weiber

❀ Created with Vellum

1

He was nothing but a shadow—a man with no name, as far as anyone else was concerned. The lone swimmer headed for the surface of Last Chance lake, dragging a computer tower by the rope it was tied to. A flashlight held between his teeth, he navigated through the dark waters and kicked his way to the top.

The second his head breached, a gunshot rang out across the water. He opened his mouth to let go of the flashlight so it didn't alert anyone to his presence. It slowly began to drift down into the depths of the lake.

He could do nothing about it, and lose the only light source he had. Or, he could use his only spare hand to grab it, losing the tower to the bottom in the process.

At the last minute, Jeff switched his grasp from the rope connected to the computer tower and grabbed the flashlight instead. Just in time. This job could wait. His life was about survival.

He turned to the tiny, metal fishing boat he'd salvaged and began to swim away from the people trying to kill him.

A woman screamed.

He twisted in the water just in time to spot a dark figure

running. The shadow streaked in front of the headlight beam belonging to a truck parked on the shore, far side. The side where people lived, worked, and recreated. Jeff lived on the opposite bank. Away from humanity. Alone, where he could keep the people he loved safe—and fall asleep at night wrapped in his honor; the knowledge he'd done the right thing. It was the only way.

Honor as cold as the water of the lake.

Another gun blast flashed in the night, and this one illuminated a dark figure by the truck. A woman, if he had to guess. By both the scream and the shadow's stature. She fell to the ground, hit by the assailant's bullet.

The cold permeated to his soul. This might have been an execution, but they weren't here to kill him.

He clicked off the flashlight and stowed it in a tiny pocket he'd sown into the leg of his wetsuit as he continued to tread water.

The truck door slammed shut, and the driver gunned the engine as he tore up the bank of the river in reverse. Job complete. She was dead.

He should swim to the boat, leave the way he'd come, and continue to remain anonymous in this town. The one where he'd grown up. Where his father had hauled them all to church in their Sunday best and then screamed and cursed at them the rest of the week for whatever infraction he'd considered unacceptable. Usually everything his mother did or said, or even an expression on her face. When he'd begun to accentuate the screams with his fists, Jeff and his brother tried to convince their mother that leaving was their only option. The day their father had taken a fist to their younger sister, she'd finally agreed.

Leaving a woman dead on the bank of the lake didn't sit right. Not at four in the morning, and not at any other time.

Jeff kicked with his legs. His body automatically turned onto its side, left shoulder down. Face toward the horizon. His right arm snapped through the water as his legs kicked in that familiar calming rhythm. Just him and the water.

As soon as his feet touched bottom, he tugged the flippers off and tossed them onto the sand. He flipped the flashlight back on and swept it across the sand until he found her.

Yellow T-shirt and worn-in jeans. Sneakers on her feet. Hair secured back with a bandana. He stared for a moment while everything in him warred between the urge to check for a pulse and the knowledge he would leave a fingerprint on the woman's skin.

He stared long enough he caught the inhale. She wasn't dead after all; just unconscious.

Jeff planted his knees in the sand beside her body and rolled her over. His flashlight beam illuminated luscious dark skin and full cheeks. She was a beautiful woman, even with the freshly broken skin stretched across a goose egg. She'd hit her temple on a rock when she fell. Knocked out cold.

Surely she had a phone on her. He'd left his back at the cabin when he ventured out earlier to dredge the lake, and its underwater secrets, looking for salvageable goods, but everyone else in the world seemed content to carry a device that tracked their every move in time and space—and evidently weren't bothered to have their conversations listened to as well.

The line of her jeans meant he didn't have to dig. She had no phone on her. Nor was there one on the sand, dropped when she fell.

He set the flashlight down and checked for a key or ID. In a front pocket, he found a folded scrap of paper. He got his thumb under a corner and flicked it open one-handed while the chill on his left shoulder reminded him of what he was missing.

What he could never get back.

His skin, exposed where he'd had to cut the unneeded sleeve off the wetsuit, bristled against the cold. He hadn't liked the way the empty sleeve had flapped around and caused drag whenever he swam. He also didn't need the sleeve getting caught up on anything while he was underwater. No one would even know he was down there, except maybe Zander. At least his friend would have an idea where to look.

No one else even knew he was alive.

Jeff angled the paper to the beam of the flashlight. Elegant handwriting, clearly female. The words were spotted with blood smears. Hers? Had she touched her head after she fell, and then put her hand in her pocket? No, she was out. She'd have been out as soon as she hit the sand.

The blood wasn't from this incident.

Quit ignoring reality. Jeff often talked to himself. It might be a sign he'd lost his grip on reality, but being in denial meant a healthy self-chastisement was warranted. On occasion. Like right now when he was clearly missing the obvious here.

He stared at the words.

This woman had his home address on a bloody paper in her pocket.

"Who are you?" His voice sounded like gravel shifting. Far too loud in the still of four in the morning when not even the birds were awake.

The unconscious woman didn't answer.

Jeff pocketed the paper back into her jeans and stowed his flashlight. He stooped down in a low squat and tugged her arm over his shoulder so her front would be across his back. He got his feet under him and steadied himself as he lifted her and started walking. It was tricky, but he managed to keep her weight on his shoulders all the way to the hidden path through the trees. The spot he'd parked his truck; out of sight.

It was two miles to the tiny cabin nestled in a clearing on the far side of the mountain.

By the time he reached his front steps, Jeff was sweating from the tension. That, and the wet suit seriously chafed. He needed out of it, but he had to get her inside first.

The door was still shut. He never locked it since he never

had visitors. No one knew he lived up here except two people, and he trusted both men.

Jeff braced her weight on his back and got the door open. He deposited her on his couch and retrieved the paper from her pocket before going back to close the front door. He started a fire from wood he'd split just yesterday. He didn't need light to change, and why look at what life had done to him. Scars. The tight skin just below his left shoulder, where his flesh had been sewn together into a stub where his arm used to be.

Every time he closed his eyes he could remember having two arms. Lifting both, simultaneously. Firing a gun two-handed. Riding a motorcycle. Playing basketball. Rock climbing.

That was the worst of it, the remembering. Not that he had to live with only one arm and re-learn everything. The hardest part was that he could recall so vividly how it felt to have two.

Until that IED had exploded.

He hadn't even been the only casualty. Plenty of people had died that day. But one, in particular, still hit him in the gut.

I'm sorry. She's dead.

Jeff shoved the drawer shut too hard and heard coins jingle on top of his dresser. He'd only ever heard her voice on the phone. And yet, that had been enough for him to want to find her as soon as the mission was over. Now he wouldn't ever get that chance.

She was as gone as his ability to operate.

As gone as his military career.

He pulled the T-shirt over his head and stuck his right arm through the sleeve. Sweats. Socks, until the fire got going. He treaded back toward the kitchen and heard a meow.

Mittens was in the laundry again.

He tugged the basket over and heard the cat tumble, along with the pile of clothes he needed to wash. At least she sat in the dirty stuff rather than nestling in a warm stack, fresh from the dryer. Then again, she lay on everything else in this cabin—

including him—so maybe he shouldn't be bothered by it. But it was the principal of the thing.

"Out."

A "rawr" was the only answer she gave. He left her to her throne of dirty socks and went to put his kettle on. Tea. Maybe soup. She would need medical attention when she woke up.

He flicked a blanket over her from the back of the couch and took his pistol from the top of the fridge and laid it on the kitchen counter while he filled the kettle.

Jeff leaned his hips against the edge of the scarred linoleum and watched her. In the light, she was no less beautiful. Lean and packing some strength in the line of her muscles. Circular face and full lips. Hair secured. She looked like she was ready for work. Practical, but there was really no way to genuinely downplay her beauty or hide the way her skin shone with that deep, resonant color.

He'd never met her before. She had no ID. Anyone else would have called the police by now, but Jeff couldn't allow his name—even his fake one—to land on any report. If he hit the radar instead of flying below it, people he cared about would be in danger.

He would be in danger.

Jeff grabbed his cell and called Zander's team doctor. There was a guy closer who wouldn't ask too many questions, but Dean's family now included a cop and there were just way fewer ties to life here in Last Chance this way. Zander lived separate and his work took him all over the world. Besides, he still owed Jeff.

The doctor didn't answer, so he left a message for a callback about a head injury. That should pique his interest. Usually their only communication was the doc calling to ask Jeff how his arm was doing.

He didn't have one. *That's how it's doing.*

The kettle whistled. He shut the burner off, and the woman stirred. He watched her wake up and flipped the latch on the canister of instant coffee grounds. Twist-top jars were a thing of the past these days. No point in them or having to do things one-handed if he didn't have to. The day he'd get his groceries, he usually dumped the entire contents into the canister before tossing the jar into the trash.

She moaned.

Jeff grabbed the gun and moved the coffee table away from her with his foot. He sat on it and faced her as she blinked. Shifted. Moaned again. She fought the glassy look in her eyes and finally realized he was watching her. He had one arm. He had a gun. She was in a cabin.

He could see each realization register in her expression before it blanked, as though a shutter fell over her features.

Someone who knew how to hide their feelings and intentions.

He held the gun loose in his lap. "Are you here to kill me?"

She'd been shot at. Probably by a rival contract killer, taking out the competition so he'd have a straight shot at completing the job.

She lifted a hand and touched her temple. Her eyes started to roll back in her head, but she fought the pull of unconsciousness and won.

"Who are you?"

She still said nothing. Just studied him with a calculating air.

"I could march you outside and shoot you. It's not like anyone would know what I've done."

But he couldn't. Nor would he. That guy, the one who would murder an unarmed, injured woman was the man his mother had left when she took her children and moved out. Not the kind he wanted to be.

"Tell me who you are."

She blinked. Her eyes were still glassy from what was probably a killer migraine. "I...don't know."

2

The man in front of her had broad shoulders. And one arm. If she stood, and he stood, they would probably be close to eye-to-eye, heightwise.

"You're just going to stare at me?"

Her head felt like it was about to split open. She continued staring at him, letting her eyes flit to the side to quickly assess her surroundings, but there was nothing familiar about this man or what looked like a small cabin where he lived. Where she lived also? She had no idea. No familiar thoughts entered into her head. Her eyes scanned the walls. Curtains were pulled over the windows, but it was dark outside. A cocoon against the world.

She started to speak. Something in her hesitated. After a few seconds, she managed to say, "Who are *you*?"

If he answered that, then maybe she would have an idea of who she was. And what was happening here.

Why did she know…nothing?

"I'm the one asking the questions."

She shifted on the couch, then sat up and put her head in her hands. Elbows to her knees. After a few long, steady breaths, she still had no clue. "Who am I?" A million other questions rolled through her head. Where was she? Who was he? What was going on? And the most prominent. "Why does my head hurt so badly?"

Even speaking seemed strange. The words rolled off her tongue in an unfamiliar way she didn't understand—her accent the same as his. What was the problem? She fought the panic rising in her chest.

"I'll get you an ice pack." He stood, but she didn't look up as he said, "I left a message with my doctor."

At those words, terror rushed at her like a crazed wolf foaming at the mouth. And this time there was no way to tamp it down. She wasn't sure if she was reliving a real experience, or if it was just a sensation. But her body acted as though it was real.

She scrambled up onto the couch, legs tucked against her chest, and backed herself into the corner. Every breath came sharp and fast.

"Whoa." His face swam in front of her. "You okay?"

"No hospital."

"My doctor doesn't work at the hospital. He's freelance."

She didn't know what that meant, and when black spots blinked in front of her face, she could no longer speak.

"You're panicking." He tugged her hand from the death grip she had on her knee and held it in his. "Take a breath and hold it. Try to slow your breathing."

Air rushed in her ears.

"Good. Take another one. Hold it. Try to blow it out slowly."

The gun lay on the coffee table beside him. Regardless of the things about herself she couldn't remember, she was positive that if she picked it up, she'd be able to eject the magazine. Then she would pull the slide back, and it would kick out the round in the chamber. Just like that, he would be disarmed.

Alternatively, she could shoot *him*.

Would that evaporate the fear?

She wasn't sure. What she did know was disarming him would shift the power back into her hands. Did she need it? He seemed strong. Whether that served her or hurt her would depend on how he decided to utilize that strength.

Given his questions so far, he thought she was the enemy. And yet, there was something about him that made *her* believe he might be a friend.

"There you go."

She lifted her gaze and realized how close he sat to her. Near enough to touch. To kill. There was a vulnerability to putting his life in her hands. Trusting her the same way she had to trust he wasn't going to grab her neck and squeeze the life from her.

Still, she didn't quite get the feeling he thought he was in all that much danger. It was more like a calculated risk. He knew what he was capable of and was confident he could overpower her anytime he wanted.

Again, something in her hesitated before speaking. "Do...do we know each other?"

He shifted back a fraction and sat on the coffee table, rubbing his palm on the leg of his sweats. "I've never seen you before in my life."

She started to speak and another roll of thunder echoed in her head. She touched her temple below the source. "Ouch."

"I'll get you ice." He took the gun and strode to the kitchen, which was in full view because this cabin was basically one living area/dining room/kitchen. The door at the far end probably led to the bedroom or a bathroom.

"I need to use the bathroom."

He turned and waved his hand in the direction of the door. "Go ahead. Coffee?"

She stood, and pain rolled through her head. "I don't like coffee." *Who am I?*

His brows lifted.

She froze. "How do I know that?"

"So you remember?"

"Ask me another question." She was unsteady on her feet, but walked to a recliner and put her hand on the back of it. A gray cat hopped up and lay down. His territory, not hers.

She moved her hand.

"Tea?"

"Yes." Satisfaction rolled through her. "I like tea."

"That's good, right?"

"Tea is very good."

He chuckled. It sounded rusty. "It's also good you remember that. Okay, then. Tea it is." He moved to a cupboard and pulled down a box. "It'll be ready in a minute. You go ahead."

She retreated to the bathroom, with its linoleum floor and basic shower curtain. The mirror had a crack in the corner. She took care of pressing business, wondering how she knew, seemingly by instinct, what to do next. Nothing in her pockets. Nothing hidden in her shoes for some purpose. Or anywhere else, for that matter.

The mirror taunted at her peripheral.

She fastened her belt. How did he do that, one-handed? She didn't want to ask when it seemed like part of him was already angry at her.

Are you here to kill me?

She wanted to ask that, too. Instead, she moved to the sink and gripped the sides of the porcelain. Rust ringed the drain of the old sink.

She had blood under her fingernails.

She wrung her hands together and stared first at the dark skin on the back of them, and then gazed at the lighter tan of her palms. Assessing, as though her hands could tell a story. Of who she was. What she was doing here. Only she didn't know what any of it meant. There was nothing familiar about her fingers. Trimmed nails, no polish. No indication she wore any kind of jewelry. Or where she'd been before she woke up on this stranger's couch.

There was nothing.

Still avoiding the mirror, she washed her hands, getting rid of the only thing that might provide an answer. But there was nothing about blood under her nails she wanted to keep.

You're avoiding the obvious. That know-it-all voice in her head persisted. Until she couldn't put it off any longer. Afraid or not, she needed to know.

She gulped in some brave breaths and lifted her head, hands back on the sides of the sink for steady support. Her whole world shifted as she met her own gaze and...

Nothing.

She stared more intently at her features while pain ricocheted around in her skull. Dark hair pulled back in a bandana. If she took that off, it would be a mess. Always a mind of its own. Stubborn hair. Stubborn jaw. *Stubborn.* Someone had said that to her. A long time ago.

The word brought a rush of grief with it.

And yet more nothing.

Dark eyes. Full lips. Strong nose. Objectively she could say she wasn't terrible looking, though she needed a shower and some makeup. Her own image didn't bring any strong emotions with it. What struck her was her lack of reaction. Because she was content with the way she looked? This was the face God had given her. Complete with a tiny circular scar in front of her ear.

The knot on her forehead looked nasty and still pounded like thunder rolling in her head.

She tugged open the mirror and found a tiny cabinet. Men's deodorant. Shaving cream and a razor. A tiny bottle of painkillers. She swallowed a couple with some water from the tap. No sign a woman lived here.

And now she was snooping.

She didn't even know her own name, let alone his, or if he would let her even live much longer. He was making tea—right after saying he would walk her outside and shoot her. No one would know.

A shiver rolled through her.

She eased the bathroom door open a crack and peeked out. Was he waiting out there to kill her?

The low murmur of someone talking filled the space. A woman's voice, but she had a low tone.

So he did have a woman living here.

A kettle whistled, and she heard the click as he twisted off the burner. "Tea's ready!"

Her whole body flinched, causing the door to close on her finger, pinning it between the door and the frame for a second. She stepped out with the pinched finger tight in the grip of her other hand. For some reason, squeezing it made it feel better. If only the same might work for her insane headache.

She stepped to the edge of the kitchen floor where wood planks met linoleum.

He handed her ice wrapped in a towel. "When you're done icing it, I'd like to put a bandage on."

She lifted it to her head and winced. "That's cold."

"Go have a seat. I'll bring your tea."

The woman's voice came from a tiny radio on the mantel, and then a song played. She'd never heard it before. That she knew of, at least.

She settled back onto the couch, and he set a mug on the table. "A few minutes ago, you said you were going to kill me. Now you're bringing me tea?"

He pulled a tiny piece of paper from the pocket of his sweats and tossed it beside her mug before he sat on the recliner, at the edge, forearm resting on his knee. She wasn't fooled that he was in the least bit relaxed, but the gun was on top of the fridge, so she didn't think she was in immediate danger.

She clumsily unfolded the paper one-handed. He probably made that look easy. On the paper was an address, written in small, curled letters. "What is it?"

"The address for this cabin. It was in your pocket."

"I was coming here?" Surely that meant they knew each

other. And yet, he didn't seem to know her. Or he was lying? How could she tell?

He shook his head. "You were at the lake. A man chased you, shot twice, and I think you must've fallen and hit your head because it doesn't appear you were shot."

She stared at the paper until her eyes burned, and she had to blink. Tears blurred the address. Did she write it and then stow the paper in her pocket for some unknown reason she couldn't remember now?

"He drove off in a truck."

She squeezed her eyes shut.

"I didn't call the police. I would have, and was about to, when I found that paper."

"That changes things?"

"No one can know I live up here. You had my address, which means we're connected."

"But you don't know how?" She needed to compose herself. This was all too fast. Too much. And yet at the same time, what she had to grasp onto was a whole bunch of nothing. No answers. No memories.

No name.

Just overwhelming fear and a giant headache.

"I've never seen you before in my life. I don't know your name any more than you do."

That sense of solidarity was a gift. "Thank you."

They were in this together. For as long as it was until he followed through on his threat. Unless it had been empty, a way to goad her into revealing too much under duress.

"I called a friend of mine."

"A cop?"

He shook his head. "He's local, a private investigator. Tate might be able to tell us who you are. He lives in town, and he gets around. *And*, he can be discreet."

Still, fear was ever-present. Like a cloud in the room she

couldn't get rid of. She nodded, though. Otherwise, how else would she get answers?

The song on the radio ended and the female DJ came back on. "Mornings with Megan continues after the news report. Police are out with their new K9 officer, searching for the body of Annabelle Filks. More on this cold case after our commercial break."

He launched from the recliner and shut off the radio, the line of his shoulders tense like concrete. His frantic movement made the cat jump off the couch.

Who was this guy, and what was he hiding?

And who was she?

Continue *Expired Betrayal* Now!

OTHER BOOKS IN THE LAST CHANCE COUNTY SERIES

Also Available in 2 collections!

ABOUT THE AUTHOR

Follow Lisa on social media to find out about new releases and other exciting events!

Visit Lisa's Website to sign up for her mailing list to get FREE books and be the first to learn about new releases and other exciting updates!

https://www.authorlisaphillips.com

Made in the USA
Monee, IL
16 April 2022

94873574R00173